Published January 2025
Published by Indies United Publishing House, LLC

Cover art by Leslie A. Piggott
Edited by: Jennie Rosenblum

Paperback: 978-1-64456-788-3
Kindle: 978-1-64456-789-0
ePub: 978-1-64456-790-6
AudioBook: 978-1-64456-791-3

Library of Congress Control Number: 2024924066

INDIES UNITED PUBLISHING HOUSE, LLC
P.O. BOX 3071
QUINCY, IL 62305-3071

www.indiesunited.net

I0594109

THE MURDER ACCRUAL

THE MURDER ACCRUAL
The Cari Turnlyle Series: Book 6

by Leslie A. Piggott

INDIES UNITED PUBLISHING HOUSE, LLC

Dedication

To my family: Brad, Abby, and Simon. Living life with you is so sweet.

Leslie A. Piggott

Table of Contents

Leslie A. Piggott

Chapter 1

Detective Genevieve Viacorte parked her Ford Expedition in the main lot. She was meeting her partner, Detective Alex Runimoss, at the trailhead near where a hiker's body had been discovered. She heard a vehicle pulling in behind her and turned to see Runimoss sliding into a spot on the opposite side. His large truck took up every inch of the tight parking space.

"How do you like driving your new-to-you truck?" she asked him after he got out.

He patted the truck on the fender. "Well, I have had some friendships rekindled through it."

It took her a minute, but she finally caught the drift. "Because they need help moving?"

He laughed and nodded in confirmation. "Yep, but in all seriousness, I like it. It has enough space for my legs for one. And enough space for everything my wife likes to buy at the gardening store."

"Even better." Genevieve jerked her head toward the trail. "Dr. Green is already here. The body is just ahead near the trail."

Alex followed her on the trail. "Do we know who it is? Dispatch said female, right?"

"That's right," Genevieve responded. "I'm not sure if they've identified her yet."

They only had to walk about a hundred meters along the trail before they reached the CSU team and Dr. Green. Yellow tape surrounded the area and a white pop-up tent was positioned near the base of the cliff. A young couple sat on a large boulder just outside the yellow tape line. Genevieve pulled out her notebook and nodded thanks to the officer standing next to them.

The young woman had tear streaks on her tawny face. Her brown eyes filled with tears again as she looked up at Genevieve. The man's dark skin was accented by a white bandana tied around his neck. Genevieve assumed he used it to keep cool in the heat. He stroked his wife's back in an effort to comfort the distraught woman.

"I'm Detective Viacorte. This is my partner, Detective Runimoss. I understand you found the body," Genevieve stated.

The young man swallowed forcefully before speaking. "Yes, I'm Devon Shaul, S-H-A-U-L, and this is my wife, Stacia. We had barely started our hike this afternoon when we saw her on the ground."

"I'm sure you told the officer some of this already, so I apologize for asking you to repeat yourself," Genevieve began. "What time did you find her?"

Stacia sniffled and wiped the back of her hand across her face. "It was around 3:30 this afternoon, right, Devon?"

Devon nodded. "We normally hike earlier in the day, but we're on our honeymoon and…"

Stacia gave him a horrified look.

He cleared his throat and continued. "We chose to hike in the afternoon today."

Genevieve smiled. "Congratulations on your marriage. I'm sorry you're having to experience trauma like this. Did you approach the body or touch it in any way?"

"We did approach the body, but we didn't touch it. I could see right away that her neck was broken. We knew she was dead, so we just called 9-1-1 and came over here to watch for you guys to arrive," Devon told her.

Genevieve made a note. "Did you see anyone else on the trail today?"

"No, at least not that I remember. We parked the car and grabbed our gear. We hadn't really reached the trailhead when Stacia saw the hiking boot," Devon responded.

Stacia bobbed her head in agreement. "I was kind of joking at first. Like, hey, you need a spare boot? And then, I looked closer and…and…" Another wave of tears kept her from finishing.

"I understand. Do you remember seeing anyone, Stacia?" Alex asked.

"I'm trying to remember. I wasn't really thinking about anything but the hike when we arrived. It's really beautiful out here and I thought we could get some good photos. It's possible someone drove away as we arrived…oh, wait! Do you think someone pushed her?!" Stacia gasped.

Alex put his hands up in surrender. "Not at all, ma'am. We are just trying to find out if there are other witnesses. As far as we know, she just fell."

Genevieve spoke up. "Just to clarify, did you see someone drive away or not?"

2

Stacia lifted her palms up and shrugged. "I really have no idea. Does the park have cameras?"

"We can ask the park ranger; they might have something at the payment booth," Genevieve remarked and pulled out one of her cards. "I think that's all we need for now. You're free to go on your way. This is my card. If you remember anything else, please give me a call."

Genevieve and Alex nodded their thanks and then stepped under the police tape. The white tent was a few paces away. They could see Dr. Green crouched on the ground next to a female body. As usual, his hair was in a state of disarray. A member of the CSU team stood off to the side with a man who looked to be the park ranger. He wore the telltale broad-brimmed hat and brown uniform. His nametag read Ted Pate. Dr. Green pushed himself to his feet when he heard them approach.

"Detectives," he said in acknowledgment. "I place the time of death between two to two-thirty this afternoon."

Genevieve looked at the woman. Her dark hair was streaked with grey and her tanned skin showed a few wrinkles. She estimated her age to be mid-fifties to early sixties, but knew it was possible her time in the sun made her appear older. She wore a forest green hiking vest over a royal blue shirt and khaki shorts. Her head was positioned at an awkward angle to her neck and Genevieve agreed it was obviously broken.

"Did you find any identification on her?" Alex asked.

"Yes, this is Elaine Frobish. She had her wallet in her front vest pocket. We found her driver's license and several business cards for Fit Winners. Have you heard of it?"

Genevieve shook her head. "It doesn't sound familiar."

"It's a fitness club for middle-aged women. Well, mostly women. I've heard they allow men if they promise not to speak unless spoken to," he chuckled. "You'll notice she has abrasions along both arms and legs as well as her face. I'd wager the cause of death is a broken neck, but I'll conduct a full autopsy once we get her back to the precinct. She's also missing three fingernails. It's possible she initially only fell part way and was trying to hang on further up the cliff. We found her hiking sticks closer to the base of the cliff face."

Genevieve looked in the direction he pointed. "Both hiking sticks are intact?"

Green nodded. "Yes, I suppose she let go of them as she went over."

"Have you identified where she went over?" Alex asked.

3

"I sent Chris and Bob up to look. It's a short hike to the cliff top. It shouldn't take you more than twenty minutes," he commented. "Let me radio them and see if they've gotten there yet."

He pulled a large black handset from his belt and put it to his mouth. "Bob, Chris, do you copy?"

"Copy, Dr. Green," Chris responded. "Bob's here with me. I think we located the place. We're photographing it now."

"Great work, gentlemen," Green said and replaced the handset.

"Is there any sign of foul play or do you think she fell?" Genevieve asked.

"I can't say anything definitively yet. Maybe she didn't realize how close she was to the edge and just slipped and fell. Whether she had help or not remains to be seen," he told her.

"Let's head up there and check it out," Alex said as he jerked his head in the direction of the cliff.

"I'll join you, if that's okay," the park ranger spoke up. "My name is Ted. I'm the head park ranger here."

They each shook Ted's hand and introduced themselves. Ted led the way to the trailhead and they followed behind him single file. The trail was well-marked with small clumps of grass and wildflowers scattered along the edge. It made a turn to the left just a few steps into their journey. Genevieve looked around Ted and saw a series of switchbacks ahead. They quickly gained altitude and reached the cliff top in less than ten minutes.

"It's a fairly easy little hike. People like to come up here to take photos or have a picnic. There isn't a lot of shade, but the view is nice," Ted remarked. "It looks like your people are just up ahead."

"Ted, did you know Ms. Frobish?" Genevieve asked him.

He raised and lowered both hands as though pantomiming a scale. "Well, I knew her, but not well. She hiked here by herself a lot, so I knew who she was."

"Do you have a lot of solo hikers? I've always been taught to hike with a buddy," Alex remarked.

"The safest way is to hike in threes, but we get some people out here on their own from time to time. Ms. Frobish was out here pretty much every week, though," he told them.

Genevieve saw Bob and Chris to their right. Bob was photographing the ground while Chris was taking an impression of a footprint. A sign near the lookout read, "DANGER! STEEP DROP!" She wanted to get a look at the footprints too, but wasn't sure what they'd photographed yet.

"Ted, hold up. Let's not step along the trail here yet. I want to make sure they photographed all of this." She hollered at the CSU team. "Bob, did you get photos along the trail here first?"

"We took photos all the way up the trail," Bob called back to her. "It's all well-documented now."

She and Alex joined him near the edge. The location looked like a popular lookout. Two rows of pine trees thinned out to an opening by the cliff. You could see down into the valley and the creek that ran through the park. It was rather picturesque. She took a step closer to look at the smattering of footprints Bob was photographing.

"It kind of looks like someone was pacing in a circle. Could they have been on the phone?" she asked Bob.

Bob grabbed his radio and clicked a button on the side of it. "Dr. Green, is there a cell phone with the victim?"

The radio cackled with static before Dr. Green's voice broke through. "There wasn't one in her vest. Let me check her other pockets...just a moment...ah, here we go. The screen is cracked pretty badly, but we might still be able to get something from it."

"Hmm...if she was pacing while talking on the phone, would she have really taken the time to try to put her phone in her pocket when she fell?" Genevieve asked.

"Seems like a stretch to me too," Alex commented. "Can I see the photos you took of the ground here?"

Bob held the camera out to Alex. "You can scroll through them with this button."

Genevieve moved closer to Alex to look at the images too. He was almost eighteen inches taller than her, so he had to lower the camera for her to see the screen. Several footprints littered the ground. She reached around Alex's hand to zoom in.

"It looks like all the prints were made by the same boot...I mean, it looks like one left foot and one right foot of the same-sized shoe," she observed and looked from the camera screen to the ground to confirm.

"Surely she wasn't the only person to hike up here today," Alex said to Ted. "I suppose she may have walked around so much she covered up all the prints before her."

"It's probably our most popular hike in the park. It's the closest to the parking lot and the shortest, unless you want to continue on exploring in that direction," Ted pointed to his left, where the copse of pine trees obscured the rest of the trail. "I suspect most people go near the edge to take photos regardless of how far they plan to hike."

"I noticed the sign warning people of the drop," Genevieve commented. "Have you had people fall from here before?"

"It's pretty rare, but yes, it does happen," the park ranger replied solemnly.

Alex zoomed out of the photo and clicked the button to see the previous photo. The next few images had a small ruler next to a footprint to help gauge the size of the print. He clicked through a few more images.

"Where is the image from the trail over to the lookout?" Alex asked Bob.

Bob reached for the camera and clicked the button a few times. "This is where we started taking photos…and this is on the switchback section of the trail…and here's the cliff top right by the edge of the trail."

Genevieve tilted her head to the right and leaned in to look more closely at the image. "But there aren't any prints here. It's pretty dry, but wouldn't there be something?"

Bob shrugged. "I would expect to see something, especially with all the prints over here, but maybe someone spread a blanket down here and inadvertently erased her footprints."

She scrunched her nose. "I suppose that's possible, but there aren't *any* footprints leading away from the area. The people having a picnic would have made footprints too. Something feels off." She turned to Ted. "Does the park have cameras near the entrance or in the parking lot?"

The park ranger nodded his head. "We have one on each side of the payment booth: one for those coming in and one for those leaving. There's only one camera for the parking lot. I'm not sure how much of the lot is visible on that one."

"We need to review the footage. I'm not sure if we're looking for possible witnesses or what at this point, but I agree with my partner. The lack of footprints here is disturbing," Alex told him.

"Let's head back down the trail. I can let you review the footage from the cameras at the ranger station," Ted replied.

"Just one second," Genevieve said to him before turning back to Bob and Chris. "Dr. Green mentioned our victim was missing some fingernails. Did you find those anywhere?"

Bob shook his head no. "We're going to try flying the drone over here to see if we can locate them. Her nail polish is pretty bright, so that might help."

6

She nodded. "Lead the way, Ted. We're right behind you."

* * * * *

The messenger bag in the front seat of Cari Turnlyle's car buzzed repeatedly. She checked her watch to see who was calling and realized it wasn't a call at all: it was a flurry of texts and emails from her co-workers. As the lead journalist at the local newspaper, the Brenington Beagle, she often got called out to interview witnesses or first responders. These messages would have to wait. She'd heard a report on the police scanner of a dead body turning up at the nearby state park. She wanted to interview the two witnesses before they left the scene.

She pulled up to the payment hut and rolled down her window. A young man in a ranger uniform smiled.

"Hi, ma'am. Welcome to the state park. Please be advised, we have some police activity near the first trailhead in the park. It's the Dacy Trail; please avoid that area for the time being. The entrance fee is five dollars. We take cash or card," he explained.

Cari didn't want to get flagged as a reporter immediately, so she feigned concern. "Police activity? Is it safe to be in the park today? I was hoping to get some exercise."

The young man shook his head. "Everything is perfectly safe. No need for alarm. Um, was that cash or card?"

Cari flashed a smile and fished her business credit card out of her wallet. It didn't say "Brenington Beagle" on it, so she felt safe using it. "Card."

He swiped the card and handed her the receipt to sign.

"Just drive straight ahead to enter the parking lot. Here's a map of the park. Please stay on the trails at all times…and leave it cleaner than you found it," he instructed her.

"Will do. Thanks," she responded as she hit the button to put her window up.

She saw the medical examiner's van parked in the lot and knew that meant the body was still present. Bob's car was parked on the opposite side of the lot. She pulled into a spot near the large map of the park and turned off the car. Behind her, a young man tossed a backpack into the trunk of a vehicle and slammed it closed. She decided to take a gamble and talk to him. The scanner had reported two witnesses and she could see a woman's profile in the front seat. Cari grabbed her bag and hurried over to their vehicle.

7

"Hi there! Excuse me, hi!" she repeated herself when the man didn't look her way immediately.

His head swung her way and he gave her a quizzical look. "Can I help you?"

"I hope so. My name is Cari Turnlyle. I work for the Beagle," she extended her hand and he shook it.

"Devon Shaul," the tall man told her. "My wife and I were just leaving. We've had a bit of a shock and she wants to go back to the hotel."

Cari nodded her head. "I understand. I was hoping to speak with you about the accident. Just a few questions. It won't take long."

Devon looked over his shoulder at his wife. "Let me check with Stacia."

Cari waited while he walked around the vehicle and opened his wife's door. He spoke too quietly for her to hear, but gestured her way a couple of times. The woman in the front seat shook her head no repeatedly. Devon looked at Cari and shrugged.

"I'm sorry, she's not up for it," he apologized. "We didn't really see anything anyway."

Cari's hopefulness faded. "Is there anything you can tell me about the victim? Name? Age? Race?"

He shrugged again. "Um, they said her name is Elaine Frobish. She's older ish, but I didn't look too closely. Maybe sixties? I'm a terrible judge of age, though. She could be forty-five for all I know. She's white, dark hair with some grey in it. Seems like she fell. That's really all I know."

"I appreciate your time," Cari said as he turned to get into the car. "Would you take my card in case you or your wife feel up for talking more later?"

He looked at her with irritation in his eyes. "I guess. We're supposed to be on our honeymoon, though. This isn't really what I had planned."

Cari swallowed and handed him the card. "Congrats on your marriage. Best wishes," she said somewhat half-heartedly.

She walked back to where her car was parked and looked at the park map. Her phone continued to buzz and ping with messages, but since none of them had her boss' name attached, she continued to ignore them. She peered beyond the large map and could see an officer positioned at the trailhead. He wasn't going to let her pass. She was about to get back in her car when she heard some familiar voices. Genevieve and Alex were following a park ranger toward the parking lot. Alex was not her biggest fan, so rather than agitate him, she ducked between two cars. Maybe Genevieve would be free to chat later.

Once they were out of sight, she got into her car and pulled her cell phone out of her bag. She had missed an email from her boss' secretary, Michelle and over ten texts from several of her co-workers. Bryson Millar had asked her to call him as soon as she had the opportunity. She touched the phone icon next to his name and waited for the call to connect.

"Hey, Cari…did you see the email from Michelle?" Bryson asked. He never made small talk.

"I haven't had a chance to read it yet, but my phone has been lighting up with messages for the past fifteen minutes. What's going on?" she asked him.

"Ollaman had Michelle send out a staff-wide email regarding an *emergency* meeting. There are rumors he's going to lay some people off. Have you heard anything?" Bryson asked in a hushed tone. She figured he must be at his desk or in the hallway and didn't want to attract attention.

"Lay people off? But why? Has something changed?" Cari asked in confusion.

"I don't want to get ahead of myself here, but I've seen things like this happen with other newspapers. When I interviewed with the Beagle last year, everything seemed to be good, financially speaking. Now, I'm not so sure," Bryson said slowly. "At my last paper in New Mexico, it started just like this. I overheard Ollaman mention subscriptions were decreasing."

"Subscriptions are always up and down though. People move away and cancel their subscription. New people move here and sign up in their place. It evens out," Cari said flippantly. "How bad is it?"

"I heard him on the phone earlier this week. His office door was open as I was leaving for the day. I just caught a few snippets. The newspaper business is not what it once was. Think about it. How many local, in-print newspapers are there any more? Even getting some of the big name, mainstream papers in print is a challenge. My cousin had something published in one of those a while back and my grandma had to go to eight different stores before she could get a real copy," he told her.

Cari brushed off a feeling of unease. The Beagle had been around for ages. Ollaman wouldn't shut it down. That was ludicrous! "When is the meeting?"

"It starts in half an hour. It's supposedly mandatory. Where are you?" he asked.

"At the state park. Some hikers found a body…it's a developing story. I'll head back now after I do one more thing. Thanks for keeping me in the loop."

She ended the call and looked back at the payment booth. She could see cameras installed likely with the intention of getting license plate images of those entering and exiting the park. She figured there was a chance it had a digital read out and wanted to get a look at the list. If Genevieve and Alex were investigating, odds were high the woman was murdered. She started her car and backed out of her spot. She pulled alongside the booth and rolled down her window. The young man inside turned to look her way.

"Can I help you with something?" he asked cautiously. "Hey, I just realized who you are! You're the journalist who has solved all those murders for the police."

Cari blushed and hoped to portray a humble expression. "I've assisted where I could. The police and detectives do the heavy lifting...so...I noticed your cameras and wondered if you get a digital list of the plates that go through here?" Cari asked and flashed a smile.

He smiled back. "It just does video footage, but we can save stills of each vehicle if necessary."

"What would necessitate that action?" she asked with her eyebrows raised.

"Well, the death today definitely will. Even if it was an accident, we'll want to get images so we can assist as needed...um, if there's an investigation."

Cari pulled a business card from her messenger bag. "Any chance I could get a copy of the images from today?"

"Um, I, uh, we, I don't think we're supposed to share people's information with the public," he stammered.

She smiled and flicked her wrist. "I'm not trying to steal anyone's identity. I'm just trying to...assist the police in whatever way I can. Sometimes I see things they miss, you know?"

He shook his head no. "Sorry. I need this job and can't risk getting fired."

"I understand. Thanks anyway," she told him and put her window back up.

She checked her watch; she was just barely going to get to the meeting on time. She couldn't imagine the Beagle closing its doors. Was her job really at risk?

10

Chapter 2

The ranger station's security office felt cramped with three adults squeezing around the small computer screen. Genevieve ran a hand over her dark hair even though it was pulled into a bun at the base of her head. She was feeling somewhat claustrophobic. Ted clicked a few more keys and the feeds from the cameras finally appeared on the screen.

"Okay, top left is the entrance camera, top right is the exit, and the bottom one is the parking lot," he explained.

"Got it. Let's back them up to half past one," Alex requested. "Green said the time of death was between two and two-thirty. It's a short hike, so hopefully, we'll see her come in."

"Frobish drives a Subaru Outback...it's dark blue and has a park pass in the windshield," Genevieve said and also read off the victim's license plate number. "The witnesses are in a Chevy Malibu, silver, so we can watch for them too."

Ted dialed the time back to 1:30 p.m. on each feed and hit play. "I'll put it on double time unless you want to watch it slower."

"Double is great, but be ready to pause it," Alex responded. "I'll watch the entrance feed, Viacorte, you take the parking lot, and Ted, can you monitor the exit?"

They both nodded in agreement as vehicles moved across the three views.

"Pause it," Alex instructed Ted. "I've got a dark Subaru entering...never mind. Wrong license plate and a dude is driving."

Ted clicked resume on the feed. Genevieve watched several other vehicles park. The occupants ranged from couples to families with young children. Alex spoke again.

"There she is. Dark blue Subaru Outback. Plate matches. See her in the parking lot?" he asked.

"I got her," Genevieve replied.

Ted paused the other feeds and slowed the playback speed to half. The three of them watched the middle-aged woman park her hatchback. She exited the vehicle and popped the trunk to remove a backpack and two hiking poles.

"Did they find a backpack with her?" Genevieve asked.

"I don't know. I'll get Green on the phone to ask," Alex said as he pulled out his phone. "Hey, Green. Does the vic have a backpack on or near her? Grey? Yeah, that's what we're seeing. Okay, thanks."

Alex put his phone away. "The ME says they found a grey backpack near the hiking poles. It had a water bottle and some snacks in it."

Genevieve checked the time stamp. "Okay, she parked at about 1:40 p.m. and walked to the trailhead. We can't see her once she gets a few steps along the trail, but we know she made it to the top. Let's see who else goes up."

Ted set the speed back to double. They watched for several minutes before a father with his young son started up the trail. Genevieve recorded the license plate so they could track the duo down and ask if they saw anyone on their hike. Two minutes later, the pair returned to the parking lot. The son had a big scrape on his leg and was in tears. His dad cleaned it up with a first aid kit, then loaded everything back in the car. They drove away. She didn't cross them off the list but figured they didn't see much in the short amount of time they were hiking. A silver Chevy pulled into the spot next to the Outback and the Shauls got out.

"That's it? No one else was on the trail?" Alex asked incredulously. "Is there another way into the park?"

The park ranger shook his head. "Not by car, and really, there shouldn't be anyone able to access it by foot either. They'd have to climb a barbed wire fence and find a way across the river on the far northwest side of the park. The fence is lined with 'No Trespassing' signs."

"If someone pushed Ms. Frobish, I'm guessing they aren't too concerned about a possible trespassing violation," Genevieve remarked. "But, hey, do you have cameras along the fence line?"

Ted sighed. "No, it's too big of an expense. We haven't had a problem with people trying to gain illegal access to the park since we put up the fence. And, honestly, we rarely had a problem before that. It's pretty challenging to get into the park that way."

"But not impossible?" Alex pressed him.

"An experienced outdoorsman could do it," Ted admitted.

"Or he got here a lot earlier," Genevieve suggested slowly. "I assume you've had people in and out of the park all day?"

Ted nodded in confirmation. "I don't know how many, but yeah, it's been busy as usual."

"If we didn't see the guy leave, maybe he's still here," Genevieve said, suddenly anxious to go check the lot again.

Alex stood up. "Let's go call in all the plates of the vehicles still here. Ted, can you get us an image of all the vehicles coming into the park today?"

Ted nodded enthusiastically. "That's pretty standard whenever we have an...event like this. It will take me some time, but I can do it."

"Do people ever camp in the park?" Genevieve asked. She willed him to say no. If that was the case, they could have to go back several days to look through images.

"Yes, but we haven't had anyone camping with a trailer or otherwise since Tuesday. The parking lot has been empty at the close of the day the last two days," he responded.

"That's a relief. Send us a copy of your video feeds and the images you save. We can run the plates easily enough," she told him and handed him one of her cards.

They rushed back out to the parking lot. Genevieve's heart sank. The lot had been much fuller when they'd walked through just half an hour ago. Only ten or fifteen cars were still in the lot. She hoped they had a clear image of all the vehicles that left while they were reviewing the footage. She looked back at the ranger station. She couldn't decide if they should go get a list of all the plates they'd missed first or figure out who was still here.

"C'mon, Viacorte. Let's get these called in. Then we can see who left," Alex barked at her.

She took out her phone and dialed the station. Her old friend Kurt answered the phone.

"Detective Viacorte, how can I help you this afternoon?" he asked.

"I need you to run a few plates for us. If anyone has a rap sheet, I need to know," she told him.

"I'm ready," he told her.

She read off the first plate and waited for him to respond.

"You found a widowed grandmother, age sixty-seven," Kurt informed her.

"Probably not her, but save her information for me," Genevieve said and gave him the next plate. Alex was at the opposite end of the lot on his phone. He gave her a thumbs down to say he hadn't gotten a good hit yet either.

"Retired couple in their fifties. What else do you have?" Kurt asked.

She gave him the rest of the plates on her side of the lot, but none of them seemed promising. Alex was walking quickly her way.

"I think my partner might have something, so I can't chat. Thanks for the help, Kurt," she said and ended the call. "What did you find, Alex?"

"One of the drivers has an assault conviction from a decade ago. He's in his forties. I'm going to boot the car. He won't be able to leave without talking to us," Alex told her.

"Do you want to get a list of the cars that left while we were in the ranger station?" she asked him.

He shrugged. "Might as well just look at those with the rest of the drivers from earlier in the day."

"What if the guy sees the boot on his car and takes off into the wilderness?" Genevieve asked.

"I'll call Green and have him send one of the officers over to keep watch," Alex offered and looked at his watch. "We can start reviewing the footage while we wait for him to get back to his car."

She nodded and walked back to the ranger station. Alex caught up to her before she reached the door. He knocked quickly and then opened it with his free hand.

"Can you send someone up to keep an eye on a vehicle for us?" Alex asked. "Yeah, I'll have Viacorte text you the plate number. It's a silver Accord."

He ended the call and then took out his notebook to get the plate number. "It's this one," he said pointing at a number with an asterisk by it. "Can you text it to Green?"

"You're such an old man. When are you going to get a real phone?" she asked.

"Not until they make me," he responded.

* * * * *

Cari hurried into the newspaper office. The email said the meeting was supposed to start at 4:30 p.m. in the large conference room. She saw Bryson walking that way and caught up with him.

"Is everyone here?" she whispered as they approached the room.

He shrugged. "I don't know. We have so many interns coming and going…I can't keep everyone straight half the time."

They pulled open the door to the conference room. Ollaman stood at the head of the table. He was giving instructions to Michelle, who was typing rapidly on a laptop. Cari and Bryson sat in two of the remaining empty chairs just as Ollaman cleared his throat.

"Good afternoon, everyone. Thanks for getting back here, those of you who were away from your desks. This won't take long, but I wanted everyone to hear it from me," he said as he flexed and released his hands repeatedly. "The printed newspaper business is a dying entity. I'm sure you're aware of how rare it is to still have an in-print, local newspaper. Many Americans read their news online, on social media, or they just watch it on TV. The Beagle has survived through generous local sponsors and subscriptions, but both of these are decreasing. Before anyone panics, I'm not giving up, but I am going to have to make a few changes. With Michelle's help, I've outlined these changes and printed a copy for each of you. I'll be having a one-on-one meeting with every employee in the coming days to explain how these changes affect you. Michelle will send you a meeting invite for those."

Several hands went up with questions. Ollaman lifted his own hands and moved them down. "I'm not going to take any questions right now. Please take the information packet home and look through it. I'll answer any questions you have in our follow-up meetings. That's all for now. Thank you."

Everyone picked up a packet from in front of Michelle and slowly filed out of the room. A lot of people looked shocked, but some were angry. Cari knew Ollaman loved the Beagle and would do whatever he could to keep it afloat. She followed Bryson to his cubicle.

"I guess the rumors were true," she said to him.

He nodded. "Yeah, this is how it begins. It's a hard business these days. Some papers have been able to transition to digital only, but it still costs money. Employee salaries, website fees, benefits…it all adds up. And if you can get the news for free elsewhere, why would you pay to get it here?"

Cari swallowed. "All valid points. I wonder what changes he's planning to make."

"I don't want to be presumptuous, but in my experience, they cut back on benefits pretty quickly. I'm guessing the internship program will go from paid to unpaid, if it hasn't already," he told her matter-of-factly.

"Benefits? Like, we could lose our health insurance?" Cari asked in a panicked voice.

He shook his head. "No, as long as he has over fifteen employees, they still have to provide some sort of healthcare package. It's just not going to be as good. Like an increase in our deductible for fewer services, that kind of thing."

Cari grimaced. "I guess I should go read through this. It doesn't sound very promising."

She stood up to walk around to her cubicle and saw Ollaman exiting the conference room. He jerked his head toward his office, indicating she should join him. She felt her hands grow sweaty; she didn't think he was going to start the face-to-face meetings today. Was he cutting her loose? He unlocked the door and pushed it open for her.

"Turnlyle, have a seat," he said as they entered his office.

She slid the information packet into her messenger bag and sat down in the chair. Ollaman's mannerisms seemed relaxed and casual, but she never felt like she read his nonverbal cues well. He cleared his throat and sat down behind the desk.

"I have a story I'd like you to piece together," he began and she looked him in the eye. "Oh, relax, Turnlyle. I'm not going to fire anyone if I can help it."

She tried to smile but figured she was grimacing at best. "Of course, sir. What's the story?"

"We've had a lot of new businesses spring up in the area over the last few months. I'd like you to put a list together, preferably by trade. Don't just include those in Brenington, do the surrounding area as well: Lander, Pfinning, and Green Mountain. Include new neighborhoods and apartment complexes too. Everything new in the last...let's say eight months. It would be great if you could get a quote from some of the owners too," he added.

Cari pulled out her notebook. "I'm going to write this down so I don't forget anything. I'm guessing City Hall probably has a record of the new builds in Brenington. They probably had to issue permits, right?"

He nodded. "Seems likely. I'm hoping if we can put together a nice article about what's up-and-coming in the area, those businesses will notice and we might be able to scare up some new sponsors for the paper."

Cari gulped. "I'll do my best, sir. What's the deadline for this?"

"A-S-A-P!" he said clapping his hands. "The sooner the better."

"Got it. I'm going to call or email the Chamber of Commerce for each of the towns before I head out for the day. I'll probably start the day at City Hall tomorrow to track down the new neighborhoods and complexes," she said and put her notebook away.

"Good plan. Thanks, Turnlyle," he said. "Did you find anything out about the body in the state park?"

She nodded. "It sounds like she fell over the edge. I talked to the couple who found her; they didn't know much. It might have just been an accident."

"Well, keep me posted as usual," he remarked and then glanced at the office door.

She took it as a sign the meeting was over and got up from the chair. She looked at her watch. It was just after five. She wasn't sure if Bob would be finished at the state park by this point. Maybe she could look over the packet and then call him to see if he could meet for dinner later. She wasn't sure what to expect inside the packet. Maybe it wouldn't be as bad as Bryson predicted.

She draped her messenger bag over her desk chair after removing her notebook from it. The number for the Brenington Chamber of Commerce was taped to her computer screen. She punched it into her desk phone and waited for someone to pick up. The line rang twice and clicked.

"You have reached the Brenington Chamber of Commerce. Our office hours are Monday thru Thursday, eight a.m. to five p.m. Eastern Time and on Fridays, eight a.m. to noon. Please leave a message and we'll get back to you as soon as we can."

A beep sounded in her ear and she returned the receiver to its place without leaving a message. She could just as easily send an email. She unlocked her computer and pulled up her work email account. Part of her wanted to ask one of the interns to compile the information for her, but she knew most of them were gone for the day. She had interacted with the BCC on numerous occasions, but was less familiar with those from the neighboring towns. She did a quick internet search to find their contact information. She started with the BCC, then copied the text before hitting send. The message only needed to be tweaked slightly for each recipient. She asked for a list of new businesses in their towns for the last eight months as well as the owner's name and contact information. She tried to envision what the final article would look like. In her mind, it could take up several pages.

Chapter 3

Genevieve yawned and rolled her head from one side to the other. They had been reviewing the video footage for close to an hour. She was writing down license plates of any single occupant vehicle while Alex gave the number to dispatch. Alex's phone buzzed with an incoming call.

"Runimoss," he said into his phone, then paused. "We'll be right there."

"Boot?" Genevieve asked hopefully.

He nodded. "Let's go talk to him. He didn't run off when he saw the boot, but it sounds like he isn't very happy about it."

They exited the ranger station and walked to the far side of the parking lot. A young man in his late teens, possibly early twenties, stood near the Accord with his arms crossed. He had on a baseball hat and khaki shorts. His brown hair stuck out from the edge of the cap and his freckled skin looked a bit sunburned.

"I thought you said the guy was in his forties. Who's this?" Genevieve asked.

Alex shrugged. "Maybe it's his kid."

They reached the young man and pulled out their badges.

"Detectives Runimoss and Viacorte," Alex said quickly. "Is this your car?"

The kid glared at Alex before he responded. "It's my dad's. Why? Did he not pay a ticket or something? I paid the entry fee."

"What's your name?" Alex asked. "Let's see your driver's license."

"Zeke. Short for Ezekiel," he said as he pulled a wallet from the cargo shorts. "Here."

"Is your dad here with you?" Genevieve asked as she looked at his license. He was twenty years old and lived in Brenington. She handed the license back.

"No. He's at work. Where else would he be? You guys keep tabs on him. You should know," he grumbled.

"What time did you get to the park today?" Alex asked him.

"Early. Like before nine," he said. "I thought I was meeting my girlfriend for a picnic, but she decided to break up with me instead. I ate the food alone in my car and then I've just been wandering the trails up there since. Then, I get back down here and find out you guys booted my ride."

Genevieve cringed. "I'm sorry to hear that, Zeke. We're investigating the death of a woman in the park today—"

"And you wanted to pin it on my dad? He served his time and he's just a regular citizen now. You guys just won't leave him alone. Every time something happens, it seems like someone is pointing fingers at him," Zeke glowered at her.

"I'm sorry you feel that way, Zeke. We're trying to be thorough. Your dad's rap sheet caught our eye. Clearly, he's not involved. We'll get the boot removed and you can be on your way. I hope the rest of your day gets better," Genevieve said gently.

Alex knelt down and punched in a code. The boot released from the tire. He put his hand out to shake Zeke's hand.

"No hard feelings?" Alex asked.

Zeke gave his hand a cursory shake and then got into his car without looking back.

"Guess we can cross that plate off the list," Genevieve said as he drove out of the lot.

"Our shift is basically over. We can look through more plates tomorrow or Monday," Alex said. "Green hasn't even declared it an official homicide yet, so I'm in no rush."

She rubbed the back of her neck. "Don't have to tell me twice."

* * * * *

Cari kicked off her shoes in the direction of her bedroom and sat down on the sofa. She pulled out the ominous packet and put it on the coffee table. She clenched and unclenched her fists a few times. Ollaman hadn't said the packet had bad news in it; maybe she was building up all this anxiety for no reason. She grabbed her water bottle and realized it was empty. She decided to refill it and *then* start reading through the information.

Her phone buzzed with an incoming call on her way back to the sofa.

"Hey, Bob! Are you finished out at the park?" she asked.

"Yeah, we're back at the lab sorting through samples. I'm going to help Chris get all of this logged and then be on my way. Want me to pick up some food for dinner?" he asked.

"That would be great. I just got home. How about pizza this time instead of Chinese?" she suggested.

"I'll call it in now. It should only take us twenty to thirty minutes to get all this logged," he told her. "I'll see you soon."

Cari ended the call and picked up the packet. The first page only had a title: Updates to Personnel and More at the Brenington Beagle. She flipped to the next page, which was a table of contents. The information was divided into three sections: Office Policies, Overtime, and Benefits. She chewed the inside of her cheek. She had been hoping Ollaman wouldn't make any changes to their benefits. She had good health insurance, which she rarely used. She knew her recent concussion, which resulted in a trip to urgent care that included x-rays, would have been much more expensive if she'd had a different insurance plan. She turned to Office Policies first.

She skimmed the text, which informed her all of the changes would be effective as of September 1, 2026. She wondered if they would have to sign new contracts. Cari didn't remember much about the original contract she'd signed. She wondered if she still had a digital copy of it. Part of her didn't really care; she liked working at the Beagle and living in Brenington. She was willing to make a few changes if it meant she could stay put. She skipped to the last section to see how their benefits were changing.

She knew they usually signed new healthcare policies on September 1 every year. She always took the cheapest option as she was young and healthy. The benefits section only took up two pages. At first, she thought that was a good sign: he must not be changing much. She read through the two paragraphs on the first page. It explained how the office was going to be below the minimum number of required full time employees necessary for the newspaper to provide a healthcare plan. She blinked and read it again, but the words didn't change. Ollaman had said he wasn't firing people, so how could this be possible? She flipped back to the first section and quickly read the different subheadings.

As Bryson had predicted, they were doing away with paid internships. She wondered if any of the college students would have to quit and find a different job because they needed the money. The junior copy editors were getting their hours reduced to part-time; only the lead journalists were retaining their full-time employee status. That included her, Bryson, and the sportswriter, as well as Ollaman and Michelle. Cari gasped. She wasn't sure people would be okay with losing their benefits this way. Things must be more dire than Ollaman indicated. She heard a key in the lock.

"It's me!" Bob shouted from outside. "I've got a pepperoni pizza and two salads."

She stuffed the packet back into her messenger bag. "I'll grab some plates and two glasses of water, unless you want something else?"

He pushed the door open and removed his key from the lock. "Do you have any beer? It's been a long day."

"I might. Let me check," she said as she reached the kitchen.

Her refrigerator was pretty empty as usual, but Bob was in luck. The six-pack he'd brought over a few nights ago still had four bottles left in it. She grabbed two and brought them to the kitchen table.

"Oh, one for you too?" he teased before seeing her face. "Hey, what's up?"

"Let me grab some plates and I'll fill you in. Ollaman dropped a bit of a bombshell this afternoon," she told him.

She pulled two plates off the shelf and two forks from the silverware drawer for the salads. They both grabbed two slices of pizza and set their salads to the side.

"Is he retiring?" Bob asked.

"No, but I suppose that's one way the news could be worse," she responded. "The newspaper is losing subscribers and sponsors. He called us all in for a meeting to alert us to some changes he's making to the business."

"What kind of changes?" Bob asked in a concerned tone.

"I'm only going to be getting a stipend for health insurance instead of being part of a group package, for one," she said grimly.

"How can he do that? You have way more than the minimum number of employees—" Bob started to object.

"No, not after September 1, we won't. He's ending the paid internship program. It will all be unpaid. He's reducing the junior copy editors' time to less than full time. There will only be five full time employees," she told him.

"Wow. You're right; that is a bombshell. Do you think people will quit?" he asked her between bites of pizza.

She swallowed her own bite. "I don't know. They might start looking for another job, though, and quit later."

"I wonder if Ollaman talked to someone who knows about money before he decided to make these changes. It's often more beneficial for small businesses to offer some sort of health insurance plan than not. There are tax benefits on both sides. It's possible the amount you have to pay will increase, though," Bob said thoughtfully.

"I don't have to pay at all right now," Cari remarked.

"What? Surely something is taken out of your paycheck each month, right?" Bob asked, surprised.

"Oh, maybe. I've never really looked at the pay stub," she said sheepishly.

"Do you get those electronically? Pull one up. Let's look at it. My dad knows all about this stuff. Well, at least for Illinois, but it can't be that different here," Bob told her.

Cari pulled out her phone and opened her email app. She had never really paid attention to the electronic pay stubs; as long as she was getting paid, everything was fine. It took a few searches, but she finally found the most recent pay stub receipt.

"Okay, here it is. You're right. They do take out money for insurance every month. I didn't even realize it," she said. "With the proposed changes, I would get to keep that money, plus get a stipend? Or would it be equivalent to what they're withholding?"

"I have no idea, but Dad will know. I can ask him," Bob offered.

"Let me take a screenshot and we can text that to him," Cari responded.

"Wait. Make sure you aren't including any personal info like an employee number or bank account or anything before you take it," Bob instructed her.

"Oh, good call," she laughed. She repositioned the info on her phone to exclude her personal information and took a screenshot. "Okay, I'll text it to both of you along with a photo of the new Benefits Package sheet. Maybe he can help Ollaman save our health insurance."

"Worth a shot. I'm sure he'll have some advice and you can pass it along to Ollaman when you meet with him," Bob replied. "Oh, look! He already responded. Looks like he needs some time to research it, but he knows where to look."

"You said you had a long day too. The hiker? Was it bad? I was only there long enough to talk to the couple who found her. They were pretty shaken up by it, though," Cari said.

Bob nodded grimly. "Her neck was broken and she lost three fingernails somehow. We flew our drone around and eventually found them about twenty feet down from the cliff top. We're guessing she was somehow able to stop herself and tried to claw her way back up, but couldn't find enough holds to do it."

Cari shuddered. "How terrifying. It seems a little strange that she'd be out hiking alone. Don't they always tell you to go with a buddy?"

Bob shrugged. "Yes, but that doesn't mean everyone listens. The park ranger said they get a lot of solo hikers."

"Was he familiar with Ms. Frobish?" Cari asked.

"I think he knew of her, but I didn't spend much time with him. Chris and I hiked up to the top to photograph the place we think she went over," Bob explained. "It wasn't entirely what I expected."

"What do you mean?" Cari asked curiously.

"It looked like someone had swept away the footprints from the trail to the lookout point. The more we looked at the ground, the more obvious it was that someone had used a branch to clear out footprints from the path to the place she fell," Bob told her. "Green probably would have declared it an accidental death if it weren't for the lack of footprints. He's got it marked as inconclusive for now."

"Interesting," Cari said and pulled her salad toward her. "I don't know a lot about Elaine Frobish, but why would someone want to hurt this woman?"

"Your guess is as good as mine," Bob replied. "Hey, are we still taking Hilary and Joel mini-golfing tomorrow evening?"

Cari nodded as she chewed a bite of salad. "Yes! Bea told me they're really excited to go again. Are you still free to go?"

"Definitely. We're doing dinner with them too, right?" he asked.

"Yeah, hopefully, it won't be a big fight to pick a place like it was two weeks ago," she grimaced.

"I'm sure it will be. They're siblings. That's what they do," Bob laughed.

* * * * *

Robby paced the floor of his home office. He caught his reflection in the mirror his wife Bea had insisted on hanging when they first moved into the house. His boy-next-door haircut, which normally looked polished and professional, was askew after numerous run-ins with his nervous hand. The dark circles under his light-brown eyes confessed his poor sleeping habits. He tried to smooth his brown hair back into place. When New Technology Systems contacted him a year ago about joining their company as CFO, he was flattered. His previous job in Florida seemed limited in regard to vertical movement and NTS offered him a chance to rise straight to the top. The signing package had everything: a bonus, a relocation package—including taking care of selling their house, great schools for the kids, and a six-figure salary. During his interview, he'd asked why the former CFO was stepping down. They'd told him the man decided it was time to retire. Everything seemed normal at first. He was not just the CFO; he also had accounting responsibilities and managed the many funds the company handled.

A few months ago, the owner of NTS called him late in the evening to ask if he could approve the transfer of funds to one of their contractors. The owner and CEO, Damien Follard, claimed the invoice had slipped through the cracks in the transfer of duties from the former CFO to Robby. If they didn't get the transfer time-stamped that night, they would be in danger of being derelict on the contract. Eager to please, Robby quickly pulled up the account and made the payment.

But then it just kept happening. Follard always had a seemingly valid excuse and as the new guy on the team, Robby was hesitant to question his boss. Sometimes he called to give Robby a heads up about an incoming payment, which Robby found strange until he realized his boss never followed up with the paperwork for it. Two weeks ago, Mr. Follard had called him during normal business hours with an invoice for a contractor. The billing code for payment was listed as HJM763841. Bea had wanted to watch *Wheel of Fortune* that night but they'd turned it on early by mistake, catching the seven o'clock news first. One of the headlines was about the unexpected death of a local small business owner, Horace J. Manwith. He was an older gentleman and he'd mistakenly stepped into oncoming traffic just as a garbage truck had turned the corner. Bystanders were quoted as saying the man had been on the phone and seemed distracted. The TV reporter said investigators were reviewing traffic cameras, but it seemed to be an unfortunate accident by all accounts. The man's initials caught Robby's eye; they matched the billing code from that morning. He brushed it off as a coincidence.

Until it happened again today. He'd been mindlessly scrolling through his phone while Bea watched TV in the same room. Her show ended and the news came on right after. A local woman had fallen to her death while on a hike in the nearby state park. The park ranger said she frequently hiked the trails alone and was a very experienced hiker. No one had witnessed her fall, but a young couple had discovered her body along the trail that afternoon. Her neck had broken in the fall. The fifty-year-old woman,

Elaine C. Frobish, had been the owner of Fit Winners, which was not only a gym, but also a certification company for aspiring fitness trainers. Robby had opened his email when he heard the woman's name. A chill went down his spine as he read the billing code he'd processed earlier that day: ECF764215.

He told Bea he needed to finish up a couple things for work and then he'd come to bed. She'd kissed him on the cheek and told him not to stay up too late. He looked at the contact on his personal cell phone: Cari Turnlyle. Part of him knew he should go to the police, but part of him was afraid he'd be in trouble for being complicit.

* * * * *

Cari was brushing her teeth when her watch notified her of an incoming phone call. She quickly spat into the sink and then accepted the call. She couldn't imagine why her brother-in-law Robby would be calling her after ten o'clock and hoped everything was okay with Bea and the kids.

"Robby? Is everything okay?" Cari asked with concern.

Robby exhaled. "I don't know, Cari. I think I might have stumbled onto something and I'm not sure what to do."

Cari's brow furrowed. "Something...bad? Illegal? With one of the kids? With Bea?"

"No, Bea and the kids are fine. It's something...something at work. I'm not sure. Maybe it's nothing," he said slowly.

"It must be more than nothing if you decided to call. How can I help?" Cari asked him. He was really being cryptic.

"Um, do you follow the news?" he asked and then laughed. "What am I saying? Of course you follow the news. You're a freaking reporter."

Cari tittered awkwardly. It was taking him forever to tell her what was bothering him. She waited for him to continue.

"Here's the deal: one of my jobs with the company is to process payments and the transfer of funds. When we bill a company for new service, the invoice crosses my desk. If we need to pay a contractor for something, the payment code goes through me," he began. "A lot of times, the codes will reflect a date for the transaction or part of the company name or possibly the employee who manages that client. They don't really have a standard system; it's something I'd like to improve as it would minimize confusion...sorry. That's beside the point.

25

"A couple weeks back, I processed a billing code for a contractor that began with HJM. I happened to watch the news that evening and a man by the name of Horace J. Manwith—"

Cari cut him off. "Horace J. Manwith! The man who was hit by the garbage truck?"

Robby exhaled again. "Okay, so you see where I'm headed. I processed another code this afternoon. It started with ECF and then I heard someone named Elaine Frobish died from a fall today. Once felt like a fluke, but twice?"

"That is concerning. Have you talked to Genevieve or someone else with the police?" Cari asked. "They are investigating Frobish's death."

"No, I…I'm worried I could get in trouble too. What if I'm approving payments for some sort of hitman?" Robby asked, fear in his voice.

Cari managed to bite back a laugh. A hitman? It seemed like a stretch. "That might be taking things a bit far. Why don't you send me the codes and the dates and times of the transactions? I can look into the background of these two people and see if there's anything else going on."

"Thanks, Cari. I'm usually a pretty rational guy and you're right, I feel like some sort of conspiracy theorist by suggesting I'm aiding a serial killer or something, but it just feels off," Robby told her.

"This is your personal cell phone, right?" Cari asked him.

"Yeah, this one is mine. NTS issued me a phone when I started, so I've always got two cell phones on me. It took a bit to get used to; I'm supposed to have the NTS phone on at all times. Luckily, no one's ever called during a movie or concert, so I haven't had to be *that guy*," he replied with a chuckle. "Keep me posted on what you find. I do keep this phone on silent during the day, but I can chat at night and sometimes during my lunch break."

"Sounds good. I'll be in touch if or when I find something," Cari told him and ended the call.

She grabbed her water glass and rinsed her mouth. She didn't want to forget about Robby's request, so she padded back out to her living room and pulled out her notebook. She wrote down Robby, HJM, and ECF. That, along with whatever he emailed her, would be enough to get her started in the morning after her stop at City Hall, of course.

* * * * *

Brenington City Hall closed at noon on Fridays. Three people stood in line ahead of Cari at the front desk. She had considered calling in her request before arriving in hopes of shortening her visit, but experience told her they might not have the information readily available.

She checked her email on her phone while she waited her turn. Robby had sent the codes, dates, and times already. He'd included three codes in his email spanning the last four months. She raised her eyebrows; she wasn't someone who kept up with the obituary section of the newspaper, but had there really been three suspicious deaths in that time frame?

"Excuse me, Ms. Turnlyle? Come back to earth! It's your turn." A voice broke into her thoughts.

"Huh? Oh, sorry!" Cari exclaimed. She looked up from her phone to see Barbara Strothers giving her a pointed look from behind the glass partitions. The older woman wore a navy-blue blazer with a white blouse as well as her signature red-framed reading glasses hanging from her neck with a string of pearls.

"Hi, Ms. Strothers. I'm here to get a list of all the new neighborhoods and new apartment complexes," she explained.

Ms. Strothers pulled her red frames up to her eyes. "That's quite a list; it seems like something new is going up every week. Let me get that pulled up and printed for you."

Cari smiled with relief. She didn't want to have to dig through records on her own to get the building information. "Does your list include the builders and contractors by any chance?"

The woman pursed her lips. "No, Ms. Turnlyle. If you want that information, you need to go down to records and pull each file on this list I'm printing for you. Records is with archives downstairs. You remember how to get down there?"

Cari forced a smile. "Yes, I remember. Thank you."

Ms. Strothers got up to retrieve the printout from the printer behind her. "Is there anything else I can help you with today?"

"I'm hoping to compile a similar list from the surrounding towns in our county. Do you know if I need to go to each City Hall to get that, or is it something I could request over the phone?" Cari asked as she took the sheet of paper from her.

"I'm not completely sure how other towns handle information requests, but it's probably easiest to call first. I've heard people say our City Hall is a bit prehistoric when it comes to technology," she said with a slight grin.

Cari smirked. She had been someone to say that very thing. "I appreciate your help, Ms. Strothers."

"Don't forget your login card," Ms. Strothers said and waved a bright pink index card at her.

"Oh, right. Thanks," Cari said.

She stepped out of the way so the next person in line could be helped. She glanced at the list Ms. Strothers had printed for her. It had three neighborhoods and two apartment complexes, so only five things to look up. She looked at her watch. It was after nine already. She felt guilty asking an intern to do her grunt work, especially now that they were on the verge of not getting paid. Still, it was good experience, and it saved her a lot of time. She could take care of the list for Brenington but have an intern do the other three towns.

Hopefully, she could find the builders and contractors for each quickly and get back to her office. She really wanted to investigate Elaine Frobish's death some more and she needed to look into Robby's problem too. She ran a hand through her curls; it was going to be a busy day.

Chapter 4

A call came in on Genevieve's Bluetooth as she drove to the station Friday morning. She saw it was her contact at the FBI, Agent Dureski and answered it. She tried to make a good impression with him every chance she got.

"Hello, Agent Dureski. What's up?" she asked.

"Viacorte. Do you have a minute?" he asked in a guarded tone.

"Of course," she responded while thinking, *that's why I answered.*

"I'm sure you caught the Frobish woman's death. Our analysts flagged it this morning. It matches some of the criteria we've been keeping an eye out for," he told her.

"Are you taking over the case?" she asked with concern.

"No. We're not directly investigating anything at this point. Right now, whoever is behind all of this doesn't know we've started to connect the dots," he explained.

Genevieve wracked her brain to try to remember what he might be referring to and it finally hit her. "You're referring to the investigation regarding New Technology Systems."

"Yes, Viacorte. Keep up. Where was I?" he paused. "Oh right. Connecting the dots. Only a few people have been read in on this; I'm never confident that someone won't leak details. We've also had some indications there might be a mole in my division, so everything is on a need-to-know basis. To be completely honest, the only reason I'm contacting you is because you have a connection to someone who's possibly directly involved," he explained.

Genevieve resisted the urge to sigh in disappointment. "I understand. I assume you mean Robby Rialto, my friend's brother-in-law."

"Yes. Tell me again what you know regarding Rialto," Dureski requested.

"I watched their kids last Friday while they were out for dinner. After the kids were in bed, I looked in his office, but I didn't find anything like a ledger. I'm not sure what I'm supposed to be looking for," Genevieve said and cringed.

"Have you tried talking to him? I thought you had confirmation something funny was going on with his job?" Dureski pushed back.

Genevieve bit her lower lip before saying something she'd regret. *It's not like you can just ask someone if they have been covering up for a murderer.* "I did hear that from his sister-in-law. I don't know what the issue is and I'm not sure how to bring it up without it being awkward."

Dureski grumbled something under his breath. "Here's the thing: this case gets bigger all the time. I've been working it for close to a year, since before Rialto was in the picture. For that reason, I don't think he necessarily knows all the details, but I think he could fill in some blanks for us," Dureski explained.

"The Frobish woman's death...you said it fit some sort of pattern. What's the pattern, if you can tell me?" Genevieve asked him as she parked her car. She kept it running so the call didn't cut out while it switched back to her phone from the Bluetooth.

"Over the last year, several small business owners have died. For example, there's this small construction firm. They do bathroom remodels and stuff like that. The owner was getting ready to head to a job site, but his car battery was dead. He was going to jump it with his wife's car, but something went wrong and he was electrocuted."

"Oh my God, how terrible," Genevieve remarked.

"I mean, that kind of thing happens more often than you'd think, but not with someone in construction. He should have definitely known how to safely jump a car battery. Hell, my sixteen-year-old son can jump a car, no problem," Dureski continued. "About a month after his death, the company was bought out by another business. Most of his workers were laid off during the buyout. The guy had kids; it's weird he didn't leave the business to one of them."

"Did anyone investigate?" Genevieve asked. *Is it really that unusual for someone to buy a business when the previous owner dies?*

"Not as thoroughly as I'd like, but that was just the beginning. At that point, nothing seemed completely out of the ordinary; it wasn't really on our radar. We identified his death as part of the pattern after the fact. This same kind of thing has happened multiple times with small business owners, not all in the same way, but all seemingly accidental deaths and followed by a sale of the business," Dureksi told her.

"But you said the other guy was in construction. Frobish owned a fitness company," Genevieve argued.

"Right. It isn't all construction and a quick look at the sales won't point to the same buyer, but we've found some things that link these purchasing companies together," he explained.

"Like one big parent company with multiple specialties? Seems like a disaster," Genevieve commented.

"Possibly, I haven't really worked out the finer details yet," Dureski told her. "When you talk to Frobish's family members, see if you can find out if anyone approached her about selling her business."

Genevieve pulled out her notebook and wrote it down. "Sure. Anything else?"

"You're a good detective. Follow your instincts. Keep me posted. And find a way to get to Rialto. I think he could be the key," Dureski instructed her and ended the call.

Genevieve slid her phone into her pocket and turned off the Expedition. She looked at the brief set of notes she'd taken while talking to Dureski. He wasn't telling her everything, which made it hard to decipher what was really happening. Without the full background, it kind of felt like they were stretching to make connections. She wasn't totally sure how Robby's company fit into the picture either. She flipped the notebook closed. Time to find some clues to how Frobish went over the edge.

* * * * *

It took Cari almost two hours to look up the builders and contractors for each of the neighborhoods and apartment complexes on the list. The two apartment complexes used the same construction company and not surprisingly, many of the subcontractors overlapped too. The new neighborhoods had some of the same subcontractors and builders as well. She found an email and phone number for the person in charge of each project and sent it to herself from the public computer. She planned to email each of them and maybe call one or two for a quote in the article.

She packed up her belongings and logged out of everything on the computer. Thankfully, there was no line at the front desk when she got back upstairs. She returned the pink index card to Barbara who scanned it to verify she hadn't printed anything. On her way out of City Hall, she called Michelle.

"Brenington Beagle, this is Michelle. How can I help you?" Michelle asked sweetly.

"Hi, Michelle. It's Cari. I have some work for one of our summer interns," Cari informed her.

"Okay, what do you need?" she asked.

"I need to get a list of new neighborhoods and apartment complexes for the other three towns in our county as well as the builders and contractors for each project," Cari responded. She turned out of the parking lot and headed toward the office.

"Okay, let me write this down. Just a second," Michelle said slowly. "Okay, got it. What else?"

"I think that's it. I already contacted the chambers of commerce for those towns," Cari told her.

"How far back should they go? A year? Six months?" Michelle asked for clarification.

"Eight months, please," she responded.

"Okay, I'll get one of them started on it. When do you need it?" Michelle asked her.

"Ollaman told me ASAP, so I guess that's when I need it. Thanks so much, Michelle!" Cari said genuinely.

"No problem. Hopefully, it won't take too long to round up this information. See you in the office," Michelle said and ended the call.

Cari pulled into the parking garage and turned her car off. She grabbed her messenger bag and headed for the elevator bay. The office building wasn't as bustling as usual, probably because it was summer and people were on vacation. She entered the newsroom and took a seat at her desk.

It took her a few iterations to get the wording how she wanted it for her email to the builders. She used the same method from the day before with the chamber of commerce emails to contact each person on the list. She didn't feel it necessary to contact the subcontractors as they weren't really part of the expansion planning process. She wasn't sure how she wanted to include that information in the article yet, so she saved it for later. The day was half over; she wanted to get onto the Frobish investigation.

Cari flipped to a new page in her notebook. She opened a browser window and looked up Elaine C. Frobish on social media. The woman had accounts on multiple platforms. Several people had posted offering their condolences to her family. She scrolled through the posts until she found one from a family member: her daughter, from the looks of it. Luna Harrison had posted a tribute to her mother's perseverance, love, and character. It sounded like they were close. Cari typed the woman's name into LexisNexis to look her up.

"Bingo!" she exclaimed.

Luna's phone number was part of the listing. Cari saved it into her cell phone so she'd have it for later. She jotted down the woman's address in her notebook. Calling her seemed somewhat inconsiderate and rude, considering her mother had just passed away yesterday. She didn't want to seem like a vulture, but she was curious to know more about Ms. Frobish. She set aside the daughter's information and looked up Fit Winners on social media next.

The fitness business had a Facebook page, so Cari navigated to the About tab and found the link to its website. An image of a very fit-looking Elaine Frobish stared back at her from the screen. She clicked on the menu and found the Contact Us tab. The web page included an address, phone number, and email address. Cari figured it was a fifty-fifty chance the business would be open today. She knew some places wouldn't open out of respect for the owner, but this was a service industry. They might feel obligated to their patrons. She gathered up her things and locked her workstation. Her stomach rumbled as she stood up from her desk. She could grab lunch on her way over to the fitness center.

* * * * *

When Genevieve got inside, Alex was just sitting down at his desk. He gave her a nod and took a sip from the coffee mug in his hand. Then he pointed at her desk. She looked over and saw he'd filled up her mug too. She draped her bag over her chair and picked up the mug.

"Wow, Alex! Thanks for filling up my cup," she said with a smile.

"I was feeling generous. Plus, we've got a long day ahead of us. I called the daughter. She agreed to meet with us in just a few minutes, so suck that coffee down," he said and stood up.

"A few minutes?! I just got here. I assume you mean our victim's daughter?" Genevieve tried to catch up.

She blew on the coffee and took a sip; it wasn't overly hot. He actually remembered to put honey in it. Wonders never cease.

"Yes, Luna Harrison. It's probably faster to walk to her house, but I'd rather drive in case we need to go somewhere else," he said and pulled the keys to the cruiser off the wall hook.

Genevieve took a drink from her mug. "Let me just see if I got that file from the park ranger."

She logged into her computer and checked her email. Sure enough, an email from Ted with an attachment sat in her inbox. She opened it and saw three attachments: two video files and one zipped file that probably had the images.

"Cool. We've got the files from Ted," she said and locked her computer. "I'm bringing my coffee. Don't drive like a crazy person."

"When have I ever done that?" Alex feigned hurt.

She rolled her eyes and followed him to the exit. "I'm no rookie, Runimoss."

They climbed into the cruiser and Alex drove out of the parking lot. He made a quick right turn that almost splashed coffee into Genevieve's lap. She barely kept the liquid contained.

"C'mon, man!" she exclaimed.

"Oh, right. Sorry, I actually did forget you brought the coffee," Alex admitted. "Mrs. Harrison lives one block west of here."

He pulled alongside the curb in front of a one-story house with tan-colored siding and cream-colored stonework. The yard was well-maintained and consisted of neatly trimmed boxy shrubs in front of the windows and some pink petunias planted around the base of a large tree. They got out of the car and walked up to the front door. A petite woman with jet-black hair and tanned skin answered the door when Genevieve knocked. She looked to be in her late twenties. Her eyes were red and her face was blotchy. She wore an over-sized yellow t-shirt and black leggings.

"You must be the detectives. Luna Harrison," she extended her hand.

"Detective Runimoss. We spoke on the phone. This is my partner, Detective Viacorte," Alex said and shook her hand.

"Please, come inside. It's a bit of a wreck, but we're coping," Mrs. Harrison told them.

A grey yoga mat was in the middle of the living room floor in front of the television. Three other mats were rolled up in the corner and some free weights were strewn around the room. The young woman closed a laptop and unclipped a white, plastic object from her t-shirt. Alex moved one dumbbell off of the sofa and took a seat. Genevieve joined him.

"Sorry, I was getting ready to record a yoga video when you got here," she told them as she set the device aside and sat across from them on the loveseat. "This is my wireless mic."

Genevieve glanced at Alex and wondered why the woman would try to record anything in her haggard state, but especially at the same time she'd said she could meet with them. He raised his eyebrows but remained silent.

"Do you live alone, Ms. Harrison?" Genevieve asked her.

"Excuse me?" Harrison gave her a confused look.

"You said 'we're coping,'" Genevieve reminded her.

"Oh, uh, I have a live-in boyfriend. He's at work. Did you need to speak with him?" she asked the detectives.

"Not at this time," Genevieve responded.

"Mrs. Harrison," Alex began.

"Please, call me Luna. Mrs. Harrison makes me sound so old. I'm not even married," she said. She pulled a hair elastic from her wrist and wrapped it around her long hair. "That's better. I really need to wash it, but with everything going on…I'm sorry. You're here to talk about Mom."

Alex nodded. "Luna, we are terribly sorry for your loss. We understand your mom owned a business in town."

Luna nodded. "Yes, it's called Fit Winners. She targeted middle-aged women but would never turn anyone away. Most of her classes were made up of women around forty to sixty years old, though."

Genevieve nodded and made a note. "Did she teach all of the classes, or are there other instructors?"

"Initially, it was just Mom. She opened the business when I was young, around the time Dad disappeared from our lives. She'd always been into fitness and is, um, *was* a licensed trainer. It was a lot of work; I think there were days she worked over sixteen hours. But she loved it," Luna said wistfully. "She was able to hire more trainers after my brother and I were done with college."

"How old is your brother?" Alex asked.

Luna blinked. "Leo lived a hard life. He never forgave our dad for deserting us. He struggled with alcoholism for many years and his liver finally gave out on him two years ago."

Genevieve swallowed hard. "I'm so sorry."

Luna waved her off. "He's all better now. No longer suffering. The last six months were really hard. I miss him, but I know he's okay now."

Alex cleared his throat. "Back to your mother. Did she always hike alone?"

Luna grimaced. "I told her that wasn't safe regardless of how experienced she is at hiking, but she never listened. She rarely went hiking with someone else."

35

"Did she have any enemies? Was anyone threatening her?" Alex asked her.

Luna paled. "I thought she fell. I thought it was an accident."

Genevieve spoke up. "We aren't certain what happened. There is some indication that it might not have been an accident. That's why we're investigating."

"I don't think anyone was upset with Mom. She was friendly, a good boss... everyone liked her as far as I know."

"Did your mother have a business partner?" Genevieve asked her.

Luna shook her head. "I don't think so. It was just her toughing it out alone, but like I said, I was pretty young when she opened the place."

Alex leaned forward. "Do you think your grandparents might have helped her get the business off the ground? Typically, there tend to be a lot of fees, plus the rent for the space, all the equipment, and so forth. It seems like she would need some help."

Luna looked perplexed. "I just don't know. I never heard her talk about anything like that. Maybe it's in her records somewhere. Have you been to her house yet?"

Genevieve shook her head no. "We plan to go there later today."

"Do you need a key? I have a spare." Luna rose from the couch as she spoke.

"We got one...um, we found her keys already," Genevieve said gently. "Does she have an alarm or anything we need a code for?"

"Yes, she does have an alarm. It's a four-digit code...um...let me think. It's her birth month and year," Luna told them.

Genevieve made a note. "Thanks. You said you were going to record a yoga video. Did you work for your mom?"

"Oh, no. This is my own thing. I'm strictly online, no in-person classes for me," Luna said pointedly.

"Did your mom ever try to get you to join her business?" Alex asked.

Luna bunched her lips before responding. "Well, I did kind of feel like she wished I would ask if I could come alongside her, but I like doing my own thing. I think she understood that."

Genevieve nodded. "Has anyone else approached you about her business since your mother's body was found?"

Luna gulped. "Approached me? Like her employees or the media or what do you mean?"

Genevieve felt Alex staring at her but ignored him. "The media or anyone inquiring about the business perhaps. Like one of her co-workers?"

"I don't think so. I've only heard from you guys and the police officers who came by yesterday to tell me her body was found," she said with a confused expression.

Genevieve nodded and made a note. Alex stood up, indicating he was finished asking questions. "I think that's all we need from you today, Luna. If you think of anything else, here's my card. Give me a call any time."

They made their way out to the cruiser and Alex clicked a button on the fob to unlock the doors. He paused with his door partway open and looked at Genevieve.

"Why did you ask about someone approaching her about her mom's business?"

Genevieve tried to remain stoic. "I'm just trying to cover all the bases here, Alex. Maybe someone has an interest in the business."

He pursed his lips and got into the driver's seat. "I guess. In some ways, it seems like she was really close with her mom, but in other ways, I'm not so sure. It's weird she doesn't know how her mom got the capital needed to start up a business."

"Should we go visit her house? See if we can find any of her records?" Genevieve suggested.

"Look up the address. I'm driving," he said and turned on the car.

* * * * *

Cari shoved the final bite of her pulled pork taco into her mouth. Several vehicles were parked in the lot outside the fitness center. The blue and white sign above the door was lit up, indicating they were open. She could see a young man seated behind a desk near the front door too. Fit Winners was between a frozen yogurt shop called Yo-Go-Go and a craft store called Crafting that looked suspiciously un-crafty. Cari hadn't visited any of the businesses before and wondered if Bea's kids had tried the yogurt place. It looked like something they'd enjoy. She wiped her mouth off with a napkin and tossed it into the passenger seat. Then she remembered Bob's most recent reaction to riding in her car and reached over to pick it up and put it into the paper bag instead. She grabbed her lunch trash and her messenger bag and got out of the car.

A conveniently placed garbage can sat near the entrance to the fitness center. Cari tossed her bag inside and then opened her messenger bag to find her digital recorder. It took a little rummaging, but she finally located it and switched it on. Then she pulled on the handle of the glass door to open it. A bell rang and the young man looked up at her. His dark hair was cut very short and his smile reached his eyes as she entered the building.

"Welcome to Fit Winners! First time here?" he asked and then paused. "Uh, do you have a change of clothes? I don't think you want to sweat in that business suit."

She flashed him a smile. "I'm not here to exercise, actually. I was hoping to talk to a few people about Ms. Frobish. I'm Cari Turnlyle with the Beagle. Did you know Ms. Frobish well?"

The smile on his face faded. "Elaine? Yeah, she was a great boss. We all knew she would be mad if we closed because of what happened, so we're all here in her honor."

Cari glanced at his nametag. *Nash.* "That's a nice thing to do, Nash. It sounds like Elaine was well-liked around here."

He bobbed his head up and down. "Definitely. She was a great boss. She helped me get into a class so I can be an instructor here too. I'm not sure if that's still going to be an option now."

"Do you know who is taking over the business?" Cari asked him.

Before he could answer a woman in her mid-forties came up to the desk from the doorway behind Nash. Her greying brown-ish hair was in a low ponytail and her fingernails were painted bright turquoise. She had a towel over one shoulder and looked like she might have just finished a class.

"My name's Tally. Are you here to try out a class or...? She trailed off after looking at Cari's attire.

"My name is Cari. I'm with the Brenington Beagle. Nash and I were just chatting about Elaine and the fitness center. I take it you're an instructor here?" Cari asked with a smile.

"I am. I was the second employee she hired. I started taking her classes about a decade ago, when all of my kids were finally in school. She helped me get certified and then hired me as an instructor," Tally explained.

"Wow, was she certified to teach licensing classes?" Cari asked.

They both shook their heads before Tally responded. "Not yet. She was working on it on the side, but hadn't gotten it finished. Wait, I recognize your name. You're the journalist who has solved all those murder cases with the police. Wait, do you think Elaine was murdered?"

Cari put her hands up. "Woah, I'm not saying that at all. I'm not sure if the police have labeled her death one way or the other yet."

Nash frowned. "But who would want to hurt Elaine? Everyone loved Elaine."

"We heard she fell or lost her footing while she was hiking at the state park. Is that right?" Tally asked in a concerned tone.

Cari bobbed her head. "That's what I've been told too. Was it normal for her to take a day off in the middle of the week?"

Tally scrunched up her face. "I mean, yes and no. She used to never do it, but if the weather was nice, she really liked being outside. She always made sure things were covered around here. Nash is a pro running the front desk and she didn't have a class to lead yesterday, so why not take advantage of a lovely day?"

Cari nodded. "That makes sense."

"You asked who was going to take over the business now," Nash reminded her. "We don't really know." He turned to Tally. "I guess this means we won't be getting the exercise pool after all."

Cari looked from one to the other, unsure what Nash was talking about. "Exercise pool?"

Tally spoke up. "Yeah, Elaine wanted to build on to the business. We have space behind where a small exercise pool could fit. It would be really great for people with joint pain, which is a lot of our clientele."

"Would it have been an outside pool?" Cari asked, wondering how that would be feasible in the winter.

"No, the addition would be enclosed. I don't remember the exact dimensions, but it's just a small pool, not like a lap pool or anything. Like an extra-large hot tub," Tally explained. "But back to who will own the business now. I suppose it could be her daughter."

"Oh! I didn't realize her daughter worked here," Cari told them.

Tally shook her head no. "She doesn't. She has her own online yoga thing."

"Had Elaine ever talked to you about coming on as a partner with her?" Cari asked Tally.

"No, and I would have turned her down. I don't need the added stress," Tally informed her. "I think she planned to maintain control even after she got to be too old to work out, which we all thought would be well into her nineties. She didn't want a business partner, at least from my perspective."

"Yeah, for sure. She was really independent; hated to be told what to do," Nash offered.

"What do you mean?" Cari asked, intrigued.

"There was this one guy who called here a few times in the past month," Nash remarked.

Cari leaned forward. "What one guy? A local guy?"

Nash shrugged. "I didn't pay attention to his number, but he could have been. He called three or more times and asked for Elaine every time. He never identified himself, but I recognized his voice. It had an edge to it."

"Like a nasally sound?" Cari asked.

"No, it was deeper. It was harsh like he was annoyed with me before I said anything," Nash explained.

"How did the conversation with Elaine go?" Cari pressed him.

Nash raised his eyebrows. "It's like the only time I've ever seen her mad. The last time he called, she took the phone from me and said, 'No means no…' uh, and added another word after that."

"I think I can infer what that might be," Cari remarked. "What do you think he wanted?"

"I'm not sure. Maybe he wanted to buy the business?" Nash suggested with a shrug.

"She'd never sell this place. It's her baby. It's what kept her going when she was out of things to lean on," Tally told her.

"What do you mean?" Cari asked.

"Elaine opened this place after her husband deserted her and their kids. He just up and left one day. No goodbye, just a scrawled note on a scrap of paper saying he didn't want this life anymore," Tally said with anger in her eyes.

"That's horrible. Those poor kids and Elaine. But how was she able to open a new business? Had she been working before?" Cari asked confusedly.

"She got a loan from the bank. First, she called all the moms on the PTA at her kids' schools. Asked if they'd sign a document saying they'd be interested in fitness classes for moms. She got over a hundred signatures just like that," Tally snapped her fingers. "Then she walked in that bank with her head held high and pitched her business. I know it seems like a long shot, but they liked it and signed off on the loan."

"Impressive. She clearly had a mind for business," Cari said. "Nash, do you think you could find the phone number for that grumpy caller for me? I'd like to try and figure out who that is."

His eyebrows went up. "Maybe. I'm not sure how far back this thing holds caller IDs."

He picked up the handset and pressed a few buttons. "Let's see. The last time he called was maybe on Monday? Yeah, it was Monday after lunch…oh, bummer."

"What is it?" Cari asked.

Nash turned the phone her way. "This is definitely the guy."

The screen read *UNKNOWN CALLER.*

"You're sure?" Cari asked trying to hide the disappointment from her voice.

"Yeah, because Mrs. Keller called right after him and that's the next number on the list," he explained. "She's a regular here."

Cari pulled out her notebook and made a note to mention phone records to Gen. This unknown caller seemed like a good lead and she didn't really want to let it go. She put her notebook back and looked at Nash.

"Nash, it seems like the police might be interested in who is behind those calls. You could call the business' phone company and ask for the information associated with that call," she suggested.

Nash blinked. "Really? Even though I don't own the business?"

Cari wasn't sure how it worked as she hadn't tried to track down an unknown caller before in this way. "Maybe? It's worth a shot. If they ask for a pin number or something, then you're probably out of luck."

Nash's face brightened "Oh! I know the pin! We had an issue with the phone lines earlier this year and I was constantly trying to get them out here to fix it. Elaine gave me the pin so I could take care of it rather than constantly having her come out to validate the call."

Cari felt the hair on her arms stand up. "Well, what are you waiting for, Nash? Call them up and see what they'll tell you."

Nash pulled a sticky note from the computer screen. Then he punched a number into the handset. Cari silently willed him to put the call on speaker.

"I'm going to put it on speaker so you can hear too," he said to Cari's delight. Tally gave him the side eye but remained silent.

An automated voice started listing several options, but Nash immediately pressed a button before it finished. Cari realized he must have been through the process enough times he already knew which option to choose. The voice told him they were seventh in line to speak with a representative and offered to have the call returned at the same number.

"I'm just going to have them call us back when it's our turn," Nash said, pressing the number one. "That way if we get a call to the gym, I can still answer it without worrying I'm missing the phone company."

Cari tried to hide her disappointment. "That makes sense. When they do call back, would you be willing to share the information with me?"

Nash shrugged. "Sure. Do you have a card?"

She fished a card out of her bag and passed it to him. "I really appreciate it. Before I go, is there anything else you can tell me about Elaine?"

They exchanged a glance, and Tally spoke. "Honestly, she's the best boss I've ever had. I really hope the business stays open. I know it won't be the same, but we'll try our best to run things like she did."

Nash nodded. "For sure. She gave this place a great vibe. She was, like, the most fit old person I know. No offense, Tally."

"You're not going to get an argument from me. I can't believe she lost her footing on the hike. She was a rock climber too, you know?" Tally reminded Nash, who nodded.

"I had no idea," Cari responded. "Do you have a wall here? Or did she practice somewhere else?"

Tally smiled. "She had a wall installed a year or two ago. It's really popular. She was so strong, and not just physically but mentally too. If she slipped, I feel confident she could have climbed back up."

"Oh, for sure," Nash remarked. "I didn't even think about her rock-climbing skills. I think you might be right. Someone must have pushed her over."

Cari gulped. "I'm sure the detectives will want to speak with everyone here too and they'd probably prefer it if you didn't post anything with the word *murder* in it while they're still investigating."

"Got it," Nash said. "Anything we can do to help."

The front door opened and several middle-aged women in spandex outfits strolled in with water bottles and mats in-hand. Cari took it as a cue to make her exit.

"Thanks again for your time. Please let me know what you hear from the phone company," she requested.

Nash smiled and gave her a quick nod before turning to greet the group of ladies. Cari made her way back out to her car and got inside. She shut off her digital recorder and took her notebook out again. Elaine, as a rock climber, shed a different light on her fall down the cliffside.

Chapter 5

A vibrating phone pulled Genevieve from her thoughts. She pulled out her phone and saw their boss, Lieutenant Grusky was calling. Alex gave her a glance.

"Hello, Lieutenant," Genevieve said and put the call on speaker.

"How did it go with the daughter?" he asked in a clipped tone.

"She was surprised to hear her mom's death wasn't necessarily an accident. She wasn't really *grieving* in a way you might expect, but I don't view her as a suspect," Genevieve commented.

"Say more," Grusky responded.

"It was a little odd. She knew we were coming over and yet she had set up her living room to record a yoga video for her business or website. She was very matter-of-fact about everything, yet seemed to be close with her mother," Genevieve told him.

"It almost seemed like she had decided she wasn't going to cry yet because she didn't have time for that right now," Alex observed.

"Yes, she also didn't know of anyone who was upset with her mother. She was shocked that we thought there was a chance someone might have pushed her off the cliff," she explained.

"That is interesting. I'm not sure if you heard, but they did find the missing fingernails. She must have been scrabbling to grab something and hold onto it. The nails were about twenty feet down," Grusky told them.

"Ouch, that hurts my hands so much. Ugh," Alex shuddered. "I want to talk to her employees next. We have a request in for her financials. We're on our way to look through her home office and see if we can find any business records there. Her daughter didn't know much about how she was able to start the business from scratch."

Grusky cleared his throat. "Sounds good. Chris hasn't gotten into her phone yet, but I'm sure it's just a matter of time."

"Any word on the autopsy?" Genevieve asked.

"I think Green is doing it right now. He put in a request to rush the tox screen through the lab. I think the chief will probably approve it, but you never know. Keep me posted," he said and ended the call.

Alex was familiar enough with Brenington that he hadn't asked her to pull up any directions. She was curious about where the woman lived so she put the address into her maps app. She recognized the area and realized the woman lived in a townhouse, not a single-family home. She wondered if they would need a gate code, though the daughter hadn't mentioned it.

"This address is for a townhouse in a subdivision. Do you think it has a gate code?" she asked Alex.

He shrugged. "I guess we'll find out. Isn't there a fob or something on her keychain?"

Genevieve grabbed her bag from the console. "Her keys are in my bag. Let me check."

She opened the side pocket and found the keychain. She flipped through the items on it. "No fob. Maybe it was in her car. Like a card or something."

"That's possible. So, what are we looking for besides her business records?" Alex asked as he steered toward the address.

"I'm not sure what to expect. I guess I'll know it when I see it," she said vaguely.

"Do you think she could have been meeting someone at the park yesterday?" he proposed.

Genevieve raised her eyebrows. "That's definitely possible. Maybe Chris will find something on her phone for us if that's the case."

They passed a shopping strip and took a right. She checked the GPS even though she was pretty sure the townhouses were just a few blocks away. The navigation screen confirmed her memory. Large green and turquoise balloons blew in the breeze outside the entrance, advertising a move-in sale. She breathed a sigh of relief when she saw the gate was open.

"We should stop by the office and ask for a gate code or card in case we need to come back when they aren't open," she told Alex.

They parked in a visitor space near Ms. Frobish's unit. The townhouses were replicas with tan paint and white trim. A community swimming pool sat in the middle of the complex. She could hear kids splashing and parents yelling for them to walk. Alex pointed at the keys. She looked at the knob before inserting the key into it.

"It doesn't look like anyone picked the lock or anything," she observed. "Did you check with the alarm company before we came over here?"

"Yeah, they confirmed no one has been inside since yesterday and whoever left used the owner's code to set the alarm," he told her.

"Which means it was probably her," Genevieve remarked. "Ready for me to unlock it?"

"Ready with the alarm code?" Alex asked as she turned the key.

"0-3-7-6," she said as she pushed the door open.

The alarm started beeping. The panel wasn't by the front door, so they raced toward the garage exit to look for a keypad. Alex beat her to it and entered the code, silencing the alarm.

"This is a nice place. I wonder what it costs to buy one, or do you rent these?" Alex asked.

"Probably some of both. Why? Are you and your wife thinking of moving?" she asked him.

"No, she would have to get rid of too much clutter to ever move. We'll probably die in our house, smothered by all her craft projects," he grumbled.

"Stop it. I like her projects. She made me a scarf last year!" Genevieve berated him.

"Whatever, but seriously, this is a nice place. Everything in the kitchen looks new: stainless appliances, granite countertops, hardwood floor. It's fancy," he told her.

"Since when did you become such a connoisseur of real estate?" she asked him as they walked through the ground level in search of an office.

"Sophia likes to watch house flipping shows on the weekends, so I sit with her," he shrugged. "That looks like it must be her office."

Genevieve looked where Alex was pointing. They had crossed from the dining room back to the hallway. The guest bathroom sat midway down the hall between two small bedrooms. One had a desk with a laptop open on it and the other had a bed and a dresser. Another door at the end of the hallway was closed. She figured that was probably the master bedroom.

"Seems like it," she agreed with him.

They entered the office and looked at the computer screen. It was dark, so Genevieve swiped a finger across the mouse pad. Nothing happened.

"Should we just bag it and let CSU look through it?" she asked Alex.

He frowned. "Hmmm…*or* we could give it a quick look."

She shrugged and pressed the power button. The machine whirred to life and the screen lit up. Genevieve pouted her lips.

"Any guess as to the password?" she asked him.

"She's close to my age. I don't see any sticky notes on the desk, but I bet there's one in the drawer somewhere," he responded as he moved past her to open the top desk drawer. "Just as I guessed. They always tell you not to do this, but who can remember a password?"

He pulled out a pale-yellow slip of paper with a series of numbers, letters, and symbols written in blue ink.

"Here, you type it in," he said and handed it to her.

She smirked and took it from him. "For a minute there, I thought you were going to surprise me with your computer savviness, but this is more on par."

"Hilarious," he grumbled.

She typed the password into the box and hit the enter key. The desktop screen appeared; it was littered with tiny file icons. Genevieve shuddered. Did no one teach these people how to take care of a computer?

"What's up?" Alex asked.

"This is a mess. She's got files all over the desktop," she told him.

He looked at the clean desktop. "What? Where?"

She pointed at the screen. "Not *that* desktop, the computer desktop location. She's saving almost everything there. It's completely unorganized and it slows down the computer."

"It does?" he asked with his eyebrows raised.

"Let me do a quick search," she said with a huff.

She clicked on the file folder near the start menu and waited for it to open. Then she typed finance into the search box. Zero results. Fit Winners yielded fifty-six results. She minimized the folder and looked at the desktop again. Several files were labeled with FW and a number, which looked a lot like a month and year combination. She opened what she assumed was the most recent one: FW0626. The folder had an Excel file, a few PDFs, and some Word documents. She opened the Excel file.

"This looks like a list of new gym members. I was hoping to find something with her financials," Genevieve said.

"Maybe she uses one of those programs that does a lot of the work for you," Alex suggested.

"Oh, good call, Alex. Let me look at her apps."

She clicked on the start menu and scrolled through all the applications on the device. Sure enough, one of them was a bookkeeping app. She double-clicked to open it.

"Bingo. Looks like her business is doing well and has been," she said as she scrolled through the entries.

"You're familiar with this program?" Alex asked, dumbfounded.

"No, not really. I'm sure Bob or Chris can decipher it better, but I'm glad to know it's on here. Let's bag it and bring it to them when we get back," she told him.

"Look in the trash. Several envelopes and papers. Looks like she tore one up," Alex observed and pulled some bits of paper out of the black plastic waste basket.

Genevieve watched as he maneuvered the pieces around. It was a typed letter, but it didn't have a letterhead. Alex hadn't found the signature pieces yet and several of the pieces with the body of the letter were missing too. She tried to read it anyway.

"Does that say something about calling in regards to her business?" Genevieve asked him.

"I think that's what it was getting at. I don't really want to dig any deeper into the trash can. See if you can find a garbage bag and we can bring all of it in for CSU too," he directed her.

"They're going to love that," Genevieve said under her breath as she walked to the kitchen.

Alex yelled at her from the opposite side of the townhouse. "I'm going through her bedroom now!"

She found a garbage bag and emptied the contents from the plastic trash can into it. She set it near the front door and then joined Alex in the master bedroom. He was opening and closing drawers.

"I'm looking to see if she has a journal or anything like that," he told her.

They searched the whole room but came up empty. It was possible the woman didn't keep a journal. Genevieve had another idea. She opened the door to the master bathroom.

"Here it is," she said, picking up a leather journal from next to the jetted bathtub.

"Good call. It's a wonder no one ever drops a book into the tub while they're multitasking like that," he chuckled.

She paged through the journal. "It's all workout plans and stuff like that. Not like a diary. It's more of a fitness journal, I guess."

"I don't think we need anything else here. Let's stop by the leasing office and see what they can tell us about the gate," Alex responded.

Before she could respond, his phone buzzed with an incoming call.

"Runimoss speaking…hey, Bob. Interesting. That makes more sense. Thanks," he ended the call and put the phone back in his pocket. "That was

CSU. They found one of those earbud thingies at the site yesterday. It paired with her phone when they charged it."

"Only one?" Genevieve asked.

"That's what he said. Maybe the other one is lost in the brush somewhere," he shrugged. "I bet she was using the earpiece to talk on the phone, which she kept in her pocket."

Genevieve nodded slowly. "That fits better. I wonder who she was talking to. I guess they got her phone to turn on if the earbud paired with it."

"If you say so," Alex said with a clueless look. "Are we done here?"

"I'm just going to bag up the rest of the trash for CSU," she told him.

"Leave it. They can send a team out to collect it later," he responded.

"Back to the station then?" she asked.

"Yep. Let's reset the alarm on our way out," he suggested.

"Good call," she responded and opened the key pad on the alarm panel. "I still want to ask about the gate entry. Let's get this stuff in the trunk and then walk over to the office."

She keyed in the code to set the alarm and they hurried back out the front door. The office was to the left of the gate. She popped the trunk on the cruiser and tossed the trash bag inside while Alex added the bagged laptop. He closed the trunk and they crossed the parking area to get to the office. A wave of cool air hit them in the face when they opened the door. Genevieve smoothed a wayward strand of hair back in place and smiled at the woman behind the desk.

"I'm Detective Viacorte and this is my partner, Detective Runimoss. We're looking into the death of one of your residents, Ms. Frobish," Genevieve said quickly.

The woman had dark, brown hair and pale skin. She wore a polo shirt with the complex's logo on the left. She chewed on her lower lip before responding. "Ms. Frobish died?"

"I'm sorry, yes. She had a hiking accident yesterday," Alex explained. "We were wondering if you could tell us about the gate to the complex."

"But you're detectives...," she said slowly as though not hearing his question.

Genevieve leaned forward and looked the woman in the eyes. "Yes, detectives. The gate? Does it have a code or a controller or a key card?"

The woman blinked several times. "The gate?"

Alex nodded, his jaw working overtime. "Yes, the gate. How does one open it from the outside?"

"Oh, right. Um, yes, a key card or if you're visiting a resident, you can enter their number on the pad and it calls their phone. Then they can buzz you in," she explained.

Genevieve wondered if the key card was still in Frobish's car, then had another idea. "Does the system log an entry every time someone's card is swiped?"

The woman's head bobbed up and down. "Yes. It records it in our computer system."

"Can you see when Ms Frobish used her card last?" she asked.

"Let me pull it up for you. Just a moment," the woman finally seemed to have regained focus. She hit a few keys on the keyboard. "Here it is. She used it at 12:30 yesterday afternoon."

"And nothing since?" Genevieve asked.

The woman shook her head. "That was the last time."

"If we need to get back in and the gate is closed, is there a way for us to call the office to be admitted?" Genevieve asked her.

"Yes, there are instructions to connect to this desk for entrance," she replied.

"Thanks for your help," Alex said.

They exited the office and walked back to the cruiser. Alex pulled the keys from his pocket and tossed them to her. She barely caught them with one hand.

"You're not driving back?" she asked in surprise.

"No, I'm kind of hungry. I forgot to eat breakfast, so you're going to go to a drive-thru and help me remedy that," he said with a grin.

She rolled her eyes. "Really?"

* * * * *

Cari sighed. Gathering information for Ollaman's article took up the majority of her day. It was already past four o'clock and she was just now getting to the information Robby had shared with her. She opened the email and read through it again. On the phone, he'd implied this had happened several times, but the list only had three codes. She already knew that HJM was supposedly Manwith and ECF was Frobish, so she started with the third code. She opened a search engine and was about to look up the third code again when she caught movement from the corner of her eye. *Ollaman.* She had the urge to minimize the screen but resisted. Frobish's death was on her docket. She turned toward him.

49

"How's the research coming, Turnlyle?" he asked her.

She grabbed her messenger bag and pulled out the sheet from City Hall. "I got this printout from City Hall with all the new builds. I haven't heard back from all of the chambers yet, but hopefully by Monday."

"What about Frobish? Anything new there?" he gave her a pointed look.

She swallowed to keep herself from snapping that it was hard to cover two stories like these at the same time. "I talked to her co-workers. They mentioned someone was hounding her on the phone and it made her angry."

She gave him the short version of the conversation.

"That is interesting. I wonder what they wanted. Back to the other story, I had Michelle make a social media post asking for local businesses to email us if they opened between last Halloween and now. She's going to forward any responses to you, so be on the lookout!" he said, punctuating the last four words by pointing his index finger in the air.

Her computer dinged several times. "That must be her now. I'll add them to my list if they aren't already there. Thanks."

"Glad to help," he smiled and then continued on to Bryson's cubicle.

She pursed her lips. She was glad he trusted her with a story like this, but also wished he'd just do it himself if it was that important to the newspaper. She went back to Robby's list and tapped her pencil on her desk. The next code, 1603124, didn't have any letters. It didn't really look like a date either. He'd listed the date with the code, so she went to the newspaper archive site to find the edition with the closest date. Nothing in that issue mentioned anyone dying, nor were there any obituaries. She went to the Beagle's social media pages and searched for relevant posts on that date too, but still came up empty.

Maybe Robby was wrong about all this. She didn't know a lot about what happened with Manwith, so she looked up his obituary next. He was survived by his wife, a brother, a daughter, two sons, as well as other nieces, nephews, and cousins. He had inherited the electronics business about thirty years ago from his father and it had grown significantly in that time. She navigated to the business website. It didn't say anything about new ownership, so maybe that wasn't the link. She went back to the obituary and wrote down the wife and kids' names. It had been almost three weeks since Manwith died, so Cari felt like she wouldn't seem too heartless if she contacted them to talk about him. She looked up the daughter's number first. Cari wasn't sure if any of the man's children had taken over the business, but the oldest child was as good a place to start as any. The young woman answered after two rings.

"Is this Kristina Manwith?" Cari asked when the woman said hello.

"Who's calling please?" the female voice asked.

"This is Cari Turnlyle with the Brenington Beagle. I had a few questions for Ms. Manwith," she responded.

"This is Kristina. I don't usually answer, but my phone didn't identify your number as a spam risk, so I hope this wasn't a mistake," she said grumpily.

"Let me start by saying how sorry I am for your loss. Were you and your father close?" Cari asked.

"I was always Daddy's little girl. I used to go to work with him every day in the summer," she said wistfully.

"That's sweet. Did you plan to follow in his footsteps?"

"Well, I hadn't thought about it a lot. I take that back; I had thought about it and hoped to come alongside him one day. I got a business degree in college four years ago and had some ideas of how I could help grow this business with him, but I didn't think I'd be the owner for another decade or more. This has all been really sudden," she said and sniffled.

Cari felt bad for bothering the young woman. "I can't imagine what it's like. I take it your dad left you his business?"

"He did. My mom said it was always his plan. The twins are just barely in college and they don't have a clue about being adults, let alone running a business," she responded.

Cari flipped back to the obituary. She had assumed Manwith was older than her parents, but his kids were all younger. She skimmed through the first two paragraphs to see when Horace married his wife Deborah or Debbie.

"I'm sure you're wondering how come all of us are so young when my parents are so old," Kristina commented.

Cari took a quick breath, startled by the woman's quick observation. "That's correct. Did your parents meet later in life or...?"

"They put off starting a family for several years. Dad wanted to be somewhat involved, but knew he couldn't do it when he was trying to take over the business from his dad. Mom tells us all the time she was worried they waited too long, but fortunately, they still ended up with the three kids they always wanted," Kristina told her.

"That's really wonderful. So, how is it going for you with the business?" Cari hoped being direct wasn't being rude.

51

"I'm in over my head, one hundred percent. This is the most overwhelming thing, well, except for Daddy dying, of course. Uncle Ben wants me to sell and split the money with the family, but Mom told me to stick to my guns. It's my business and Daddy wanted me to have it," she said confidently.

"Wow, that does sound overwhelming. Has anyone approached you about selling or how did that idea come up?" Cari asked her.

"Honestly, I'm still sorting through paperwork and his financials with his lawyer and accountant. If someone is trying to buy it, I haven't gotten to that piece of paper yet. My dad was pretty old school. I actually just threw together a website earlier this week. He barely had a Facebook page for it, so I'm trying to get us into the twenty-first century as quickly as I can," she told Cari. "Um, what was it you wanted to know about Daddy?"

"Nothing specific really," Cari tried to scramble for a valid reason and remembered Ollaman's article. "I've been working on an article about new businesses in the area and yours came up, I guess because it's changing hands or whatever."

"Oh, that makes sense," Kristina commented. "What can I tell you?"

"When was the business founded?" Cari asked.

"1953. I'm pretty sure they just did radio repairs and maybe sold radios and car batteries back then. That was before all the big box stores. I'd have to look up the actual inventory," Kristina explained.

"1953? So, that was your great-grandfather who founded it?" Cari asked for clarification.

"That's correct. Clyde Manwith," Kristina told her. "Do you have any other questions?"

"I can't think of any right now, but if you think of anything else I should know about the business, please don't hesitate to call me," Cari responded.

"Will do. Thanks for the call," Kristina said.

Cari ended the call and wrote down a few more notes. She wanted to talk to Debbie, the wife and Uncle Ben, the brother too. It sounded like there was some dissension in the ranks. First, she needed to get an update from the intern who was gathering information from the neighboring towns.

* * * * *

As they drove back to the station, Genevieve's mind wandered back to her earlier conversation with Dureski. She wanted to show him she was competent, but he didn't give her much information about the case. She tried to remember everything he'd mentioned: businesses changing hands, a construction company, and some sort of connection to Robby's company. She knew his company did something involving technology, but her limited interactions with the family hadn't helped her figure out much more than that. She needed to take a few minutes and read—

"Earth to Gen!" Alex called out from the passenger seat.

She flinched. "What?"

"I've been going through various theories on our case and I thought you were listening, but you just agreed that it could be related to global warming. Are you with me now?" he grumbled.

She inwardly rolled her eyes at him. "Yes, what's your take?"

"I'm not sure. Everyone we talk to seems to only have nice things to say about her. What do we know about her ex-husband?" Alex asked.

"Nothing really except he wasn't a good dad or a good husband. Seems like he left them high and dry," Genevieve remarked.

"Agreed. Maybe he heard she was doing well and came back to try to get into her good graces," Alex suggested.

"I'm sure we can get his name and look him up. Something tells me he won't be involved, though," Genevieve hypothesized.

"It does kind of feel like he left and never looked back," Alex agreed. "The daughter's response was not what I expected. She seemed completely unfazed by her mother's death."

"She was odd in several ways, but I don't think she killed her mom. Maybe she's in shock and just processing her grief," Genevieve suggested.

"Maybe. I agree with you. She was weird, but she doesn't strike me as a killer. She didn't seem upset in the way we usually see family members, though," Alex observed. "If it weren't for the crime scene, I'd think she just fell."

"The crime scene suggests someone else was there and they tried to sweep away their footprints. Maybe someone knew she'd be there. It sounds like she went hiking there fairly regularly and by herself, so she must have been in good shape," Genevieve responded.

"Exactly. She was in great shape and she was barely over fifty, which is really the new twenty," he continued.

Gen snorted. "Mmkay."

"What is it you always say to me? Shut it. Fifty is *not* old. Where was I?" Alex asked.

"Exactly," she laughed and felt him glare at her.

53

"Anyway. As I was saying, Frobish losing track of her surroundings and falling over the edge doesn't work for me. We need to see who she talked to on her phone last and for how long. I hope they can get into her phone, but if not, we can always go through the phone company. We need to look at text messages too," he told her.

"I told you already. I think they got into her phone, remember? The earbud they found paired with it," Genevieve reminded him.

"Oh, right. So, I think maybe she was on the phone with someone, and she was pacing up there while she talked to them," he rationalized.

"And, what? They told her to jump off the cliff?" Gen frowned in disbelief.

"No, but her footprints were isolated. Someone must have brushed all the prints from the trail to the overlook area. They couldn't just erase their own, but they ended up making it look even more suspicious. I really think someone else was up there," he told her.

"Well, hopefully, her phone and call history can tell us more about who that might be," she responded as she pulled back into their parking lot.

"Let's go in and see what they have on her phone before we go to her business. It's possible one of her employees wanted more from her...maybe a raise, or more hours, or to be a partner. We also don't know where she got the money to start it in the first place. Maybe that will be on the computer," he said and pointed toward the trunk where they'd stowed it.

Genevieve turned the cruiser off and undid her seatbelt. She helped Alex remove the evidence from the trunk and then locked the vehicle. Alex's long stride carried him up the steps quickly, so she hurried to stay with him.

"Let's take this down to CSU and see what they have on the phone," Alex said once they were inside.

Genevieve scrunched her nose when they reached the basement. It always held a faint smell of the autopsy room even though the heavy doors remained closed. She swallowed, trying to keep the smell out of her mind. Alex held the door to CSU for her and they carried the items inside.

"Trash is supposed to get picked up, not brought back in," Chris joked when he saw them enter.

"Sorry, man. We found some things of interest at the victim's home and thought they deserved a look," Alex informed him.

"Like what?" Bob asked, wheeling his chair around from his desk.

"For one thing, some sort of letter inquiring about the victim's business. It was torn to pieces, so we're hoping you like puzzles," Genevieve said with a grin.

"I don't like smelly, garbage puzzles," Chris complained. "But we'll sift through it. What else is there?"

"We found her laptop and wanted you to see what you can make of her financial records. There's an app on the laptop for them," Genevieve explained. "The password is on a sticky note inside the laptop."

"Perfect. Top notch security, right there," Bob laughed.

"Let me show you what we found on her phone so far," Chris offered.

They crowded around his computer screen. A cell phone with a cracked screen was connected via a cable to the side of his laptop.

"She used her phone a lot. I went through her call log from the past month and she had calls to her daughter Luna...uh, I know it's her daughter because the entry is saved as 'Daughter-Luna' in her phone," he pointed to the computer screen. "She called her business every day. She also got a call every day for about ten days from an unknown number, which she eventually labeled with a, um, colorful nickname."

Genevieve looked at the expletive on the screen and chuckled. "I guess that's one way to do it. Did she get texts from this person?"

"If she did, she deleted them already. The phone company will have records of them, though," Chris told her. "Grusky already put in a warrant request for the records. We'll probably have them later today."

"Awesome," she responded and leaned in for a closer look at the screen. "Any other frequent callers or callees?"

Chris quickly scrolled through the list. "Not really."

"I'll start looking through her laptop now," Bob said. He added his name to the evidence log and then sliced through the red tape on the bag holding the laptop.

"Her laptop is a bit of a disaster. For someone with a successful business, she doesn't seem very organized," Genevieve told him.

"Thanks for the warning. I'll start with the financial records and let you know if I find anything interesting," he remarked.

"I sent over the video files from the state park. Did you get them?" Genevieve asked Chris.

"Yeah, it's on the list. You said we're looking for single occupancy vehicles, right?" he asked her.

"Yeah, and if you can get the owner's name, address, and so forth, that would be great," she responded.

Alex looked Genevieve in the eye and flicked his head toward the exit. "Unless you need anything else from us, we're going to go check out her business."

"Careful, they might sign you up for a membership, Runimoss," Chris teased. "Doesn't it target middle-aged people?"

Genevieve laughed as Alex glared at the younger man and exited the room. "I think the target audience is actually female. See you guys later."

She caught up to Alex on the stairs. "Slow down, old man."

"Who you calling old?" he grumbled. "I'm nowhere near middle-aged."

She looked at her watch and cringed when she saw it was after five already. "We need to get over to the fitness place quickly. Grusky isn't approving overtime right now whether it's a murder investigation or not."

Chapter 6

B ryson Millar jumped in the elevator just as the doors started to close. Cari stepped to the side to give him some space. Bryson pressed the G for garage again to get the doors to close.

"How is that article about local businesses coming together?" he asked her.

She sighed. "It's a big project. I see why he wants to do it, but the number of businesses and contractors and so on…well, it's a long list. I tasked one of the interns with making me a list from the neighboring towns." She tapped her messenger bag. "They emailed me their findings right before I clocked out for the day."

"Good call. You're working on that business woman's death too, right?" he said and put out a hand to hold the elevator doors open for her.

"Thanks. Yes, it's a lot of back and forth, which is why I enlisted the help of an intern for the other story. What does Ollaman have you working on now?" she asked as they walked to their cars.

"History of Brenington. I guess the town turns four hundred years old this fall. I'm compiling info alongside the chamber of commerce people regarding the founding of Brenington and its expansion," he told her.

She raised her eyebrows. "Well, good luck with that."

He chuckled. "I might need to enlist an intern for help too."

"See you next week," she said and waved goodbye.

Her cell phone buzzed as she unlocked her car. "Hey, Bob. I just need to swing by my apartment to change clothes before we pick up Hilary and Joel."

"Same. Maybe we should come up with a dinner plan so we can avoid a sibling battle?" he asked.

"The mini golf place has hot dogs, right? Isn't that okay?" she asked as she pulled her car onto the street from the parking garage.

"Does your sister let them eat hot dogs?" Bob asked with concern.

"Oh, hmm…should we get permission for that?" she asked and wondered again why Bea let her watch her kids.

"Probably so. She might already have an idea. Worst case, I know she lets them eat pizza, so we can grab one on our way back to their house," he suggested.

"That's a good idea. Let's be sure to get the alarm code from Bea this time. That was a little awkward two weeks ago," she laughed. "Traffic is light, so I'm almost home."

"Luckily, we know a couple of people in the police department," he chuckled. "Okay, I'll pick you up in five."

"See you then. Love you," she said with a smile.

"Love you too," he said and ended the call.

Cari navigated the last few blocks to her home on autopilot. She couldn't stop thinking about her conversation with Robby the previous evening. She had two possible cases based on Robby's billing codes so far, but it all still felt a bit like a conspiracy theory. She wished she could have called Manwith's wife and brother before the end of the day. Something about her conversation with the man's daughter raised her hackles and she wondered if the other two family members could shed some light on it.

"I could do it tomorrow..." she thought aloud as she got out of her car.

She looked down and realized she was rubbing her locket. Her self-soothing habit always made her want to call her grandmother, who gave her the necklace when she graduated from high school. Cari opened it and looked inside. Her six-year-old face laughed alongside her grandmother in a field of sunflowers.

She glanced at her watch. Bob would be at her apartment any minute and she hadn't changed clothes yet. She grabbed her messenger bag from the passenger seat and pulled her phone out of it. She could multitask.

"Is that my Cari?" Her grandmother's voice brought a smile to her face.

"Hi, Grandmother! I was just thinking about you," Cari said as she hurried up the stairs to her unit.

"It sounds like you're working hard. Where are you off to now?" she asked.

"I'm running inside my apartment to change clothes. Bob is on his way here to pick me up, so we can get the kids for mini golf tonight," she explained and unlocked the apartment.

"Oh, that's right! It's date night for Bea and Robby. That sure is nice of you two to take the kids every now and then. I know they all enjoy it," Grandmother said kindly.

"Well, Bob loves those two kids and they are pretty fond of him too," Cari said as she kicked off her shoes and pulled a shirt off its hanger.

"What else is on your mind, my dear?" Grandmother asked knowingly.

Cari hesitated. Robby had called her in confidence and she didn't want to worry Grandmother unnecessarily. It *would* be helpful to get another person's perspective, though.

"Are you still there?" her grandmother asked with concern.

"I'm still here. Sorry!" she exclaimed as she switched the phone to speaker and tugged on a pair of jean shorts. "I got a bit of a strange request or story lead recently. I'm not sure what to make of it."

"Tell me more," Grandmother replied.

"Well, this person thinks he might be inadvertently assisting in paying off a hitman or something to that effect," Cari said. Saying it out loud made it sound even more ridiculous.

"Someone local?" Grandmother asked in a shocked tone.

"Uh, yes, someone in the area," she said vaguely. "It just seems like a stretch given the type of company they work for and everything. I think they might be a little paranoid."

"I can tell it still has you curious though. It can't hurt to dig into a little bit, can it?" Grandmother suggested.

"I suppose not..." Cari trailed off.

"But..." Grandmother prodded.

A knock at the door interrupted the conversation. "Oh! There's Bob at the door. I'm sorry to cut this short. I'll try to call you tomorrow, Grandmother. I love you!" she said and shoved a foot into her sneaker.

"Come on in, Bob!" she called out from the bedroom.

"I love you more, sweetheart. Have fun!" Grandmother ended the call.

Cari slid her phone into her back pocket. She heard Bob unlocking the apartment door.

"I'm almost ready. Be right out!" she hollered.

"You left your keys in the door again," he told her with a grin. "I did still have to unlock the door, so at least you locked it this time."

Cari looked up to see him in the bedroom doorway holding up her key chain. She blushed. "Whoops. I guess I was doing one too many things on my way inside just now."

"Was that Grandmother on the phone?" he asked.

"You got me. I hadn't talked to her in a day or two and wanted to say hi," she told him. "Ready for some mini golf?"

"I'm planning on winning. I can't let Hilary beat me again. That was embarrassing!" he laughed good-naturedly.

59

She took her keys from his hand and pulled him into a kiss. "You're a good sport, Bob Hursley, but I don't know that *winning at mini golf* is ever going to be on your resume."

Once they were in his car, Bob started drumming his fingers on the steering wheel. "What's on your mind, Bob?" Cari asked him.

"Work. The Frobish case. Chris and I spent the day looking through the woman's phone records and her laptop. Did you know she basically fundraised to get her start-up funds?"

She nodded. "That's what one of her employees told me. I guess she had a lot of people who believed in her and wanted to support her."

"Which makes it harder to imagine someone wanting to kill her," he said with a hint of frustration.

"Did Green rule it to be a homicide officially?" Cari asked with intrigue.

"Off the record?" Bob asked with a gleam in his eye.

"For now," she said, only half-joking.

"I don't think he's officially ruled that to be the case, but I think it's inevitable," he responded. "The park ranger told Genevieve and Alex an experienced hiker could possibly enter the state park from the northwest side. I guess there's a barbed wire fence and a creek or something you have to cross. He said they haven't had an issue since they put the fence up, though."

"Oh, they have cameras on the fence?" Cari asked.

Bob shook his head. "He told them there weren't cameras. I'm not sure how he can verify no one is entering that way, but they said he sounded certain of it."

Cari started to respond when her phone buzzed with an incoming call. She recognized the number to the Frobish woman's business. *Maybe Nash had a phone number or name for her!*

"I have to take this. I'm sorry," she said sheepishly. "This is Cari. Is this Nash?"

"Yes, ma'am. I got a phone number for you from that angry caller if you still want it," he told her.

"Awesome. Can you text it to me at this number?" she requested.

"I got you," he said. "Just one second…entering your number…and his number…and send!"

Her phone buzzed with a notification. She checked her watch to confirm. "Got it. Thanks, Nash. I really appreciate it."

"Well, I hope it helps. Oh! Someone's coming into the gym, so I gotta get back to work. Later," Nash ended the call.

Bob glanced her way. "Get a lead on something?"

"Maybe. I got a phone number for someone who was harassing the victim," she told him.

"Are you going to call it?" he asked, his eyes darting to the clock on the dashboard.

She looked at the clock too. "We have about ten minutes until we get to their house, right?"

"More or less," he agreed.

"Maybe I'll just call and see who answers. It might be a business line or it could be a personal number. I'll work up a story of why I'm calling while it rings," she said as she touched the number on the screen.

She put her phone up to her ear as she waited for it to connect. She frowned when she heard the tell-tale sound of a number no longer in service.

"Well, I guess that's a clue in and of itself," she said dejectedly.

"No longer in service?" Bob guessed.

"Yep. It must have been a burner or something. I wonder if Nash got a name. He had to cut the call short because someone came into the gym," she explained.

Bob looked at her knowingly. "Well, send him a text and ask already!"

She smiled at his encouragement. "Done. Cross your fingers we get something from him."

Bob held up his crossed fingers. "What's your take on it?"

"Her death?" she asked and he nodded in confirmation. "I'm not sure. On the surface, it definitely seems like an unfortunate, yet careless fall." She paused when her watch buzzed. "Rats. Nash doesn't have a name."

"That's a bummer. Back to your assessment of the case…when do you ever leave something at just a surface glance?" he prodded her.

"Fair, and you're right. I feel like there is more going on between that and…" she trailed off, not wanting to get into Robby's predicament.

"What? More changes at the newspaper?" he asked with concern.

"Ugh. I haven't hardly thought about that today. No, it's…well, Robby called me last night," she said slowly. "And don't say anything. He hasn't told anyone else."

"This sounds serious. What is it?" Bob asked with his eyebrows raised.

"He's noticed a weird, uh, pattern with his billing codes and some deaths—" she began.

"Deaths?!" Bob exclaimed.

"Seriously, he's pretty freaked out about it, so you can't say anything or act like anything is weird. He's probably just being paranoid," she said, trying to ease the tension.

"I'm still unsure how billing codes are resulting in…death…wait…does he think he's authorizing a payment for a hit or something?" Bob asked uncertainly, glancing her way.

Cari bit her lip and nodded slowly. "He does. I guess he's been asked to approve some payments at odd times with codes that match the initials of some locals who have died in some sort of accident. It's kind of a stretch, but I told him I'd look into the codes and see if I could make anything from them. He thinks one of the codes is related to the Frobish woman's death."

"Has he talked to the police?" Bob asked.

Cari realized they were already on Bea and Robby's street. "No, and he's afraid to. If it's nothing, then he's thrown undue suspicion on his company. If it's valid, then he might be seen as an accessory. He wants to get some evidence one way or the other first. I shouldn't have said anything. That was unprofessional of me. He's a source and I shouldn't share that with someone."

Bob pulled into the Rialto's driveway and turned off the car. "I'm not going to leak this to the department or something, but be careful with it, Cari. If he's right, looking into this could alert a very dangerous person."

Cari laughed uneasily, trying to diffuse the uncertainty in her mind. "Like I said, he's probably just being paranoid. He's a numbers guy. He's trained to look for patterns and probably sees things that aren't there all the time."

Bob pursed his lips but didn't respond. Cari looked at the window and saw two little faces staring out at them. She smiled and waved.

"Ready for some putt-putt?" she asked as cheerfully as she could.

* * * * *

The parking lot outside of Fit Winners teemed with activity. Genevieve watched a group of teenagers exit a frozen yogurt business while harried moms with young children and full grocery carts trudged across the asphalt toward their vehicles. Several middle-aged women power-walked through the crosswalk toward Fit Winners. She wondered if a class was about to start.

"It's like Grand Central Station here," Alex grumbled as he searched for a parking spot.

"Just make another lap. I think the mom with the three kids was almost finished loading her groceries into her car," Genevieve told him.

He circled the lot again and just as she predicted, the minivan was pulling out of a spot. Alex steered their cruiser into it and sighed.

"I thought everyone was doing curbside pickup these days. Why is this place so busy?" he complained as he got out of the car.

"Maybe they all admire your 1980s way of life and can't resist shopping in person," she said with a grin.

"Funny," he mumbled.

He opened the door to the fitness center and held it for her. She smirked at him on her way by. Women with yoga mats bypassed the front desk for a hallway marked 'locker rooms'. The young man at the front desk was on the phone. He looked up when the door opened and held up a finger to indicate he'd be right with them.

"Welcome to Fit Winners! How can I help you today?" he asked after ending his phone call. "Is this going to be a membership transfer? You both look like you're in incredible shape."

Alex pulled out his badge in response. "I'm Detective Runimoss and this is my partner, Detective Viacorte. We wanted to talk with some of the employees here about the owner, Elaine Frobish."

The young man's face clouded. "We're all in shock about Elaine. She was the best boss. I honestly thought she'd live to be over a hundred. She took such good care of herself. I can't believe she's gone…sorry, I'm rambling. My name is Nash. I run the front desk…in case that was in any way unclear."

Genevieve smiled. "Thank you, Nash. How long have you worked here? Forgive me, but you seem pretty young."

"Right back at ya, sister," he said and then cleared his throat when Alex glared at him. "Uh, I've been here six years. I take night classes on Tuesdays and Thursdays at the university. Elaine was really flexible with my schedule. I used to work fairly sporadically, but I decided to save a little more for the future by working closer to full time here and being a part time student. It's working for me so far."

"You mentioned Ms. Frobish was a good boss—" Alex started to say, but Nash interrupted.

"I said she was the BEST boss. I'm not sure if that's important. Sorry," he mumbled to another icy stare from Alex.

Genevieve intervened. "Did everyone like working for Ms. Frobish?"

Nash bobbed his head up and down. "Yes. Everyone loved her and not just her instructors, but the members too. You can feel it, right? The place has a great vibe. Elaine made that happen. I don't know what we'll do without her."

"You're saying she got along with everyone?" Alex asked for clarification.

Nash frowned. "Well, almost everyone. You came at just the right time, actually. The Beagle reporter was here earlier and she suggested I request phone records...well, anyway. There's this guy who had been calling quite a bit recently, but the caller ID always showed *unknown*. I don't know what he wanted, but Elaine got pretty angry when he called."

"I think I'm following your train of thought, Nash. Are you saying you were able to get the phone number?" Genevieve asked.

"Yes, I got the records and just called the reporter with the number when you were arriving. I wrote it down, but the company emailed me all the phone records for the last two months. I can send you the file if you have an email address," he offered as he handed Genevieve a sticky note.

She glanced at the phone number. "That would be great. Let me get you my card. It has my email and phone extension. My cell is on the back."

Nash took the business card from her and started typing on the computer keyboard. "Perfect. You should get it any second now."

Genevieve got her phone out and saw the email icon show up at the top of the screen. "Got it. We'd like to visit with some other employees while we are here. Is anyone else free right now?"

Alex took the sticky note from her and tilted his head toward the front corner of the business. "I'm going to call Chris before he leaves for the day and see if he can find the owner of this number."

Genevieve looked at Nash. "Any other employees, Nash?"

"Oh, right. Um, let me get you a list of all our instructors. Only two are here right now and one is teaching a class. I'm sure everyone will be cooperative. Like I said, we all loved Elaine," he told her.

She waited while he typed on the keyboard some more. "You can email me the list rather than print it."

"Awesome. The printer is a little low on ink anyway. We're mostly digital here. It's faster and easier," he said as he typed away on the keyboard. "And...sent. What else can I help you with today?"

"You said there were two instructors here right now, but only one teaching. Can we speak with the other one while we're here?" she asked.

"Of course, let me just text her to come out. I think she's just getting ready for her class that starts at six. She is friends with a lot of the women in the class and…I'll just text her real quick," he said when he saw Alex return with a grumpy look on his face.

"Chris is going to run the number and get back to us," Alex told her.

"Courtney will be right out," Nash informed them.

A woman in her fifties with almond-shaped eyes and ink-black hair entered the lobby. She was wearing black capri leggings and a black, cropped, form-fitting top. She smiled and held out her hand.

"I'm Courtney. Nash says you're with the police department?" she introduced herself.

"Nice to meet you, Courtney. Yes, we're detectives with BPD, Viacorte and Runimoss," Genevieve explained. "We're very sorry for your loss. Do you have a minute to talk about Ms. Frobish?"

"Sure. Nash, I think we could use the office, right? Do you have the key handy?" she asked him.

"For sure. Here you go," he said as he pulled a key out of the top drawer.

They followed Courtney to an office near the entrance to the workout room. Genevieve could see the class in session doing some sort of Pilates together. A hand-made sign outside the office door read "Captain Fitness" and had a child's drawing of a woman possibly doing jumping jacks. The corners were dog-eared and several pieces of tape held it to the wall. She saw the name Luna scrawled near the bottom of it.

"Here we are," Courtney said after unlocking the door. "Have a seat. What questions can I answer?"

"How long have you worked here?" Alex asked her after he sat down. Genevieve pulled out her pocket notebook.

"I was one of Elaine's first employees. Our daughters were in school together. I guess it's been what, almost twenty years?" she said with her hands raised off the desk.

"Do you know how Ms. Frobish obtained the start-up capital for the business? Did she get a loan or have a family member help her or something like that?" Genevieve asked.

"Oh no. Nothing like that. She basically begged for it from everyone she knew. She pitched her business idea to all of us moms and we loved it. She asked for people to commit to signing up for a membership. She got our signatures and she took them to the bank. They were impressed and they gave her the loan. She had it paid off pretty quickly too, I think. She was smart. She took just the right amount of risk and it paid off for her," Courtney explained.

"So, as far as you know, she didn't have any debt to anyone associated with the business?" Alex asked.

Courtney shook her head. "Not that I know of. She had a celebration when she paid off that loan. That's when she started to expand some. She hired another instructor or two and eventually, we got Nash out there full time. It's been great. Until, well, we don't know what's going to happen now. I guess it will go to her daughter. None of us have heard."

"Did anyone not get along with your boss? Any dissension in the ranks?" Genevieve questioned her.

Courtney raised her eyebrows in shock. "Oh no. Not at all. People loved working here. We constantly got applications even though we were rarely hiring."

"The initial loan? Do you know what it covered?" Genevieve asked.

"Some of it went toward the rent at first, and some of it covered the equipment. Like yoga mats, Pilates balls, hand weights…that kind of thing. She initially had one evening class Monday through Thursday and one morning class Monday through Friday. She was closed on Friday evenings because she figured people were less likely to come to a class on Friday night. She had three classes on Saturdays and Sundays. She was in *great* shape then. After a month or two, she was exhausted. She took me on as her first employee to teach a class on Saturday and Sunday," she told them.

"It sounds exhausting to do all that and be a mom. We spoke with her daughter earlier. Do you know what happened to Ms. Frobish's husband?" Genevieve asked her.

"He just left. Said he didn't like being a dad. Too stressful or something. She came home from grocery shopping one day and he was gone. He'd cleared out their bank account too. It was a real mess for her," Courtney said with a frown.

"Did she ever hear from him again?" Alex asked.

"I don't think so. He didn't show up for the kids' high school graduations or college graduations either. I don't even know if he's still alive," Courtney said with a shrug.

"Frobish's daughter's last name is Harrison. Did she marry at some point or why is it different?" Genevieve asked.

Courtney nodded in understanding. "Yeah, that's confusing. The kids had their names legally changed to Elaine's maiden name when they each turned sixteen. They didn't want to be tied to their dad in any way. Elaine didn't want to deal with the headache of changing everything for herself though. She kept his last name all this time. Not that Garrett cared, the jerk."

Genevieve made a note to look up Garrett Frobish and see where he lived now. She wondered if he was behind the harassing phone calls. Alex nodded his head, signaling he was out of questions.

"Thanks for your time, Courtney. If you think of anything else, please don't hesitate to call us," Genevieve said. "Here's my card with all my contact information."

Courtney took the card and slid it into a nearly invisible pocket in her leggings. They stood up and exited the office. Courtney locked the door behind them and gave the key back to Nash. Genevieve heard a phone vibrate and saw Alex take his cell from his pocket. He pointed at the door and rushed out.

"Thanks again for your cooperation. Please let us know if you think of anything else," Genevieve told Courtney and Nash.

She could see Alex's shoulders droop and wondered who was on the phone. She hoped it wasn't Chris with bad news. The phone number seemed like a decent lead. She pushed the door open and caught up to him on the sidewalk.

"Thanks, Chris. Appreciate it," he said and ended the call. "The number was to a burner and it's deactivated. It was the same number she was talking to the afternoon she fell."

"Which makes it even more suspicious," she remarked.

* * * * *

Fireflies danced in the darkness as Cari and Bob walked out to his car. The front door to Bea's house opened just as they reached the vehicle. She looked back to see if they'd left something behind and saw Robby standing on the porch. He waved her over. Bob nodded knowingly and got into the driver's seat to wait while she walked back to the porch.

"Hey, I just wondered if you made any progress on, uh, the codes we talked about," he said quietly and then held up a small metal rod. "I told Bea I wanted to check the tire pressure."

Cari gave him a quizzical look. "Doesn't your car alert you to that on its own?"

"Yes, but she wasn't driving, so she doesn't know that it's fine," Robby explained. "It was the first thing I could think of."

"Okay, well, I haven't necessarily found a connection, yet. I talked to Manwith's daughter, who inherited the company. She mentioned his brother was upset about that, but that's as far as I've gotten. Has something else happened?" she asked him.

"No, I'm probably just making myself paranoid, but ever since I talked to you, it feels like I'm being watched," he said uneasily.

"At work or where?" she asked.

"I don't know. I just have this strong feeling of uncertainty, like someone is looking over my shoulder or listening to my calls or monitoring my computer activity," he said and swallowed.

"That sounds like anxiety. Maybe you should tell Bea about your fears or…it's never too late to go to the police," Cari suggested gently.

"No. No police," he said firmly. "I want to know that I'm not imagining all this before I consider talking to any law enforcement on this."

Cari held her hands up. "Okay, okay, I get it. I'll keep you posted. Try to relax. This might all be nothing. You only have three suspicious codes, right?"

Robby blinked once and nodded. "Yeah, Frobish, Manwith, and one other. Did you identify that one?"

She shook her head. "No, I couldn't find a relevant death in the time frame around that code. Was there anything different about that payment?"

He exhaled. "I didn't really look."

She took a step toward him. "You never told me how much money was involved in these payments. How big are we talking?"

He ran his empty hand over his hair and back forward. "I told you I didn't look. I could double-check, but if someone's monitoring my activity, it might make them more suspicious."

Cari swallowed. "I understand, but maybe you're just feeling anxious and letting your fear get the best of you. Everything is still as it was before we talked, right? You're okay, right?"

He nodded. "I'd better get back in there before Bea gets suspicious."

"Talk to you later, Robby," she said and waved goodbye.

Bob was reading the news on his phone when she got into the car. He slid his phone into his pocket and started the car. She buckled her seatbelt and sighed.

"More codes?" Bob asked with curiosity.

She shook her head. "No, he's just worried. He thinks someone is watching him or keeping tabs on him. Like, now that he's said something about what he suspects, someone else was alerted to his activities."

"Sounds like a recipe for poor sleep," Bob remarked as he drove out of the neighborhood.

"Right? Hopefully, I can shed some light on something one way or the other soon. I'm planning to work on it some more tomorrow," she told him.

Bob gave her a nervous glance. "Just how many codes are we talking about here? Three, four…?"

Cari grimaced. "He only gave me three codes, which, I agree, is not very many, just barely enough to say there's a pattern. He thinks he's already identified two of the codes, but the third code was only numbers, so I couldn't make any sense of it."

"How large of an area did you check, just out of curiosity?" he asked her.

"I did our county and the two others nearest us," she told him.

"So, you were able to include the city," he said and then shrugged. "Maybe it is all in Robby's head."

"I'd like to hope so, but I'm not sure a lack of evidence will necessarily feel like a no to him," Cari remarked. "I thought maybe he'd be more relaxed after a night out with Bea, but he still seems pretty tense."

"I'd suggest he do something fun with his family to destress, but those kids are competitive!" Bob laughed.

"Hey, I can't remember, who won at putt-putt tonight?" Cari said with a gleam in her eye.

"Very funny. You know you won. I can't believe Hilary beat me again. Are you sure you didn't give her a few extra mulligans?" Bob asked.

Cari laughed. "She beat you fair and square. Hey, at least you were a few strokes ahead of Joel still."

"He's only seven!" Bob exclaimed.

"Well, we all have our strengths. You can't be good at everything, Bob," Cari told him.

"We should take them to an escape room next time. I can definitely be good at that," he suggested.

"That's a good idea. I bet they have some for kids around here somewhere," Cari agreed. "I'll ask Bea next time we chat and see if they've ever done one before."

"You said you were going to make some phone calls tomorrow, but do you have any other plans?" Bob asked as he turned into her apartment complex.

"Are you asking me out on a date, Hursley?" she ribbed him.

"If I was, would you say yes?" he teased her back. "Oh wait, tomorrow is Saturday. We're volunteering in the morning, right?"

"That's right. Are you picking me up, or...?" She left the question hanging.

"I might be in the neighborhood, if you need a ride," he said with his eyebrows raised.

"Sounds like you're fishing for a sleepover," she laughed.

"I mean, I'm already here..." he said encouragingly.

"Well, are you going to park or what?" she said with a gleam in her eye.

Chapter 7

After a six-mile run, Genevieve went up to the roof of her apartment building to work in the raised bed gardens. She found the task relaxing and it also helped her to think through her cases. She pulled out her tools from the small shed and took a seat on the ground next to one of the beds. A few weeds had sprouted in the bed since her last session with the garden, so she quickly pulled those and set them aside. Her mom always called them opportunistic plants. Regardless of their name, they could still choke out her tomato plants if they were allowed to grow. She plucked several nice-sized tomatoes from her plants and placed them in the basket she'd brought upstairs with her. She looked at the bed where she'd planted a few carrots and onions; she was pleased to see them growing well too. She might have enough to make a few jars of marinara sauce.

She thought back to her conversation with Dureski. He'd mentioned other related cases but didn't tell her who or where. He had also said something about businesses changing hands, but Genevieve still thought it was probably normal for a business to take on new ownership when an unexpected death took place. She wondered if she could tease out the other cases on her own. She didn't know how frequently a business changed hands or which city or county she should search, though. She still had too many unknowns and not enough answers. It felt like someone had emptied out four puzzles onto one table and you needed to get them all put together at once. She needed more information, but didn't even have the search parameters to look for it. That was probably how Dureski wanted it, if she was being honest with herself. She'd promised to keep him updated, so she pulled out her phone to tell him what they learned from Frobish's employees.

"Viacorte, tell me you found something useful," Dureski said when he answered her call.

"Maybe. We spoke with Frobish's employees last night. The front desk person told us someone had been calling to harass her the last few weeks. She got pretty agitated by their calls, but they were persistent," Genevieve told him. "Unfortunately, it seems like he was calling from a burner phone, so we're going to have to find another way to figure out who he is."

"Text me the number. Maybe we can find something on it," Dureski instructed her.

She glanced around to be sure she was still alone and then put the call on speaker. She found the phone number and copied it into a text message. After hitting send, she turned the speaker phone function off.

"Done," she told him.

While she waited for him to respond, she moved to her other raised bed to look at the carrots and onions. A couple of the carrots looked like they were ready to be harvested. She gently pulled them from the bed and placed them on top of the tomatoes. She started to dig around an onion when Dureski spoke again.

"Got it. Thanks. We'll see what we can find out about this number. Anything else?" he asked.

"No. Everyone we've talked to has only said good things about the woman. They loved her," she paused.

"What?" Dureski asked when she didn't continue.

"Well, when we went to see her daughter, she didn't seem sad. It was a little odd. It almost seemed like she was more frustrated with us that we showed up when she wanted to record her yoga workout than she was sad her mother had died," Genevieve explained.

"That is odd behavior. We didn't find anything suspicious regarding the daughter, but I'll have my people take a second look. Thanks, Viacorte," he said and ended the call.

She stared at the phone screen for a few seconds before slipping it back into her running belt. She wished he would share information with her too. She might be able to help him solve this case. She stood up and brushed the dirt off her clothing. She needed to take a shower, then she was going to make some marinara sauce with her vegetable harvest.

* * * * *

Cari checked her watch again and almost sighed. Her shift at the soup kitchen wasn't passing by as quickly as it usually did. She couldn't stop thinking about Robby and his codes. Twice, Regina had to clear her throat to remind Cari to keep up with their guests. She kept zoning out, caught up in her thoughts.

"Is everything okay today?" Regina asked when they went back to get a refill on the pancake batter.

Cari gave her a half-hearted smile. "Yes, I'm sorry for being so distracted." She paused, not wanting to share Robby's concerns. "We've got some changes coming up at work and I'm kind of balancing two stories at once on top of that."

"Sounds stressful. Good changes or bad changes?" Regina asked with concern.

"Some restructuring. It's worse for some than others," Cari responded vaguely.

"It always is. I hope it works out for you in the end," she said encouragingly.

Cari set the bowl of batter back on the counter by her work station. She smiled when she saw a familiar face approaching the front of her line.

"Dorothy! How have you been?" Cari asked the older woman as she ladled more pancakes onto the griddle.

"Hungry right now," Dorothy laughed and rubbed her stomach. "But I'll probably make it another day."

"I'm glad to hear it," Cari told her. "It's good to see you."

Dorothy smiled warmly. "You too, Cari. Don't burn those pancakes."

Cari laughed, but looked quickly at her griddle. Thankfully, nothing was burning. Dorothy liked to tease her about cooking pancakes after watching Cari's first effort almost a year ago. She smiled at the memory and went back to flipping and serving pancakes. She hadn't seen Dorothy in a few weeks as she'd participated in the 5k the previous Saturday morning. Her ladle scraped the bottom of the bowl. She looked up and realized they'd served all the guests in line. She released the ladle back into the bowl and took the items back to the kitchen so they could be run through the commercial dishwasher. After washing her hands, she removed her apron and added it to the laundry pile.

Bob was just entering the dining area from the garden when she exited the kitchen. He quickly crossed the room and joined her.

"Are you finished? Want to get brunch?" he asked.

She looked at her watch and then quickly glanced around the room to see if anyone could overhear them. "I really need to call a couple people regarding the thing I told you about with Robby."

"Dinner instead?" he asked in a somewhat pleading tone.

She grabbed his hand and tugged him toward the exit. "Count me in. Are you cooking, or am I?"

"You cook?" he asked and quickly leaned away to avoid her punch.

"Not funny," she said laughing.

"What sounds good?" he asked as he pulled out his keys to unlock his car.

"Surprise me," she responded.

"By the way, my dad called a little bit ago. I told him we were volunteering, but not together. He said to call him back any time. He had some ideas about Ollaman's proposed cuts," Bob told her as they got on their way back to her apartment.

"Let's call him," Cari responded. "I hope Ollaman is willing to take some feedback."

Bob hit a few buttons on his steering wheel and a dialing sound filled the car. His dad picked up after two rings.

"Bob! Thanks for calling back. I take it Cari is with you now?" Jack Hursley asked.

"Hey, Jack. Thanks for taking the time to look through the financials for me. I really appreciate it," Cari told him.

"No problem. I really think your Mr. Ollaman should reconsider cutting health insurance from his employee package. It's not really going to save him much money and he does have the option of not subsidizing it with company funds," Jack said over the speaker.

"Wait, does that mean we would still be paying for our health insurance?" Cari asked uncertainly.

"Yes, but if he arranges a package for the employees, there will almost definitely be a discount on the price. It's better than each of you finding something on the market alone," he responded.

"Oh, that makes sense. Any advice on how to suggest this to him?" she asked hopefully.

They heard a hissing sound as Jack sucked air in between his teeth. "Well, I never worked in HR, so you're on your own there. Good luck with it!"

"Thanks, Dad," Bob said. "We'll talk to you later."

"Happy to help," Jack said. "Margie, call him yourself if you want to ask that..."

Bob clicked the hang-up button before they heard any more of the side conversation. Cari fidgeted in her seat. She figured Margie wanted to know if they'd made any wedding plans, yet, just like her own mom asked every time they spoke. Thankfully, they had reached her apartment complex. Bob pulled into an empty parking space and unlocked the car doors.

"I'll call you later to let you know when dinner will be ready," he told her after they shared a quick kiss. "Love you, Cari."

"Love you too, Bob. Thanks!"

She climbed the steps to her unit and unlocked the door. She was ready to get to work on Robby's case and wanted to call Debbie Manwith as well as Horace's brother, Ben. Her gut said Debbie would be more amenable to talking. She filled a glass with water and sat down at her table where she'd left her messenger bag the previous evening. She pulled out her laptop and booted it up.

Kristina had given Cari a good phone number for both her mother and her uncle. She found the two numbers in her notes and entered Debbie's into her cell phone. She mentally crossed her fingers the woman would answer.

"Hello?" A woman's voice spoke cautiously into the phone. "Who is this?"

"Mrs. Manwith? This is Cari Turnlyle with the Brenington Beagle. Can you hear me okay?" Cari asked.

"Yes, I'm Debbie Manwith and I can hear you just fine. Is this about Horace?" the woman asked.

"Yes, ma'am. I'm terribly sorry for your loss. I spoke with your daughter earlier this week and she gave me your number," Cari explained.

"Kristina mentioned you might be calling. She said you wanted to know about the business, though. I don't know much about it. Horace didn't really bring work home as they say. He just spent all his time there," Debbie told her bitterly.

"I understand. Did he talk about how the business was doing or if he was having any trouble with anyone at work?" Cari asked.

"I can't imagine he was unhappy at work. He slaved away there day after day. It was a rare weekend when I could talk him into taking time off to spend with the family," she told Cari. "He mentioned something about wanting to add a floor to the building so he could expand into some new product lines, but I don't know if he was serious about it."

"I haven't gotten to read a lot about his business yet. He sold electronics? Like televisions or something else?" Cari asked her.

"Oh, not televisions. It was more of a specialty electronics store. He sold all the components you could use to build your own computer or laptop. He also did repairs to all sorts of electronics. My daughter has a great mind for business, but she doesn't know electronics as well as her father did. She's got a lot of catching up to do," Debbie said matter-of-factly.

For someone who claims to know little about the business, she sure has a lot of opinions.

"Surely there are some employees who are skilled in that area too?" Cari asked out of curiosity.

"I'm sure there are. I wouldn't know," Debbie mumbled.

"Kristina mentioned her Uncle Ben having an interest in the business…" Cari floated the thought, hoping Debbie would pounce on it.

"Ben can cram it if he thinks he deserves any of that business. It was Horace's business, not Ben's. It's always passed to the oldest offspring for the last three generations. This one should be no different. Just because Kristina is young, doesn't mean it shouldn't still be hers," Debbie said fiercely.

"Did Horace get along with his brother Ben?" Cari asked gently.

"I always thought so. I never knew Ben had an interest in the business at all. Here's the thing: it's not like this is some sort of out-of-date patriarchy malarky. Horace's grandfather, the founder of the business, had two sons. The younger son loved music. He was a wonderful musician, but he had no mind at all for business. The older son was a tinkerer. He took stuff apart and put it back together. He was always finding old broken radios or lamps or who knows what and disassembling them, fixing them, and putting them back together. His dad saw clearly the older son should inherit the business. However, he didn't want to leave the younger one out to dry, so he set up a trust. A third of the annual profit went into the trust. It earns interest, or so I understand and *that* money goes to the musician's family. It just expanded from there. A new trust was established when Horace took over for his dad and Ben gets the interest from it. Once we recover from losing Horace…" Debbie swallowed loudly and then exhaled. Cari heard her swallow again and sniffle a few times. "Sorry, it still hits me like this at least once a day. Where was I?"

"You were talking about the trusts," Cari reminded her.

"Right, we'll get trusts set up for the twins. No one's getting left behind or short-changed. Besides, Ben had his own career. He was a vet. He had benefits…a 401k. He's fine. He's being greedy and I don't know why," Debbie said slowly. "What other questions do you have?"

Cari typed the word 'greedy' into her notes on her laptop next to Ben's name before she responded.

"I think that's it. I appreciate you taking the time to speak with me, Mrs. Manwith," Cari told her.

"Call me Debbie. Mrs. Manwith sounds like an old woman."

You're not lying. Cari thought.

"Well, thank you, Debbie. If I think of any other questions, I'll give you a call," Cari said.

The call ended and she set her phone on the table. It seemed like Benjamin Manwith might not be so forthcoming with information. In fact, Cari thought he might respond with hostility. She took a deep breath and let it out slowly. She could handle a grumpy old man. She punched his number into her cell and waited for him to pick up.

"You better not be calling to ask me for money, 'cause I'm not giving anything. I don't care who needs it," a grumpy voice said into her ear.

"Hi, sir. This is Cari Turnlyle. I'm with the Brenington Beagle. I'm not calling to ask for money. I was hoping to chat with you about your brother Horace and his electronics business," she said as cheerfully as she could.

"Well, it's not his anymore, now, is it?" the man grumbled. "It's his daughter's."

"Right, I read the business was changing hands. I'm very sorry for the loss of your brother, sir. I'm sure that came as a shock," Cari said graciously.

"Idiot walked in front of a garbage truck. People need to get off their phones and pay attention to their surroundings," he growled.

Cari paused, not wanting to debate phone usage with him. "I understand you're a veterinarian?"

"Retired. People still call me about their pets, though. I retired early. I thought Horace might take me on as a partner. Then, he went and got run over," he said glumly.

"Had you and Horace discussed going into business together?" Cari asked.

"Harumph," he grumbled some more. "I'm sure you already talked to Debbie, so you know I get a dumb stipend or whatever, but this was our family legacy. I wanted to be a part of it as a second career."

"I understand. Was Horace not interested?" Cari asked again.

"Well, we hadn't really discussed it at length. I knew his two sons weren't going to be up for taking over when he was ready to retire and his daughter, well, she's a girl. No offense," he said quickly.

Cari bit her lip to keep from spitting out a retort. "Doesn't Miss Manwith have a business degree?"

"Useless. Anyone can get a degree. I know business and that electronics store is a good one. I could have really ex…" he trailed off.

"Did you say you wanted to expand it, sir?" Cari asked.

"I-I, uh, I said it's a good business. Profitable," he said slowly.

Cari felt like he was lying, but kept it to herself. "Of course. I appreciate your time, Mr. Manwith. Again, I'm very sorry for your loss. Best of luck to you in retirement."

She ended the call before he could complain anymore. She was tired of his grumpy demeanor, but the call had been informative. She was pretty certain he'd started to say he wanted to expand the business. Debbie Manwith had mentioned something similar, but Ben's statement had a different ring to it. She wondered what the story behind the expansion really was.

* * * * *

Blanching and peeling tomatoes was hard work. Genevieve scored the last tomato at its base and lowered it into the boiling water with her slotted spoon. She fished the previous one out and started peeling the skin off of it. Once the tomatoes were finished, she would start sauteing the onions, carrots, and bell peppers. Making sauce took some time, but it was worth it in the end.

She set the tomatoes aside and started cutting up the other vegetables. She'd barely made it through the onions when her cell phone buzzed with an incoming call. *Dureski, checking in again.*

"Agent Dureski. Did you find something on the number already?" she asked as she bent her neck to squeeze the phone between her ear and her shoulder. She wanted to keep chopping her vegetables.

"We weren't able to get a name on it, but we did verify the calls placed from the phone came from the same area," he explained.

"Any chance the number was tied into some of the other cases?" she pressed him a bit. Maybe if she was assertive, he'd share more information with her.

"That's a good thought; I had the same one. I have my analyst scanning the other victims' phone records for the same number. Maybe we'll get lucky with one of them," he told her. "Still, we can't be certain that the person behind the phone calls is also responsible for the deaths. He could be calling the shots, or he could be taking orders from someone else."

"That's true. You have mentioned other related cases a few times; are they all in the area?" she asked, hoping to squeeze something else from the tight-lipped agent.

He didn't answer immediately. Just as she was about to resign herself to remaining mostly in the dark, he spoke.

"They're all in my jurisdiction. All in New York state," he told her.

She grabbed a pen from the counter and scribbled a note on a paper towel. Maybe she could connect some of the dots without asking him for more information.

"Is there a point when you'll pull all these investigations into your purview?" she asked and set her knife down before she cut herself trying to do too many things at once.

"You're wondering if I'm going to take your case from you?" Dureski asked pointedly.

"I guess I am, sir," she said with as much courage as she could muster.

"It's entirely possible, Viacorte. I don't like to get into jurisdiction battles. I prefer to work alongside local law enforcement, but there may come a time when I have to take over. It wouldn't be because I question your competence. You're obviously very insightful. Keep it up, Viacorte. I'll be in touch if I find out more," he said and ended the call.

She set her phone down and picked the knife back up. Now she knew each of the cases involved the death of a small business owner in the state of New York. The business changed hands a month or so after the owner's death. Those were search parameters she could possibly work with. Obviously, having the victims' names would be more helpful, but maybe she could identify them on her own.

* * * * *

Rather than put Robby in a tough spot by calling him, Cari texted him to see if he was free to chat. When he first approached her about the codes, he'd made it sound like there were more instances. Then, he only sent her three codes. She felt like there had to be more, or he wouldn't be so nervous. She thought about her conversation with Benjamin Manwith. Maybe he had tried to help coordinate the expansion, but his older brother decided the cost was too high and called it off. She needed to talk to some of Manwith's employees. It's possible one of them had a similar experience to Frobish's Nash and fielded a call from an aggressive caller. She searched for the address and its hours of operation. It was Saturday, so they were open until the early evening. She grabbed her bag, phone, and keys and headed outside to her car.

The business was located less than ten minutes from her apartment. She was halfway there when a call came in over the vehicle's Bluetooth.

"Hey, Robby. Thanks for calling," she said quickly.

"Sure thing. Did you find something?" His voice was barely over a whisper.

"Are you not free to talk right now?" she asked him. "I can barely hear you."

"I'm in the garage, but Bea is playing Monopoly with the kids right on the other side of the door. I begged off playing and told them I needed to organize the garage," he whispered.

"Well, turn on some music or something so they don't think you're talking to yourself," she commanded. "Honestly, you should really talk to Bea. I don't like sneaking around behind her back."

She heard Bon Jovi come in faintly over the Bluetooth and grinned. "I didn't realize you were a fan of 80s music."

"My mom played it in the car all the time when I was growing up," he explained. "I'm not ready to talk to Bea about this yet. If it's nothing, then I'll look crazy."

Cari sighed. "When you first called me, I got the feeling this had happened multiple times, but then you only sent me three codes and dates."

"Three *is* multiple," he countered.

She scowled. "C'mon, Robby. There have to be more or you wouldn't be so freaked out. And don't think you're hiding this well from Bea. She mentioned it to Grandmother a month ago. She's noticed you have frequently had to take calls late and you're in a bad mood after you do it."

Robby was silent. Cari started to wonder if he ended the call. "I'm sorry to be so blunt. Are you still with me?"

"Yeah, I'm here. I'm frustrated. I hate this. I thought this was going to be a great job, but it feels wrong in so many ways right now," Robby complained.

"I need the other codes if I'm going to be able to help you," she prodded.

"Fine. I can't look them up until Monday. If someone is watching me within the network, then they'll be extra suspicious if I look something up on the weekend," he told her.

"First thing Monday, then," she said firmly.

"I'll do my best," he said quietly and the call ended.

She grimaced and pounded her palm into the steering wheel. *Did he want her help or not?* She had reached Manwith's business and pulled into the parking lot. "Batteries+" was lit up on the electric sign above the door. A small plaque in the window indicated the business was founded in 1953, just as Kristina had told her. A banner covered the lefthand window and informed potential customers they could get their cell phones and tablets repaired inside starting at $25. Cari pulled open one of the double glass doors and felt the cool air from inside. The display case housed several boxes of prepaid cell phones and gift cards for both iPhone and Android users. Every battery size you could think of was displayed on the wall to her right. Rows of shelving held what she assumed were computer parts. A middle-aged man sat behind a table with a cash register in the middle of the room. His grey hair stuck out in tufts above his ears and his bifocals kept sliding down his face. He watched her walk up the aisle without smiling.

She extended her hand. "Hi, I'm Cari Turnlyle with the Brenington Beagle. I'm doing a story on some of our local businesses and hoped you had a minute to chat."

He gave her a half smile and shook her hand. "Well, I'm not the owner and wouldn't it have been faster for you to call?"

She tried to keep her smile from faltering. "It probably would have, but I've never visited this business before and thought I could write about it better if I stopped by instead. I understand the owner's daughter is in the process of taking over?"

He nodded and looked her in the eye. "This place is only in business because we have a cracker-jack repair guy who can fix any contraption on the market. Well, within reason. He's not a miracle worker. But if your kid throws your phone on the sidewalk and the screen cracks, he can get it back good as new really easily. Or if they drop their tablet or iPad or whatever they are, he can fix those too. Only thing I've seen him stymied on is the laptop that went into a creek. It was just too wet. He could have rebuilt it, you know? But it would have cost more than just buying a new one. He was able to get the young man's files off of it, though, so that seems pretty darn good."

Cari smiled and wondered if he was intentionally not answering her questions. "That is impressive. Have you worked here a long time?"

That question resulted in a smile. "Since I graduated high school. I was on the football team with Ben, so he helped me get the job."

"Oh, I didn't realize Ben ever worked here," Cari commented.

"Oh, he didn't, but he talked to his dad and his dad hired me on. It's been a good job and Ben's brother was a good boss too. He kept me on after his dad retired," the man told her.

"Do you just work the cash register or do you ever answer the phone too?" Cari asked him, noticing the landline near the register.

"I do both. We can put people on hold if we're helping another customer. I'm not very good with electronics or technology, but I'm pretty strong. I was a linebacker on the football team back then, so I started off unloading freight here and getting stuff on the shelves. Now that I'm older, they just park me here," he told her.

"That's great to have such stability in your job," Cari complimented him. "Do you ever get any grumpy or angry people on the phone?"

He looked over both his shoulders before he answered. "Well, I did take a few calls a month or so back from a guy who really wanted to talk to Horace. He was really unfriendly. I sent the call over to Horace's office line. After the fourth time, Horace asked me to just tell him to stop calling."

Cari felt the hair on her arms rise. "Did he call again?"

The older man shrugged. "If he did, I didn't take the call."

"Did the man identify himself on the phone?" Cari asked.

The older man pulled out a spiral notebook from the desk drawer. "I write down the names of anyone who asks to speak with the manager or owner. Let's see, that was a month ago, so let me flip back..." he paused. "Oh, I remember now. I asked for his name and he said he'd give it to Horace, which I didn't really like, but I decided it wasn't really my place to say if the man could talk to Horace or not. He blocked his phone number too, so I couldn't even record that."

Cari resisted the urge to let her shoulders droop. "I read that the business has been in the family for over three generations. Horace's daughter will be the fourth generation, right?"

"She will be. I'm trying to be polite to her and all, but I've never worked for a woman before, well, unless you count my ball and chain..." he guffawed.

Cari tried to smile at his joke but doubted she pulled it off when he cleared his throat a second later.

"My apologies; Beth tells me it's rude to call her that too. Anyway, I've never had a female boss before, so I'm trying not to offend her. She's always been a kid in my eyes...been coming up to the shop since she couldn't even see over the countertop here. I think she'll do just fine if she can put up with me," he grinned.

Cari did smile this time. "I'm sure it feels overwhelming to her right now, but it sounds like the business is familiar to her. Other than the one caller you mentioned, did anyone else not get along well with Mr. Manwith?"

He looked at her funny for a second. "Oh, you mean Horace. I was thinking his dad at first and that guy didn't get along with a lot of people, but he kept his customers happy for the most part, so I guess it worked out. Horace? He worked like a dog. He was here all the time. I guess the only person who didn't like that was probably his wife Debbie."

"Understandable," Cari remarked. "Well, thank you for your time, sir. I hope everything with the transition of ownership goes smoothly for you."

"I'm sure it will be fine. Or it won't and I'll retire," he guffawed again.

Cari waved goodbye and walked back out to her car. It sounded like there was a decent chance the same person had called this business owner too. She wondered what the two businesses had in common. Or maybe it was a connection between the owners. She felt like the answer was just beyond her grasp.

* * * * *

Genevieve stirred the simmering vegetables while she read through her notes from their time with the park ranger. He had mentioned something about people getting into the park from a back route. She wasn't sure how to access the area behind the park as she'd only entered through the front gate. Park ranger Ted had given them his number for any follow-up questions, so she decided to call him and see if he could give her directions. She punched in the number with her left hand while she stirred with her right hand.

"This is Ted," he answered cheerfully. "Is this Detective Viacorte?"

"Yes, I'm sorry to bother you on a Saturday, but I was thinking about something you said on Thursday. You said it didn't happen often, but people used to try to access the park from the wilderness beyond the park's borders. I wanted to check it out as a possible entry point, but I'm not sure how to get back there," she explained.

"Ah, well, it's pretty challenging to get back there, which is why I said it was rare. You have to climb some boulders and navigate several steep switchbacks," he told her.

"From the park side or the wilderness side?" she asked.

"Well…both. The park side is a little easier because we have a nicely marked trail part of the way. On the wilderness side, you have to get across a stream first. Then, there's a pretty high barbed wire fence to get over once you reach the park's boundary. Everything over there is part of the Strahan family's land," he responded. "You and your partner seem to be in pretty good physical shape. This is a pretty long hike, over seven miles round trip. Were you wanting to go out there today?"

Genevieve smirked. Alex would never agree to work like this on a Saturday. "Would you have time to be a guide?"

"Oh, yeah. Today is my day off, but I love hiking. I'd be happy to lead you guys up there. What time should we meet?" Ted asked her.

Genevieve bit her lip. "I think it's probably just going to be me. Detective Runimoss has pretty strict work-life boundaries."

Ted chuckled, then cleared his throat. "Well, that changes things. We need three people to do the hike in case someone gets hurt. Safety first."

"Oh, right. I think I can find us a third hiker," she said slowly, thinking of Cari. "What time works best for you?"

"How about two o'clock? I can meet you at the main entrance," he suggested.

"That works. I'll call you back if I can't find someone to join us. Thanks, Ted," she responded.

"Happy to help. See you soon," he said and ended the call.

Genevieve hoped Cari would be free in the afternoon. She knew she would be up for chasing a lead. She found her name in her contacts list and hit the call button. She could hear road noise when her friend answered and wondered where she was driving.

"Hey, Gen! What's up?" Cari asked.

"I know you're looking into the Frobish woman's death and wondered if you were up for a little sleuthing with me," Genevieve told her. "Where are you right now?"

"I'm in the car. I was just…out running errands," her friend said vaguely. "What kind of sleuthing are you suggesting?"

"Well, the park ranger suggested someone could possibly enter the park by hiking in from the back by trespassing, more or less," she explained. "I wanted to see if there were any signs someone had been back there."

"Count me in," Cari said quickly. "What do I need to bring?"

"He said it's a pretty challenging hike, so wear some good shoes and bring some water. I'll have some sunscreen and bug spray," she told Cari.

"No problem. What time? Bob is making me dinner tonight, but I'm sure that will be after five," Cari mentioned.

"I'll pick you up at a quarter to two. We're meeting him at the main entrance to the park. It's about seven or so miles, round trip," she explained.

"Got it. I'll be ready to go. Thanks for including me, Gen," Cari said and ended the call.

Genevieve pumped her fist. *Success!* She wondered if she should let Alex know about her plans. Sometimes he got irritated if she called him on the weekend about a case; other times he was frustrated if she kept him out of the loop. She turned off the vegetables and looked at her phone. Better to stay on Alex's good side. She hit talk on his number.

"Gen, it feels like you're making a habit of working on the weekends. We definitely aren't *besties*, so I know you aren't calling to invite me to the movies," Alex grumbled into her ear. "What's up this time?"

She smiled. "Well, Grandpa, I was thinking about the back entry to the park."

"I thought there wasn't an entry in the back? Oh, I see, the trespassing entry. Go on," he instructed her.

"I called Ted and asked him if he could show me the back fence. He said I had to bring someone along because we need to hike in threes," she told him.

"Oh, come on. Don't tell me you're including me in this. No overtime, remember?" he complained.

"Don't worry. I called Cari. She's going to join us. I just wanted to let you know, so you don't feel left out on Monday," she explained. "Oh, and before I forget, I asked my FBI contact to run that number we got yesterday."

"And?" he asked, suddenly more interested.

"They agreed it was probably a burner. They did get hits on towers in our area for the number, but haven't tied it to a name yet. I'll keep you posted," she told him.

"See you Monday, Viacorte," he said. "Be safe out there on your little hike."

"Will do. Bye, Alex," she said and ended the call.

Genevieve looked at her pot of marinara sauce. She probably had enough for two jars to freeze and one to save for a meal this week. It had taken several failed attempts to perfect ladling the sauce into the jars, but she could finally do it without burning herself or spilling most of it on the floor or counter. She finished getting the sauce into three jars and set them aside to cool completely. It was just after noon, so she had time to eat some lunch before gathering her hiking gear and picking up Cari.

She made herself a sandwich and then logged into her laptop. She wanted to look up Garrett Frobish and see what he'd been up to recently. Like she told Alex, she didn't think he was involved, but they needed to eliminate him as a suspect. The employee said he'd run off to Florida, so she included that in her search parameters. Frobish wasn't that popular of a name, so her search only gave her a few results. She was able to eliminate all but one after looking at their ages. Garrett Frobish, formerly married to Elaine Frobish, had died in a traffic accident nearly a decade ago. *That settles that.*

Chapter 8

Cari decided to spend some time on Ollaman's new business article. She had almost two hours to burn until her hike with Genevieve and the park ranger, so she might as well get some work done. She pulled up the list of businesses and started to organize them by product or service. Five new restaurants, a laundromat, and a book store had opened in the last eight months. Cari debated about including the book store as new; the previous structure had burned down last fall, but it did have a new owner and a new building, just not a new name. Some of the new businesses had taken over existing buildings, but two of them had been built in the newer part of town in what everyone called the warehouse district.

She logged into her email to get the lists the intern sent her the day before. She repeated the process of sorting the businesses on the three lists in a similar fashion. The intern had wisely created a spreadsheet to tabulate all the names and Cari decided to just add the info from Brenington. The spreadsheet had multiple column headers including the business name, whether it was new or changing ownership, the city, the owner, and any builder or contractor information. As she scrolled down the sheet, she noticed the contracting company Pierce Construction and Landscaping showed up multiple times. In the last eight months, they'd been hired to work on twelve of the new projects. The name seemed familiar, so she switched to her email to see who did the landscaping for the new neighborhoods in the area: Pierce again. Ollaman would definitely want to highlight such a prosperous company. She opened a search engine to find their website.

Pierce Construction and Landscaping, or PCL as their website commonly referred to it, was owned by Randall Pierce. He looked to be in his fifties and was originally from Canada. In the biography section, Pierce was described as a boy-next-door and a bit of an All-American even though he was technically Canadian. After getting a degree in construction science and some sort of special certification called LEED, he worked for a well-known big-box store as the head of their landscaping division. Frustrated by the one-size-fits-all attitude of the large business, he started his own company to do things his way. His desire was to offer affordable landscaping to both commercial and residential clients in the area. The website emphasized supporting local businesses and the community through sponsoring youth sports teams and other charitable donations. The business' primary focus was landscaping, but they also took on simple construction jobs like wheelchair ramps, raised flower beds, fire pits, as well as outdoor kitchens. Cari thought building an outdoor kitchen sounded complex, but she had about zero construction skills. She selected the tab called Personal Reviews and began skimming the quotes of happy customers.

> *Pierce brought new life to our business. I couldn't be happier.*
> *Randy Pierce does fantastic work. Whatever you need, he can do it.*
> *If you're looking for a landscaper, look no further than Pierce. They'll treat you right.*

The business was also endorsed by the Brenington Chamber of Commerce. Cari went to their contact page to find a phone number or email. Michelle had given Cari a list of the newspaper's current sponsors but she didn't remember seeing PCL on the list. She found the list and scrolled through it. Sure enough, PCL was not a current sponsor. She wondered if Ollaman had missed them or if the business had turned him down. She hadn't contacted the subcontractors individually yet, so she formulated a personal email to Randall Pierce to give him a brief overview of her article and to ask if he had time for an interview.

She checked her watch and gulped. Genevieve was going to arrive any minute and she hadn't changed clothes yet. She slammed her laptop closed and hurried into her bedroom to get ready for the hike.

* * * * *

Just when Genevieve had about given up on her friend coming outside on time, Cari rushed from her apartment. She quickly locked the door behind her and hurried down the stairs to the Expedition, shoes in hand. Genevieve smirked. She remembered her little brother making similar exits from their house when they were young.

"Sorry, sorry, sorry! I completely lost track of time," Cari apologized as she climbed into the large vehicle.

"Glad you're able to join me. The park ranger said we had to have three hikers and Alex wasn't interested," Genevieve told her. "I brought an extra water bottle, some sunscreen, and a canister of bug spray. I already put on sunscreen. You can put some on while we drive. Do you need anything else?"

"Water! Whoops. I filled that up but must have left it inside. Thank goodness you're organized," Cari said gratefully. "I just need to send Bob a text. He's making dinner tonight and he's supposed to let me know what time to come over."

Genevieve smiled at her friend. "That's sweet. So, have you guys set a date yet?"

Cari groaned as she thumbed off a text to Bob. "Not you too! Our moms are constantly asking us the same thing. I mean, we've only been engaged a little over a month."

Genevieve put a hand up in surrender. "Fair enough. Just making conversation."

"I know. Sorry for snapping. Man, things are just stressful lately," Cari remarked. "Ollaman's got me working two stories…and…"

"And, what?" Genevieve asked with concern wondering why her friend trailed off.

"I, um, well, I guess it isn't really a secret," Cari began.

Genevieve felt the hairs on her neck rise. *Maybe Cari knew something about Robby's company.*

"Ollaman is restructuring the benefits and stuff at the newspaper. He's changing the intern program to unpaid and possibly dropping our health insurance package, too. I guess the sponsorships have dropped off some as well as subscriptions. People don't read the newspaper like they used to. You can get most of your news basically for free," Cari explained.

"I hadn't thought about that. I guess it's true. I think the local kids and their parents like seeing their names in the paper, though. Surely that counts for something?" Genevieve asked.

"Well, I'm sure it does to a point, but money is tight for everyone anymore. People might choose to just buy one issue if their child is in it rather than have a yearly subscription," Cari theorized.

"That's true, but your job is okay, right?" she asked as she turned down the road to the state park.

"Yeah, all of the full-time journalist positions are safe, at least for now," Cari told her.

"Hopefully, Ollaman can stir up some more funding," Genevieve said encouragingly.

"Fingers crossed. That's what one of my articles is sort of focusing on, in an indirect manner," Cari said and explained her other story.

"Ah, so he's hoping some of these new businesses will like the *free* advertising and feel inclined to support the newspaper?" Genevieve guessed.

"That's his hope," Cari confirmed.

Genevieve's mind wandered to Robby and what Dureski had told her. Cari had confided in Genevieve that Bea was troubled by something with Robby's job. She wondered if Cari had learned any more.

"Hey, you told me a while back that something was bothering Bea about Robby's job. Did she ever tell you what it was?" Genevieve asked in what she hoped was a casual tone.

Cari's hand went to her locket and Genevieve silently berated herself for being nosey. After a few more seconds, Cari finally responded.

"I think she was, uh, just frustrated with how many hours he was having to work. He has a lot more responsibility now than he did in his old job, so I think it's been, um, an adjustment...for both of them," Cari said as she crossed her left leg over her right.

Genevieve was trained to read people and their body language, but even an untrained eye could see her question had made her friend uncomfortable. Cari's body language also told her Cari was either holding something back or lying. She decided not to press her on it and just nodded in understanding. It probably had been an adjustment for the entire family.

Cari uncrossed her legs after a moment and then cleared her throat. "Do we have to pay to enter when we're here for official police business?"

Genevieve laughed and put her window down. "Day pass, please," she said to the ranger in the booth.

After paying, she pulled into a parking spot. Ted was waiting for them near the trailhead she'd hiked earlier in the week. She got out of the car and waved.

"That's the park ranger over there," she told Cari. "Let me just grab my backpack and we can join him."

She pulled her backpack out of the backseat and took out the bug spray. After coating herself liberally, she handed the canister to Cari. She waited while Cari sprayed her arms and legs, then returned the can to the backpack.

"Right this way," she directed her friend.

Ted looked nonplussed when they reached him. "Ladies, this is a pretty challenging hike. It might take over an hour and we're going to have to climb over some rather large boulders."

"Sounds fantastic," Cari said enthusiastically. She held out her hand. "I'm Cari, a friend of Genevieve. Thanks for being our guide."

"Ted," he said and shook her hand. "If you're ready to go, then let's get hiking. The trail is clearly marked, so why don't I take the rear? Detective Viacorte, you lead the way."

Genevieve stepped past the park ranger and started up the now-familiar trail. She was fairly certain he picked her to be in the lead because she was the shortest member of the group. She was ready to prove herself, if she needed. They reached the top of the cliff in about ten minutes.

"Hold up. Does anyone need to rest?" Ted asked.

"I'm fine," the two women said in unison and then laughed.

"Well, grab a drink of water. You don't want to get dehydrated," Ted instructed and took a drink from his canteen.

Genevieve turned to Cari so she could get the extra bottle of water from the side pocket of the backpack. She took a swig from her bottle and then returned it to its place. Cari shoved the spare bottle back into the pocket.

"This next stretch is flat for a bit, then it starts getting into the switchbacks," Ted told them. "Ready, Detective?"

Genevieve nodded and continued past the lookout point along the dirt trail. A few wildflowers dotted the grasses alongside the trail. If she'd been out for a leisurely hike, she might have stopped to take photos. They had barely reached the first section of switchbacks when Ted called out again.

"Need a break?"

Both women told him no and continued hiking the trail. Genevieve typically stopped for water about every fifteen to twenty minutes. She knew it had only been about ten minutes since they reached the cliff top, so she looked ahead on the trail. An outcropping of rocks sat to one side of the trail. They could sit on those and be out of the way if anyone else was coming back down the trail.

"How about we stop for a water break by those rocks up ahead?" she called back to Ted and Cari.

Cari gave a thumbs up. "Great idea."

A few minutes later they each took a seat on a rock to get a drink. Ted pulled out a bandana and wiped it over his face. After taking a few drinks from her water bottle, Genevieve stood up and put her backpack on again.

"You're really determined to get to the back of the park," Ted commented.

"If it's a possible entry point, we need to check it out," Genevieve told him. "If the fence is undisturbed, then we'll have to look for his entry from somewhere else. No one lives in the park, so he got in somehow."

The rest of the hiking trio stood up and Genevieve continued up the trail. The switchbacks were somewhat challenging as the elevation increased fairly quickly. After another fifteen minutes, the trail straightened out. They were over halfway up the mountain now and had almost reached the boulders Ted mentioned. She decided to stop for water again when they made it to the tall rocks.

"We need to have another water break soon, Detective," Ted said from the back of the line.

"Agreed. I thought we could stop by the first boulder ahead," she told him.

Rather than sit down, she stayed on her feet to drink this time. The hike had been challenging, but she didn't want to waste time chatting. Cari followed her example and took a couple drinks before returning the water to the backpack. Ted took off his ranger hat briefly to wipe the sweat off again. He nodded he was ready to keep moving.

Whoever developed the trail to the top had cut through some of the large rocks to make passage on the dirt possible. Other times, just a portion of the rock was carved away and Genevieve had to pull herself up onto it and then slide down the other side. Cari was a few inches taller than Genevieve, but most of the rocks were too tall for her to step up onto as well. Ted was able to step up onto the carved-out section and then step down to the trail on the other side. They'd been hiking for over forty-five minutes and Genevieve was starting to breathe a little harder. This was like a full-body workout. As she slid down the opposite side of another boulder, she felt a stinging pain on her right arm and immediately gripped it. A sharp edge of the boulder had scratched her. Thankfully, it wasn't bleeding.

"Okay up there?" Ted asked.

"Just a scratch. Let's stop for water again once everyone's on this side. I have a first aid kit and can clean it up a bit," Genevieve responded.

She set her backpack down and opened it to find her small first aid kit. Cari slid down to the path and stayed to the left to avoid getting scratched. She grabbed her water from the backpack while Genevieve used an antiseptic wipe on the scrape.

"Need any help?" Ted asked as he stepped down onto the trail.

"I think I've got it. I'll put some ointment on it and it should be fine," she responded.

She squeezed a little antibiotic ointment onto her left index finger and rubbed it along the scratch. It wasn't deep, so she decided not to bandage it. She packed up the kit and then took a moment to drink some water.

"We've got about five more of these boulders to navigate. After that, it levels off some to the fence. We aren't above the timber line here, so it's pretty wooded the whole way. The trail will turn before we reach the fence, but you should be able to see it through the tree growth," Ted told them.

Genevieve swung her backpack on and continued to the next boulder. She had hoped to show the park ranger that she was a skilled hiker by reaching the fence in under an hour and a half. Her mild injury had taken some time to care for, though. She pulled herself over the next five boulders and felt mental relief when she slid down the last one. It had to be easier going down than going up; at least she hoped it was. They marched along the tree-lined trail for several minutes. Thankfully, the trail was clearly marked, or Genevieve could easily imagine getting lost. All the trees looked the same. Eventually, the trail made a sharp turn to the left. She slowed to a stop and tried to peer through the tree branches.

"Is this where we access the fence?" she asked Ted.

"Yes. If you push back these branches a bit," he demonstrated as he spoke. "See? There's the fence just beyond this row of trees."

Genevieve looked where he indicated and saw the tall chain-linked fence with two strands of barbed wire on top. She looked up at Ted.

"And it's okay if we leave the trail to get a better look at it?" she asked for permission.

"Lead the way, Detective," he said, gesturing toward the fence.

She carefully pushed the branches aside and held them for Cari to grab before moving forward. She walked slowly and watched the ground as much as the branches. If someone had been through here, they might see footprints or other evidence. Wild grass grew in patches under the large trees. As she neared the fence, she noticed some grass looked trampled. She stopped to take out her phone.

"The grass is broken off in places up here. I want to get a photo before we disturb it," she explained as she took photos.

"Oh no!" Ted exclaimed when he reached her.

She followed his gaze and realized his cause for alarm. The fence pole nearest them had plastic zip ties securing the chain-link fence to it rather than the metal loops that traditionally held it together. Someone had cut through the links and then tied them back together. The rest of the fence still looked relatively new and didn't have any bends in it, but the section nearest them was warped as though someone had folded it back to enter through the gap. Whoever cut the fence had only zip-tied a few of the links rather than all of the cuts. Something caught Genevieve's eye.

"Look at that," Cari said at the same time. She started to reach out to grab it, but Genevieve put a hand on her arm.

"That could be evidence. I need to photograph it and then we have to get someone from CSU up here to collect it properly," she told her friend.

A small piece of black fabric was caught on one of the cut links. Genevieve photographed it from a few angles. She wondered if whoever left it behind had also gotten scratched. The CSU team could analyze it and would be able to swab it too. It might have some DNA on it, so it was worth trying.

"Some of the cut ends are rusted. It hasn't rained in the last few days, so these were cut before Thursday," she observed. "How often did you say the fence is checked?"

Ted took off his hat and ran a hand over his head. His cheeks were flushed and Genevieve wasn't sure it was just from the hike. He grimaced.

"Honestly, I don't know. It's something that's supposed to be checked at least weekly. It's assigned weekly, anyway. I assumed it was being done. I need to radio this in, if you'll excuse me for a moment," he said and pulled his radio off his hip.

Genevieve motioned to Cari. Beyond the fence, she could see a creek with more trees past that. She wanted to continue the hike and see what other evidence they could find, but knew it would be better for CSU to collect it. She strained to look for clues. It seemed like the grass was matted down a bit in a path toward the creek. She couldn't make out any footprints though.

Cari raised her eyebrows. "Are we going to keep exploring on the other side?"

Genevieve grimaced. "As much as I would like to, we can't. We don't want to disturb any evidence. I need to call this in to Grusky and see how he wants to proceed. Have you heard from Bob yet?"

Both women pulled out their cell phones and simultaneously frowned. They were in some sort of dead zone and neither phone had a signal. Genevieve tried raising her phone over her head in the hope it would get a bar or two but didn't succeed.

"I'm going to have to borrow Ted's radio or ask him to relay a message," Genevieve said.

They looked in his direction. He had just clipped the radio back to his belt. He walked back over to them.

"I spoke with the ranger on duty today. They checked the log book and it said we've had someone up here checking every week. Obviously, that's not true. I'm going to be meeting with them on Monday to discuss what was really happening," he said grimly.

"Ted, I need a favor. Can you radio your ranger again and ask them to call Brenington PD? They'll need to get dispatch to put a call out to Lieutenant Grusky regarding this fence. We need to get some people out here," she told him.

Ted put up his hands. "That was a lot. Let's relay it one sentence at a time."

Genevieve recounted her request sentence by sentence. The ranger on the radio said she'd be in touch once she talked with BPD. She hoped it didn't take too long; she'd feel bad if she made Cari late for her dinner with Bob. She looked over at her friend. Cari was walking in circles, seemingly trying to get a signal on her phone. She tripped on a tree root and almost fell.

"Watch your step!" Ted called out to her.

Cari gave a thumbs-up with one hand as she slid her phone into her pocket with the other. Genevieve waved her over.

"It probably won't take as long to get back down, right?" she said encouragingly.

Cari nodded. "For sure. Down is always faster than up."

"Ted, what's on the other side of the forest? Is there a road at some point?" Genevieve asked the park ranger.

He pulled a map from his hiking vest and unfolded it. "Here's the state park," he said, drawing a circle with his index finger. "And Brenington is down here. The forest stretches on about eight to ten miles to the north and west. There's a county road just past that, but you have to pass through the Strahan's farm to get to it."

Genevieve pulled out her notebook. "Strahan, you said?"

"S-T-R-A-H-A-N," he confirmed with the spelling.

"I wonder if they've had any evidence of trespassers lately," Genevieve remarked. "Do you know them?"

Ted nodded. "I can give you their number, sure."

He pulled out his cell phone and unlocked it. After scrolling for a few moments, he touched the screen.

"Are you an iPhone user?" he asked her.

"Yes, sir," she said holding up her phone.

"Let me airdrop it to you," he said as he punched some buttons on his phone. "Oh wait, I need to turn my Bluetooth on. I don't have a signal up here."

Genevieve heard Cari clear her throat and wondered if she was trying to keep from laughing. "I've got mine on, so ready when you are."

Ted hit a few more options on the phone and Genevieve's finally lit up with a notification. "Got it. Thanks, Ted."

"This guy breaking in through the back of the park...it seems premeditated, huh?" Ted asked her.

Genevieve bit the inside of her cheek. It was one thing to discuss an active case with Cari, someone she could trust. Ted, at best, was law enforcement adjacent.

"It's kind of early to speculate," she responded vaguely. "We don't even know if this was his ingress point."

She fidgeted with her thumbnail as she spoke. It was her nervous habit and she did it without even noticing sometimes. She caught Cari staring at her hand and stopped herself. Cari's eyes darted away, which made Genevieve feel even more awkward. She looked back at Ted; he'd raised his hands in surrender.

"Message received," he said with half a smile. "I've lived here for over twenty years. It seems like we've really had an increase in suspicious deaths in the last year or two. Have you noticed that too?"

Genevieve started to respond when Cari choked on her water. She looked her way and Cari had a hand up to indicate she was fine. She took another drink.

"Sorry about that. It went down the wrong way." She cleared her throat and coughed again. "I think I got it out now. Phew."

Ted's radio crackled. He turned up the volume as he removed it from his belt again.

"This is Ranger Ted. Can you repeat that?" he requested.

"I spoke with Lieutenant Grusky just now. He's sending out two people from their CSU team. He asked that you continue to secure the location until they arrive. Over."

"Roger that. Over," Ted responded.

Genevieve checked her watch. It was almost four o'clock now. It would probably take the two CSU people an hour to hike up to their location. She hoped the delay didn't make Cari late. She looked over at Cari, who smiled, but her knee was bobbing rapidly.

"You okay on time, Cari?" Genevieve asked her.

Cari looked at her watch. "I'm fine. I mean, it's possible they're sending Bob out here too."

"I thought you said he wasn't on call?" Genevieve reminded her.

"I don't think he is, but sometimes things change, right?"

* * * * *

His cell phone blasted out his boss' ring just as Bob finished washing the Brussels sprouts. He dried his hands on the kitchen towel and reached to answer the call.

"This is Bob," he said quickly.

"Hursley. It's Dr. Green. I need you to join Luvenon out at the state park again. I'm sorry to call you out on your weekend off, but I couldn't get Judith or Sarah to answer," Dr. Green told him. "Viacorte went out exploring and seems to have found something of interest."

"No problem, sir. I'll head over there now. Does Chris have our gear or do I need to stop by the station?" he asked.

"Luvenon has everything. He'll be waiting for you at the main entrance. Thanks, Hursley," Green said and ended the call.

Bob wondered what Cari and Genevieve had discovered. He texted Cari to tell her he was meeting her now instead of the other way around, but the message remained unread. Maybe the signal was spotty at the park. He put his colander of sprouts in the refrigerator and hoped he would be back soon to roast them.

He tried to call Cari once he was on his way to the state park, but the call went straight to voicemail. *No worries; I'll see her shortly.* The traffic was light, so he reached the parking lot in less than ten minutes. After paying the gate attendant, he taped the receipt to his windshield as instructed and then parked by Chris' vehicle. His co-worker was waiting for him at the trailhead. Even though Dr. Green said Chris would have everything, he'd still brought a backpack with some water and granola bars just in case.

"Hey, Bob. Heard you had to come out instead of one of the ladies. Sorry about that," Chris said when he shook Bob's hand. "I got directions from the park ranger. We've got quite the hike ahead of us. It might take more than an hour to get there."

Bob raised his eyebrows. "No kidding? Guess we should get started then."

"Follow me," Chris said and turned toward the trail. "The park ranger said we should have three people for the hike, but I promised her we wouldn't get hurt."

"Here's hoping," Bob said with a laugh. "What evidence are we collecting up there?"

"I guess someone cut through the fence in the back of the park. It's supposed to keep out trespassers, but no one has been checking it lately. Detective Viacorte found some fabric out there. She has no idea if it's relevant or not, but there is some indication of more evidence on the other side of the fence."

"You said it takes at least an hour to get to them?" Bob asked.

"That's right, maybe longer if we're slow," Chris said. "You brought water, right?"

"Yeah, I brought some granola bars too," Bob responded.

"I know the head park ranger is with Viacorte up there, but the female ranger said there were three people. I can't imagine she was able to drag Runimoss out here," Chris mused.

Bob blushed and was glad Chris couldn't see his face. "Uh, she didn't. Cari is with them."

Chris stopped and looked back at Bob. "The journalist? Your fiancée?"

Bob nodded. "You know what Cari's like; she's always chasing the next story. I guess hiking in threes is a big deal to the rangers out here; he told her he wouldn't take her up there without a third hiker."

"Fiancée. That is a life step. I'm not sure I'll ever get there. When are you guys getting married?" Chris asked.

Bob cringed. "We, uh, haven't set a date, yet. It's only been a month or so."

"Right on. I guess some people are engaged for years or whatever before they make it official, right?" Chris asked him.

Bob hoped it wouldn't be a years-long engagement. "Yeah, I suppose it's different for everyone."

They reached the lookout point they'd photographed two days before. A family of four was taking photos of each other, oblivious to the two men passing by. Chris continued up the trail.

"Let me know if you need to take a break. I'm probably going to drink water while I walk, unless I get winded," he told Bob.

"Luckily, I'm still kind of in shape from that 5k last weekend," Bob chuckled. "This is easy compared to that."

Chris didn't stop until they reached the boulders. Bob gratefully took off his backpack and sat down on one before getting a drink of water. It had taken them a little over half an hour to get there. Chris remained standing while he drank from his water bottle.

"These boulders are going to be a bit more challenging. Viacorte's pretty short. I bet she really struggled here," Chris commented.

"She's pretty strong, though...and very determined," Bob remarked.

"True. She showed us all that at the race. I can't believe both of them beat me. Runimoss is never going to let me forget it," Chris laughed. "Ready to keep going?"

Bob put his water away and stood up. "Lead on. We've got to be getting close, right?"

"Yeah, after these boulders, it's a lot easier and not too much further," he said as he stepped onto the first one. "Hopefully, we'll reach them in the next ten to fifteen minutes," Chris responded.

Bob found himself grunting as he maneuvered over one boulder after another. He was going to be really sore tomorrow. He sighed with relief once he stepped back onto the regular trail until he remembered they were going to have to go back the same way. He could hear voices through the trees and knew they must be close.

"CSU-on-site!" Chris called out, then turned to Bob. "I didn't want to startle anyone, but they should be expecting us."

"Good call," Bob agreed and checked his watch. "It's almost five o'clock. We made pretty good time."

Up ahead, three figures emerged from the wooded area. Bob waved in acknowledgment. He wondered how far beyond the fence line they needed to travel to collect evidence. While he wasn't super familiar with the area, he didn't think there was another road very close by. Genevieve waved them over as Cari hopped up from her perch on the boulder.

"Bob, I wondered if you might get called out," she said with a big smile. "Good to see you again, Chris."

Genevieve pointed toward the fence. "There's a piece of fabric that got snagged by the fence. I think you should swab the section for DNA. I have an evidence kit if you need it," she told them. "If you look beyond the fence through the trees, you can see places where the undergrowth is matted down, like someone walked on it. Obviously, I can't say how recently."

Chris pulled off his backpack. "I have everything we need in here."

Bob returned Cari's smile and then joined Chris by the fence to collect the evidence. The black fabric was fairly nondescript. He thought it looked synthetic, but they'd have to look at it under the microscope to be sure. Chris took out a DNA swab for the fence tine. He rubbed it over the metal end sufficiently and then sealed it into an evidence bag. Bob handed him the bag with the small piece of fabric.

"I'll put these in the digital log from my phone," Chris said as he set the two items on a rock.

"Good luck. There's no service up here," Genevieve told him.

"Shoot. I guess I'll just photograph it for now and get it logged later," he said with a grimace.

Cari had sidled up next to Bob and gave his hand a squeeze before releasing it. He smiled at her before returning his attention to Genevieve. She was still gesturing at the creek.

"Do you see what I mean? Someone was definitely up here," she said to them and walked toward the fence.

The park ranger was sitting on a rock nearby. He nodded in their direction, but didn't initially get up. Bob remembered his name was Ted.

"Ranger Ted?" Bob asked, which brought the ranger to his feet.

"Yes, sir. How can I help?" he responded.

"It sounds like we need to get on the other side of this fence to possibly collect more evidence. Should we cut these zip ties again or do you have another access point?" Bob asked him.

Ted took off his hat and scratched his head. "Well, there's not a gate. This fence was installed jointly by the Park Service and the Strahans. He probably wanted it more than we did. We didn't have a need to get to the opposite side and we didn't want to make it easy for people to sneak into the park...so...no gate."

Chris pulled out a set of wire cutters and a box knife. "I guess this is our key, then. How far through the woods are we going?"

"Well, hold up. We're running out of daylight as it is. You're never going to make it to the road before dusk. In fact, we're just barely going to make it back to the parking lot before the sun starts to go down. I think it's best to wait until morning to start collecting your evidence." He put his hands up when Chris and Genevieve started to protest. "I know you came all the way out here, but we all hiked that trail. It's not easy. It's not safe to do it in the dark. I'm guessing I'm the only one here with a head lantern?"

Bob saw Cari nod in confirmation along with him. Genevieve turned her head, a look of frustration on her face. Chris rummaged through his bag and hissed something inaudible.

"Yeah, I don't have one either. Must have forgotten to put it back in here after I used it last. Dang. Detective Viacorte, this is your case. Are we coming back out tomorrow or waiting until Monday?" he asked Genevieve.

"More than likely, it will be Monday. The department is trying to avoid overtime whenever possible, and Runimoss is happy to oblige in that regard," she explained. "I'll check in with Grusky once we get back down."

"Aren't you concerned the evidence will be lost in that time?" Chris asked.

She shrugged. "It's already been forty-eight hours. Not much more we can do. I don't think the person is going to come back to make sure they didn't leave anything behind. Right now, we aren't even sure we're looking for someone. Green hasn't declared it a homicide yet, has he?"

Chris looked from Bob to Genevieve to Cari and then Ted. "Uh, I don't think he issued a press release yet, but he did declare the Frobish case a homicide earlier this afternoon. You might have already been on the trail by that point and out of signal range."

"I'm sorry you two had to come all the way up here just to turn around and go back, but as much as it pains me to say it, I agree with the ranger. It's safer to come back a different day," Genevieve said.

"What kind of access do we have from the other side? Can we use an ATV to get out here?" Chris asked the park ranger.

His face paled a bit. "ATVs can really destroy the vegetation of an area…but it does seem ridiculous to carry evidence out on foot when it's probably eight or nine miles in one direction."

"Eight or nine *miles*? We're for sure using some kind of motorized vehicle to get out here," Chris remarked. "Does the park have something we can borrow? A gator or something?"

Ted nodded. "Let me know when you need it and I'll make sure you have access. Is everyone ready to hike back down?"

"Let's get moving. I'll lead," Chris said and turned around. "Holler if you need a break."

Chapter 9

A yawn escaped Cari's lips and she gave Bob a sheepish look. He smiled good-naturedly. It had been a long day.

"Thanks for helping me cook dinner. I'm sorry we're eating so late," Bob told her.

"I'm not sure how helpful I was, but the food is delicious," Cari responded between bites. "It helps that I was starving."

"This fish tastes even better when you grill it, but the apartment won't let me have a grill. Fire hazard," he shrugged.

He opened his mouth again but didn't say anything. He looked down at his plate and forked another bite of fish. Cari wondered what was on his mind. She took another bite while she waited for him to speak, but Bob continued eating. She decided to bring up Robby again. She'd already given him the basic outline of what was happening, so she might as well take advantage of his insight.

"I talked to Robby again. I think he's holding out on me," Cari said slowly.

"Hmm…" Bob said with a nod.

"When he told me about this whole thing, he made it sound like this was happening over and over again. Multiple times, but then he only sent me three billing codes," she explained.

Bob just nodded. Cari wasn't sure he was really listening.

"I looked into the three codes and one of them seems meaningless. The other two might be relevant, but I think the police could be more helpful. He still won't talk to them. He hasn't even told Bea about his theory," Cari said with concern. "But if it's just the three codes, then it's probably nothing. He promised to look again on Monday. My gut says he has more to give. He's afraid someone is watching him, like digitally…do you think that's rational?"

Bob made eye contact this time, but then shrugged. "How big is his company?"

Cari shook her head. "I have no idea. It seems big, but I've never asked."

"A lot of larger companies keep track of their employees' internet usage," he remarked. "Just like certain websites and apps are blocked at schools."

"That's true." She took a drink of water. "While we were waiting for you and Chris to arrive, Ted made a comment about several suspicious deaths in the area recently. It kind of caught me off guard. Maybe Robby is onto something with these codes. I don't know what to think."

Bob didn't say anything but raised his eyebrows. Cari felt like he seemed irritated. She wondered why. Rather than ask, she just kept talking.

"I think I might be a bit dehydrated. That hike really took it out of me. Those boulders were no joke."

Bob put his fork down and pushed his plate toward the center of the table. "It was a hard hike. I'm beat. Church tomorrow?"

"Sure. What time?" Cari asked after wiping her mouth with a napkin.

"Let's do the late service. I don't want to set an alarm," he confessed. "I'll pick you up at 10:30."

"Sounds good," she stood up and grabbed her plate.

"Don't worry about the dishes. I'll do them later," Bob said with a yawn.

"Okay. You don't have to tell me twice," she said with a grin, but Bob didn't really laugh.

"I just remembered you didn't drive here. Let me grab my keys," he said as he got up from the table.

"Is everything okay?" she asked him with concern.

He grabbed her hand. "Yeah, everything's fine. I'm just...really tired."

"I could stay...?" she offered half-heartedly. "Then you don't have to drive me back to my place. I don't have anything to wear to church in the morning, though."

Bob ran a hand over his face. "I don't mind driving you home. We'll both sleep better in our own beds, right?"

"You're probably right," she said and smiled. "Thanks for playing chauffeur for me."

He nodded and opened the door to his apartment. She stepped outside and waited for him to lock the door. They yawned in unison.

"Are we old now? We aren't even thirty yet!" Cari laughed.

"One of us is closer than the other," Bob answered.

"That's right. You're only like two months from a new decade, huh?" Cari acknowledged as she got in his car.

He nodded again. "I sure feel old after today."

Cari smiled and patted Bob on the shoulder. "I wasn't sure we were ever going to get back to the trailhead. It was hard work getting up there, but equally challenging to get back down."

Bob nodded in agreement. He rubbed his face with his hand. The day had been really long for both of them. Cari caught herself falling asleep on the short drive to her apartment. She yawned again and rubbed her face. She just needed to stay awake a little bit longer.

Bob gave her a quick kiss at her doorstep before hurrying back to his car. Cari wondered again if something was bothering him. He seemed distracted. She found herself rubbing her locket and checked her watch. It was too late to call Grandmother now. She could call in the morning. For now, she was going to sleep.

* * * * *

Cari's legs screamed at her when her alarm woke her up the next morning. She reached to silence her alarm and realized her arms were sore too. Maybe she didn't drink enough water during the hike and her muscles were protesting because of it. She'd barely managed to peel her clothes off the night before and slip into her pajamas. Her skin felt grimy and tacky after the grueling hike. She'd feel better after a hot shower. Her locket caught her eye as she dragged herself out of bed. If she wanted to chat with her grandmother, she needed to call now. She picked up her phone and commanded Siri to make the call. Grandmother answered on the second ring.

"You're up early this morning, my dear," her grandmother observed. "Are you going to early church?"

"No, we're going to the later service this morning. We took a pretty long hike in the state park yesterday and it really wore us out," she explained.

"You and Bob?" Grandmother asked.

"Bob, Genevieve, Chris, the park ranger, and me," Cari told her. "Genevieve wanted to see if someone had gotten into the park by trespassing. Turns out she was right."

"This is in relation to the poor woman who fell last week?" Grandmother asked with concern.

"Yes, possibly. It's still early," she paused.

"What's bothering you?" her grandmother asked.

"You always know when something's off with me," Cari said with a smile. "Bob seemed a little, well, off himself last night. He wasn't very talkative and kind of gave off an irritated vibe."

"It's rare for Bob to seem irritated. Maybe he was just tired," Grandmother told her.

"Maybe. He just didn't respond much to most of what I said," Cari said uncertainly.

"Well, Bob is a planner. I get the impression he likes to know what's happening and when," Grandmother pointed out. "Have you asked him about it? Maybe he wants to start making some wedding plans but feels like you aren't ready yet."

Cari gulped. "It was just ten days ago he said we could take as long as we need. Surely, he hasn't changed his mind already."

"He's probably just tired, dear. What were you trying to talk to him about anyway?" Grandmother asked.

Cari hesitated. She didn't want to share Robby's secret. "Just the case. You're probably right. I bet he was tired."

"Well, I've got to get going or I'll be late for church," her grandmother told her.

"Okay, love you, Grandmother," Cari said warmly.

"I love you more," she responded.

Cari set the phone aside and headed into the bathroom to shower. She still wasn't convinced Bob was just tired. Maybe she should just ask him when he picked her up for church.

The shower refreshed Cari's mood. She started up her coffee pot and then stuck an English muffin into the toaster for some breakfast. It had taken some effort to tease all the tangles out of her curly hair, but she finally had it in a presentable state. She had a little less than half an hour before Bob said he'd be at her apartment. She was glad to have a relaxing morning for once. Her phone pinged with a notification; Ollaman had sent her an email.

She opened her email app and selected the message. It was a calendar request for a meeting the next morning. She accepted the request and made sure it added to her phone's calendar correctly. The request included a statement telling her the meeting would be in regard to the new HR changes. She wasn't looking forward to it, but hoped she could convince her boss not to alter their healthcare plans as Jack had suggested. Ollaman was stubborn, so she set her chances at fifty-fifty.

Bryson's comments about the changes rolled through her mind. She'd never considered the newspaper business to be unstable or something that wouldn't continue to thrive, but maybe she was naïve. The more she thought about it, the more she realized Bryson was right. It was becoming rarer for towns to have their own newspaper. All she'd ever wanted to do was write for a newspaper. It was overwhelming to think her dream job was becoming obsolete. A knock at the door pulled her from her thoughts. She put her empty coffee cup in the sink and rushed to the door.

"I didn't mean to make you come inside. I kind of lost track of time," she told him when she opened the door.

He smiled. "No problem. We aren't in a hurry. Are you ready to go, though?"

Cari pulled him into a hug. "Come in for a second. I just need to grab my purse...and a water bottle."

"How are your legs today? Mine are so sore. I almost fell out of bed," he said with a laugh.

"I'm pretty sore too. Hopefully, it won't last long," she said as she gathered her things. "Okay, I'm ready."

"Great," Bob said as he turned back to the door.

She grabbed his hand and squeezed it as they stepped outside. He seemed back to normal today; maybe he wasn't irritated with her after all. She locked her door and followed him to his car.

"You mentioned Chris was going back to the station to log the evidence and start analyzing it. Did you hear anything from him?" Cari asked with curiosity.

"He said the swab tested positive for biological materials, so he started the process to get a DNA profile from it. We don't have anything to compare it to yet, so I'm not sure how it will help us," Bob informed her.

"What about the fingernails? Was there anything usable on the nails you located with the drone?" Cari asked as Bob drove toward the church.

"We did get some epithelial cells from two of those, but it takes a lot of time to extract DNA from the skin cells. Green wanted to do the autopsy first. It's possible the cells are the victim's and won't really help us," Bob told her.

"It's a start," Cari said encouragingly.

Bob nodded as he pulled into a parking space. Cari looked around the lot; summer break definitely put a dent in church attendance. As they walked toward the entrance, her mind wandered to their wedding. She tried to picture having the ceremony inside, but couldn't quite imagine it. Maybe an outdoor wedding fit her personality better?

* * * * *

Genevieve's thumb hovered over the call button for a few seconds. Unable to press it, she set her phone on the table. She went back to her notes to make sure she was ready to call Dureski with an update. Maybe she was just a cog in his network, but she wanted to be a noticeable one if she could. She settled her thoughts and unlocked her phone again. Now she was ready.

"Dureski," he said into the phone. "What do you have for me, Viacorte?"

"Couple things, sir. The park ranger informed us of an alternative entrance to the state park. It's not a legal entrance; people have to get through a fence and trespass on someone else's property as well," she explained.

"Obviously, breaking the law is not a problem for this guy. I don't need a history lesson. Just tell me what you found," Dureski barked.

Genevieve bit back an apology and plowed on. "We found a breach in the fence line as well as a scrap of fabric and possible DNA left behind."

Dureski whistled. "Hmm…I have one other case with DNA, but the perp wasn't in the system, so it was a dead end from the looks of it."

Genevieve made a note. "We also found epithelials under the victim's nails, uh, the broken off nails. The lab guys are working on extracting DNA. Hopefully, we'll have those results tomorrow."

Dureski stayed silent. Genevieve worked up her courage to ask him for information. It didn't have to be a one-way street.

"Did anything come up with the burner number? In other cases, that is?" she asked with as much confidence as she could muster.

"The, uh, the burner…oh right. Actually, yes. The number showed up in another victim's call records. It's a little reckless on his part," Dureski observed.

Genevieve added it to her notes. "Are there other numbers on the records which overlap?"

"These are great questions, Detective, but I don't need your assistance on the larger case. Keep working on Frobish. Call me with updates," he retorted and ended the call.

Genevieve pouted. She thought she was really making progress when the agent clammed up again. Wasn't more information better? She wished he was more willing to trust her, but for now, she'd just have to keep proving herself.

She looked at her notes. She needed to call the Strahans and see if they'd had any trespassers. It seemed like they would have reported it, at the very least to the state park if not the police, but maybe it wasn't a priority. She found the contact Ted had air-dropped to her and hit the call button. It rang several times before someone answered.

"Hello?" a gruff voice reverberated in her ear.

"Is this Malcolm Strahan? This is Detective Genevieve Viacorte with the Brenington PD. I'm calling in regards to the fence line that runs between your property and the state park," she explained.

"You sound a little young to be a detective," Strahan remarked. "What do you need to know about the fence?"

"In the course of an investigation, we discovered a portion of the fence had been snipped and folded back to allow access to the park. Have you had anyone trespassing on your land?" she asked.

"Someone cut my fence?" he barked. "Georgia! Georgia, where are you?"

Genevieve pulled the phone away from her ear a bit as the man shouted at Georgia to join him.

"Okay, just a sec…gotta find the speaker button. Got it. Georgia, this is a detective on the phone. She says someone cut our fence," he said pointedly.

"The fence between here and the park?" the woman sounded young. Genevieve wondered if it was his daughter speaking.

"What other fence can get cut?!" he grumbled. "Your boys were out there on the ATVs the other day. What day was it? Wednesday? Thursday?"

Genevieve silently willed it to be Thursday. Maybe they saw something.

"It was last Thursday," Georgia said quietly.

"Call them in here," he demanded.

"Owen? Landon? Grandpa needs to talk to you…" her voice rang out. "Yes…right now."

"Boys. Sit down. Don't lie to me. I got the police on the phone right here. Isn't that right, Detective?" Strahan asked in a commanding voice.

"I'm still on the line, yes," Genevieve said quickly, regretting the direction the call was taking.

"Did you cut a hole into my fence?" he asked loudly.

"It wasn't…it's not really a hole," a small voice said slowly.

"Grandpa, we're really sorry, but we were shooting our arrows and one of them went through the fence. We had to get it back," another young male voice explained with a tremor.

"We repaired it straight away, sir. We borrowed your wire cutters and some zip ties and closed it back up right after we got the arrow out," the first voice spoke again.

Genevieve's shoulders drooped.

"Is that how you got the scratch across your back? You're lucky you just got a tetanus shot at the doctor's a few weeks ago. You could have really had some problems…and I'm not talking about with me," Strahan said firmly. "You boys know better than to be going into the state park. You shouldn't have been anywhere near it. You had to cross the creek to get over there and I've told you it isn't safe to be playing around there without an adult with you. If you fell in, the current could carry you down to the waterfall before you even blinked twice."

"We're sorry, Grandpa We won't do it again," the young boys assured their grandpa.

Genevieve heard some muffled speaking between possibly the mother and her sons.

Strahan cleared his throat. "Is the state park considering pressing trespassing charges?"

Genevieve blinked. This conversation had not gone at all as she expected. "No, sir. The park officials were assisting the police with a different investigation. Are you certain no one has trespassed through your land?"

"The only people who have been on my land are my workers and those two hooligans I call my grandsons. I have motion sensors set up to alert me if someone crosses onto my property. The road ends at the entrance to my farm. If someone tries to pass through the cattle guard, an alarm goes off. If someone touches the fence, an alarm goes off," he explained.

"How high is the fence? Could someone possibly vault over it?" Genevieve asked, even though the idea felt preposterous.

Strahan guffawed. "Like a pole vaulter? That's a good one. The motion sensors scan along the perimeter of the fence. Someone could definitely try to vault over it, but I'd see them. Now, as to the fence I share with the state park, I don't have cameras set up over there, which is why I was unaware the two boys had gotten into any trouble. I didn't think they would ever attempt to cross the creek. I'll pay to have the fence repaired. Please give my apologies to the state."

"Thank you for your time, sir. Have a good day," she responded and ended the call.

Her theory of someone accessing the park through the Strahan's property had just been eliminated. Whoever sent Frobish over the cliff got into the park somehow. They must have arrived much earlier than she and Alex had assumed. They would need to review more of the video feed. She had been putting off going through the images and footage. It was tedious work, but they needed to do it. She sighed in frustration.

She wasn't supposed to be logging overtime hours, and she'd already bent that rule by dragging CSU out to the park again the day before. She went through the tidbits Dureski had shared with her about the other cases. The same burner phone had called two of the victims: Frobish and someone not long before her. One of the victims had owned a construction business, but Genevieve had no way of knowing if that was the person who died more recently or not. The overlap with the burner phone seemed like something she could pursue. Chris had gotten the phone records for that number; maybe she could see if there was another number the phone called with some frequency in the same time frame. She closed the laptop. She needed to call Chris and let him know the DNA they'd collected was irrelevant. At least they didn't need to search the entire Strahan property for more evidence.

* * * * *

Mae's Corner proved to be a popular lunch spot for the after-church crowd. Cari and Bob had lucked out and arrived just before the rush. Cari looked over the menu even though it looked like it hadn't changed since her last visit. She'd tried their chicken salad sandwich during her most recent visit to the diner, but decided to order an egg salad sandwich this time.

"What are you going to get?" she asked Bob.

"I've heard their BLT is really good, but I kind of want some fried chicken and mashed potatoes," he responded. "What about you?"

"Egg salad sandwich," she responded.

"Here comes the waiter, so I guess I need to decide," Bob remarked.

Cari smiled at the familiar face. The owner's grandson, Justin, had been her waiter multiple times.

"Ms. Turnlyle, good to see you again," the young man said to her. "What can I bring you to drink?"

"Just water for me," Cari told him.

"I'll have water too," Bob said with a smile.

"Are you ready to order or do you need another minute?" Justin asked.

Cari looked at Bob who nodded. "I'd like an egg salad sandwich, please."

Justin made a note and turned his gaze to Bob. "And for you, sir?"

"Justin, this is my fiancé, Bob. Bob, this is the owner's grandson, Justin," Cari interrupted.

"Nice to meet you. Uh, I'll get the BLT. I've heard it's the best one in town," Bob requested.

"Good choice…and nice to meet you too," Justin said and collected their menus. "I'll be right back with your waters."

"On the way into the church today, it struck me that we haven't really talked about where we'd like to get married," Cari observed. She could tell from the look on Bob's face her comment caught him completely off guard.

"Yeah, I guess we haven't. Did you have a place in mind?" he asked.

Cari shook her head. "I tried to imagine us getting married at our church, you know, like, in the sanctuary and I just couldn't see it. I sort of always thought I'd get married inside a church, but now, I don't know. Maybe outside would fit us better."

Bob nodded contemplatively. "We could do a destination wedding. Go to Hawaii or something."

Cari felt her heart race at the idea. "Oooh! That could be fun!"

"On the other hand," Bob said matter-of-factly. "A lot of our friends and possibly even family might not be able to attend a destination wedding."

Cari smiled. "I love how rational you are. And you're right. Maybe we'll save Hawaii for a different trip."

"As long as we're being rational, having the ceremony outside also kind of limits the time of year we could have it. No one wants to be outside for half an hour or more in December," Bob remarked.

"Maybe we could do late spring or early summer?" Cari proposed.

"Are we set on an outside venue?" Bob asked for confirmation as Justin returned with their drinks. They nodded their thanks and continued the discussion.

Cari shrugged. "I don't know. It seems like there are a lot of risks when you try to plan for an outdoor event. You need a backup plan if the weather is bad. It kind of adds to the stress."

"Maybe this is why people hire wedding planners," Bob laughed.

Cari joined him. "Maybe so. I could ask Michelle if she knows anyone. It seems like something she'd be familiar with."

"That's a good idea. Keep me posted on it," he requested. "Who knows? Before the end of the month, we might even have a date to satisfy our moms and everyone else who keeps asking."

Cari put her hands palms up. "I know, right? We go from dating to engaged and everyone's ready for the wedding right away. One thing at a time, friends."

"Here is your egg salad and your BLT," Justin said, startling Cari. "Can I get you anything else?"

"These look great. Thanks," Bob told him.

"I'm so hungry. I think I'm still playing catch up from yesterday," Cari said after swallowing her first bite. "This sandwich is really good. How is yours?"

"It definitely lives up to the hype," Bob said between bites. "Since we're talking about the wedding...did you want a big wedding or something smaller?"

"Smaller," Cari responded immediately. "I don't think I know enough people for a large wedding anyway."

"Same for me. It might be easier to find venues if we aren't expecting a big crowd, too," he said thoughtfully.

"Maybe so," Cari agreed. "I was kind of shying away from talking about wedding plans; they just kind of intimidated me, you know? But this is fun. I like planning our future together, Bob."

He gave her a big smile. "Me too, Cari."

* * * * *

After Cari got home from lunch with Bob, she went back to working on the new businesses story. She started by logging into her work email account to see if anyone had responded to the messages she'd sent. Her inbox had several unread emails, so she started sorting through them to see what she could delete and what she needed to read. She smiled with satisfaction when she saw Randall Pierce had already responded. She double-clicked on the email.

Ms. Turnlyle,

Thank you for reaching out. I would be happy to provide an interview for your article. Please call me at your convenience.

Sincerely,

Randy Pierce

She decided to give Ollaman a call even though it was Sunday. It seemed like he would want to pounce on a potential new sponsor right away. The man rarely took a day off, so Cari knew he'd answer her call.

"Turnlyle, what's the story?" he asked her.

"Hi, Mr. Ollaman. I've been sorting through all the new businesses and builders and neighborhoods for the article you assigned me. One contractor's name has come up repeatedly and I thought you'd want to know. His name is Randall Pierce. He owns—"

"Pierce Construction and Landscaping. I'm familiar, yes," Ollaman interrupted in an annoyed tone.

"Oh, great. I didn't see the business name on our current sponsor list and after reading about his company, it seems like they'd make a great sponsor for the newspaper. He's all about supporting local businesses and being involved in the community, which fits right in with what our newspaper does," Cari said hopefully.

"I'll look into it," Ollaman said gruffly and ended the call.

Cari stared at her cell phone for a few moments before setting it on the table next to her laptop. She had expected Ollaman to congratulate her on identifying a new sponsor, but he didn't even say thank you. More than that, he sounded irritated she would suggest them as a sponsor. She wondered if Michelle knew more about it. She needed to ask her about wedding planners anyway, so she sent the woman a text.

Sorry to bother you on Sunday. Have a minute?

She watched as the message quickly switched to read and the three dots appeared, indicating Michelle was typing.

Sure. What's up?

Rather than continuing to text, Cari touched the call button. She wanted to hear the tone of Michelle's voice when she brought up the landscaping company. The other woman answered immediately.

"Hi, Cari. Working on the weekend?" she asked with a laugh.

"Sort of," Cari confessed with a smile. "I actually have two questions for you."

"Ask away," Michelle responded.

"Has the Pierce Construction and Landscaping company ever been a business sponsor for the newspaper?" she asked.

"Mmmm… Pierce…I don't think so. We get a lot of checks and EFTs and I don't recognize the name as one that we get a recurring payment from. Why?" Michelle asked her.

"Their name came up in my research and they seem like a great company. I guess you don't know if Ollaman has ever approached them about being a sponsor?" Cari mused.

"Oh, I have that list too. Let me see," she said slowly. "I need to get my laptop. Just a moment."

"Take your time," Cari told her.

"That would be great if we could take on a new sponsor. I'm pretty bummed about the changes Mr. Ollaman gave us. The healthcare coverage is a big disappointment. My husband is on my insurance plan. He's an entrepreneur and does odd jobs in the community, so we either have to pay out of pocket or have him as a dependent on my plan. Sorry, I'm just venting," she said with a hint of sadness. "I've got the file pulled up now. Pierce, you said?"

"That's correct," Cari confirmed.

"I don't see anything with that name on this list. Great find, Cari!" she said with enthusiasm.

Don't get too excited. Ollaman wasn't. Cari thought. "Thanks," she said, trying to sound cheerful.

"What's your other question?" Michelle asked.

"Oh, right. I almost forgot," Cari said nervously. "Uh, Bob and I were talking about planning our wedding and realized we don't really know a lot about how to do it. Any chance you know a good wedding planner?"

"Squeeee!!" Michelle cooed. "I *love* that you asked me this. I have a great friend who is fantastic at wedding planning. I'll text you her info. Her name is Aspen Wilson. I promise you will not be disappointed with her. Ohhh! How exciting! So, you picked a date then??"

Cari cringed. "Uh, no. Do we need to pick a date before we speak with her?"

Michelle giggled. "Oh no. Not at all. I'm so excited for you two. Okay, I just sent you a pic of her business card. Happy planning, girl!"

"Got it. Thanks, Michelle," Cari said after seeing the text notification pop up on her watch.

"See you tomorrow," Michelle said and ended the call.

114

Cari looked at the photo of the business card. Aspen had a website, so Cari typed the address into the web browser. It looked very professional. She had customer testimonials as well as images from some of the events she had planned for her clients. The landing page had a form she could fill out to request a meeting. Cari entered her information and clicked submit. *Here goes nothing.*

Her phone buzzed with an alert. She looked at her watch and saw a response from the wedding planner. Cari figured it was automated, but when she opened it, she realized Ms. Wilson had emailed immediately in response to the form submission. She had scheduled Cari and Bob, if he wanted to join them, for a meeting on Wednesday morning. She texted Bob with the calendar information and then set her phone aside. Making plans with a wedding planner made everything feel much more real.

Chapter 10

Ollaman had scheduled Cari for her benefits meeting at 9 a.m. Monday morning. She'd barely had time to get coffee and settle in at her desk when her calendar reminder went off. She grabbed her notebook, the HR packet, and a pencil. Hopefully, he hadn't already made up his mind on everything. She walked over to his office and knocked lightly.

"Turnlyle, come on in," he said cheerfully.

The sunlight glinted off of his shiny head. She resisted the urge to squint and took a seat in the empty chair across from his desk. He clicked something with his computer mouse and then looked up.

"Okay, this should be pretty quick, depending on how many questions you have," he told her. "Let me just run through a few things and then I can address any of your concerns. You brought the packet?"

"Yes, sir," she said and held it up.

"Not a lot is changing for you, except for how we're handling health insurance. I couldn't justify the expense of a large healthcare package for everyone, so I'm switching to a stipend instead. It shouldn't be a big change. You'll be getting more or less the same amount to buy your own coverage instead of the Beagle covering a portion and you covering a portion in pre-tax dollars," he explained.

"Sorry to interrupt, sir," Cari said timidly. "But I did a little research about health insurance and it seems like it's more profitable for everyone for a corporation to use a company healthcare package rather than a stipend. There are tax credits and other incentives, plus everyone will actually have insurance instead of electing not to buy anything."

"What people choose to do with the stipend is not my concern," Ollaman retorted. "I'm sorry, Ms. Turnlyle, but this is what I have to offer."

Cari swallowed. "I understand."

Ollaman went through some of the other changes in the packet. He had signed the Beagle up for a collegiate intern program where the college participants could get paid through the program's grants rather than the newspaper's funds. Cari wondered if they got to select the interns or if they were just assigned, but she didn't ask. She felt like she'd already challenged him too much for one morning.

"Any other questions?" Ollaman asked as he flipped the packet back to the first page.

"No, I think I understand the changes. By the way, I'm requesting a meeting with that landscaping company for some time this week. It seems like they'd be a great sponsor for the newspaper."

"Let me handle that. I've been in touch with them previously and they weren't interested in being a sponsor," Ollaman informed her. "Any updates with the Frobish woman?"

"I thought I had a promising lead, but the phone number was attached to a burner that's since been discarded," she told him.

Ollaman cleared his throat. "Well, keep at it…I know the health insurance change is frustrating, Turnlyle. Sometimes we have to weather some storms in the newspaper business. It's always up and down. It'll come back up."

Cari nodded once. "I hope so. Thanks for the meeting."

Ollaman tilted his head toward the office door. "Well, I have a full day of these meetings, so if there's nothing else…?"

She shook her head and stood up. "I'll forward the email I got from the landscaping company to you so you can follow up."

Ollaman nodded, but was already back on his computer. He waved his goodbye without looking up. Cari resisted the urge to shrug and let herself out of his office. She wanted to get back to her investigation.

* * * * *

Robby carefully eased the door to his office closed. He reminded himself he usually kept his office door closed, so closing it would not raise suspicion. Still, his frayed nerves kept him on edge as he logged into the company network to access his files. He had a good memory and could usually rely on it, especially when it came to anything related to numbers and dates. If his memory served, he had five codes to find. He scrolled through the ledger and found one of the dates. NTS had a lot of clients; he approved multiple payments a day, but he knew this code had a T and a W in it. He scanned the rows of numbers and finally found it: TTW041526. He jotted it onto a sticky note with the date and started to look for the next one.

117

Approaching footsteps in the hallway startled him. He minimized the account window and went to his email. Several messages awaited his attention, but he couldn't focus on reading any of them. He listened and the footsteps continued past his office. He ran a hand over his face and enlarged the account screen again. He needed to be faster so he could stop looking over his shoulder. He quickly found the next two codes and added them to the sticky note with their respective dates. He was over halfway finished. The oddly-timed payment requests had occurred a little more than once a month since he started with the company.

Robby's company cell phone rang from its position on his desk just as he found the next code. The sound made him jump and almost resulted in the phone getting knocked to the floor. He quickly answered it and tried to keep his voice even.

"NTS. Robby Rialto speaking," he recited as always.

"Robby! Glad I caught you," his boss, Damien Follard said easily. "Have a minute?"

"Of course. What can I do for you?" Robby asked while trying to slow his breathing.

"We've got a new potential client coming in today. I was hoping some of us could join him for lunch. Can I count you in?" Follard asked.

Robby swallowed before he responded. "Certainly. What time and where?"

"We've got a table for 12:45 at The Silver Spoon. We can walk. Meet in the lobby at 12:25," Follard informed him.

"I've got it on my calendar," Robby said and added a reminder to his computer's calendar. "Anything I should know about the client?"

"I'll send you their portfolio after I hang up. Our software came highly recommended to them, so it should be an easy sell," Follard explained. "See you in the lobby. Don't be late."

Robby started to respond, but the call ended before he could say anything else. He looked through the small window in his office door. He tried to ignore the paranoid feelings racing through his head. No one was watching him through the window. No one was spying on him. He was a good and reliable employee. He took a drink of coffee and set the mug back on his desk. Just two more codes, including the one he'd found right before Follard called and he could go back to his regular work day. He opened the ledger again. He knew Cari thought he was imagining things to some extent and he didn't think he'd explained the situation to her adequately.

Most of the time, payment requests came through via email or their accounting system. Project managers would submit an invoice for payment. NTS had its own codes for each line item, but the companies sent invoices using their coding system, so they weren't all in the same format of letters first followed by numbers. He didn't need to open each of the payments to get all the details; Cari only needed the date and the code he'd been sent by Follard. The codes he had mentally marked as suspicious hadn't been submitted through the accounting system or via email first. They had all been done over the phone or by Follard coming to his office and relaying the information. In some cases, he'd just noticed deposits in the account when he arrived in the mornings. Those seemed to show up on the same day Follard asked him to process these other special invoices, though sometimes it would be the morning after. He located the final codes and wrote them down for Cari. He snapped a photo of the sticky note and then texted it to Cari. He tried to decide where he could hide the note. Should he shred it or put it in his wallet? He didn't want it to fall out at an inopportune moment. He folded it half twice and then slipped it behind his wedding photo. Robby checked his watch. He had about three hours before the lunch meeting. Breathing a sigh of relief that his covert work was complete, he closed the ledger and got back to work.

* * * * *

Cari's foot tapped out a nervous rhythm from under her desk. She felt foolish for thinking she could change Ollaman's mind about the health insurance. Health insurance hadn't really been on her radar until an unfortunate experience in a kayak left her with a concussion. She was just starting to get claim statements from the ensuing medical visits and was thankful for her insurance coverage. Tears clouded her vision and she angrily wiped them away. She should have gone to Ollaman with a more detailed plan that showed him how everyone could save money. Rather than dwell on it, she opened her email application again. She forwarded the message from Randall Pierce to Ollaman and sighed. Her mind was still inwardly debating how the conversation could have gone better. She closed her email program and locked her computer. She needed to get some air and reset her outlook.

She slid her cell phone into her pocket and walked toward the breakroom. Instead of turning right down the hallway, she went left and opened the door to the stairwell. Her footsteps echoed in the concrete corridor as she made her way down to the exit. When she reached the base of the stairs, she took her phone out and called Bob.

"Hey, Cari," Bob said. "Is everything okay?"

She took a deep breath, not really noticing the background noise on his side of the call. "I met with Ollaman. He won't budge on the health insurance. It's basically a done deal. I'm going to have to start finding my own coverage."

"Ah, that sucks. I'm sorry," Bob said gently. "Have you looked at your finances? I'm sure Ollaman included information about how to continue on your current plan or modify it to a plan that costs about the same, right?"

Cari bit her lip. "I haven't looked at any of it. I really thought I could change his mind, but I guess that was a pipe dream."

"At least you tried," Bob offered.

"I guess so. He said we're in a down cycle right now and it always comes back up..." she trailed off.

"But you're worried it won't?" Bob asked.

"I am. Bryson told me this was how it started when his previous newspaper went out of business," Cari told him. "I mean, if you think about it, how many local newspapers are still in publication?"

"I honestly have no idea," Bob confessed.

"It's becoming less and less common," Cari told him. "I love working as a newspaper journalist. I can't imagine this job no longer being around."

"Well, don't get ahead of yourself," Bob cautioned. "Why don't you come to my place again tonight? We can order some food in and look at your options."

"Okay. Thanks for listening, Bob. I'll let you get back to work," she said gratefully.

"Love you, Cari," Bob said.

"Love you, too," she responded and ended the call.

Rather than climb the stairs back to the newsroom, Cari walked out to the parking garage to take the elevator. She pushed aside her frustrations with the upcoming changes. Her watch buzzed with a text notification. Robby had texted an image. She hoped it was the remaining codes. She opened the text on her phone and looked at the image. He'd sent her a photo of five more codes with their corresponding dates. The elevator doors opened and she hurried to her desk.

After unlocking her computer, she logged into the database to search obituaries again. The first code, TIW041526 was from January. The newspaper ran obituaries and she could sort them by date and see if any of the initials matched Robby's list. She tried not to get her hopes up as she set the parameters for the search, but she pumped her fist when a named matched the initials: Thomas Isaac Washburn.

After skimming his obituary, she went to the web browser to search for more information on how he died. She found a short article by the Associate Press. The man had discovered his car battery was dead one morning when he tried to leave for work. He attempted to jump the battery using his wife's car, but had somehow electrocuted himself. Cari's hand shot up to cover her mouth. His wife had discovered his body over half an hour later. She'd been in the shower when the accident occurred and only went outside because she heard a car running in the driveway. Washburn had owned a local construction company called New York Construction. Cari opened a new tab to look up the business. Under the About tab, she read about the company being founded by Washburn, but after his shocking and unexpected death, the business was under new ownership. The new owner was quoted as saying he aspired to abide by the high standards Washburn had always set in his business practices. Goosebumps peppered her arms when she compared the date of Washburn's death with the code's date. They were identical. She didn't know a lot about car batteries, but figured someone could rig something to cause another person harm.

If the math held, then there could be at least two more deaths within these codes. Even identifying three names made her feel uneasy. She wanted to talk to Robby but knew he would be extremely rattled if she tried to call him at work right now. Finding this third link made his theory seem much more valid. She knew he needed to take this to the police, but wasn't sure she could talk him into it. She couldn't violate his trust by sharing it herself either. She pursed her lips and got back to the list.

* * * * *

Genevieve arrived at the station extra early in an effort to beat Alex to their desks. She knew he got irritated when she worked their cases during their off hours; it made him feel like he was playing catch up. She pumped her fist in victory when she didn't see his truck in the parking lot. She could get them both a cup of coffee first.

She bypassed the detective bay for the breakroom and filled two cups with coffee. After adding milk and honey to hers, she grabbed the two cups and walked quickly to her desk. Alex was just entering the station. She raised the cup of coffee in greeting.

"Returning the favor, huh?" he said with a laugh when he took the coffee from her.

"Don't get too excited. It's still from the breakroom," she laughed. "Listen up. I did a little weekend work—"

"Ugh, you're killing me, Smalls," Alex groaned. "Why can't time off be time off for you too? You make me look bad."

She rolled her eyes. "As I was saying…we hiked to the back of the park on Saturday and found the fence had been cut. I called CSU out and they logged a couple pieces of evidence."

"Wow, I thought that was a wild goose chase for sure," he complimented her.

"Well, it kind of was. Turns out, it wasn't what I thought," she said and explained about the young Strahan grandsons.

"Ha ha ha, I bet they get to help fix that fence," Alex laughed. "What else?"

She shrugged. "That's it. I was really hopeful when we found DNA, but it wasn't relevant."

Suddenly, Lieutenant Grusky burst from his office and slammed the door behind him, making Genevieve jump. Alex laughed for the third time in the same number of minutes. Grusky reached their desks and gave him the side eye. He was holding a small sticky note.

"Something funny, Runimoss?" he asked.

"No, sir. What's up?" Alex asked sheepishly.

"CSU got a hit on the DNA from the fingernails," Grusky informed them.

"That's awesome. Who are we picking up?" Alex asked.

"No one, yet," Grusky said slowly. "The match is to another case; a cold case from a different precinct. I just got off the phone with their lieutenant. They can pull the murder book for you to review."

"In New York?" Genevieve asked for clarification, goosebumps rising on her arms.

Grusky nodded. "Here's the investigating officer's phone number. Give him a call to sort it out."

He passed the note to Alex and turned back toward his office. "Keep me posted," he called over his shoulder.

His door slammed closed again and Genevieve flinched. "Does he always need to slam the door lately? What is up with that?!"

Alex smirked. "Who knows? Maybe he got in trouble for it being open or unlocked or something, so he's overcompensating now? Maybe he has pent-up frustration from home?"

She frowned. "I wish he'd knock it off already. I guess he wants you to call the detective since he gave you the note."

"Maybe the guy's old school," Alex offered.

"More old school than you?" she teased him.

"Watch it, runt," he ribbed back and grabbed the phone receiver off his desk. "Let's hope we can go review their case today. We're kind of running out of leads here."

She nodded and waited for him to make the call. Grusky told them it was a cold case, but maybe he was exaggerating and it was the same case Dureski had mentioned on the phone. She watched as Alex punched the numbers on his desk phone keypad. He put the call on speaker once it started ringing. A raspy, male voice answered after three rings.

"Detective Benson," the man said gruffly. "Is this Brenington PD?"

"Detectives Runimoss and Viacorte," Alex confirmed. "We got a DNA match on one of your cold cases and wanted to come by to discuss the case with you."

"Yeah, our lieutenant swung by and told us. You coming right now?" Benson asked.

"If that's okay with you," Alex responded.

"Sure. See you in a few," Benson said and the call ended.

Genevieve took the last drink of her coffee and tossed the empty cup into the trash. "This could be the break we need."

"It's possible," Alex said as he stood and grabbed the keys to the cruiser.

"You're driving again?" she asked and pouted.

He handed her the keys and grinned. "I guess I could give you a turn."

"You're just worried you'll have to parallel park," she grumbled.

"Possibly," he said and held the door for her.

She gave him the side eye. "I know I said I was over being mad at you holding the door for me, but I didn't say I liked it any more than I did before."

"Maybe if you grew a few inches, you'd get to the door first," he teased her.

Her hazel eyes flashed at him. "Oh, another short joke. So witty."

* * * * *

Cari felt like she was really gaining momentum. Even though she hadn't convinced Robby to speak with the police yet, she hoped having a third name to add to the list might end his reluctance. Since she couldn't call him, she plugged ahead with her research. The next code was all numbers with a date in January, not long after Robby started at NTS. She frowned. Robby had surprisingly clear handwriting for a man, so there was no mistaking any of the characters. She decided to skip it and go on to the next one.

She looked at the list again: AQR085164 from late March. She adjusted her parameters and hit enter. Cari scanned the names in the results and homed in on the name Aaron Quincy Roth. As with Washburn, the man had died the same day the code was generated.

Roth died after an accidental drowning. He'd been fishing at a nearby lake and had slipped in. Her arms suddenly felt chilled. The water must have been really cold in March. The man owned Socket to Me, which was a local hardware store. She looked up their website. It had a banner across the top in red and white which read: Now under new ownership. The business sold hard-to-find tools and gadgets but started with socket wrenches. She wondered how hard it was to find a socket wrench, but rather than question the business model, she made a note about Aaron Roth in her document.

Before she could move on to the next code, her desk phone rang. She grabbed the receiver.

"Turnlyle, how close are you on finishing the new business article?" Ollaman asked after she said hello.

She cringed. She'd barely touched the article today. "It's coming along. I'm in the process of organizing the businesses by category and collecting quotes from some of the owners."

"I've got some free time tomorrow as these meetings are going faster than I expected. Send me your research and I'll finish it up. I'll keep you on the byline," he added quickly.

Her eyebrows shot up in surprise. "Oh, uh, sure, okay. I'll send it right over. It might take me a few minutes to put everything together."

"No problem. Thanks, Turnlyle."

"Sir—" she started to ask a question, but he'd already hung up his phone. She wanted to know if he'd had a chance to talk to Randall Pierce and if he'd signed on as a sponsor.

She minimized her document with Robby's codes and opened her email. She'd received a few responses from some of the business owners while she'd been searching through the obituaries. Cari decided to forward each of the messages to Ollaman but thought she should blind copy Michelle on each of them in case his occasional struggle with technology led to any of them getting lost or deleted. Rather than surprise the woman with numerous emails, she grabbed the desk phone receiver and punched in her extension.

"Cari, what's up?" Michelle asked.

"Ollaman wants to take over the new business article, so I'm going to be sending him my progress in the next few minutes," she paused. "Sometimes, he, uh, has some issues…"

"You're sending them to me too. Good idea. I'll keep them sorted accordingly in case any go missing," Michelle assured her. "Plus, I still have the responses we got from the social media posts."

"Awesome, thanks," Cari responded.

"I'm surprised he thinks he has time for that," Michelle mused. "He's been working ten-to-twelve-hour days lately trying to get everything done for the transition in addition to his normal weekly stuff."

"Huh, that is strange, but I'm happy to pass it off. The Frobish story is taking a lot of my time as it is," Cari told the other woman.

"I'll be watching for your emails," Michelle said. "Good luck with the other story. Hey, did you hear back from Aspen?"

"I did, but I just realized I never confirmed the time was good for Bob. Clearly, I need a wedding planner to keep me on track," she laughed.

"Well, good luck with that too," Michelle responded.

"Thanks," Cari replied and hung up the receiver.

She scanned her work inbox for any messages responding to her request from the previous week and forwarded them to Ollaman and Michelle. She created a new message and attached her documents with the lists of businesses, contractors, neighborhoods, and apartment complexes. She double-checked her email for any other related messages, but didn't find any. While she hoped Ollaman appreciated her thoroughness, she really hoped some of it generated some more income for the newspaper. Her stomach rumbled, reminding her it was time to take a break for lunch. She hadn't packed anything that morning, so she decided to hit up Larry's for some tacos before getting back to Robby's list.

* * * * *

It had taken almost an hour to drive to Detective Benson's precinct from Brenington. Genevieve tapped out a nervous rhythm with her foot. She wished the other detective had told them more over the phone, but

125

they'd find out soon enough. She smiled as they approached the station when she saw they had a parking lot and she wouldn't have to parallel park.

"Looks like you could have driven here after all, huh, Alex?" Genevieve asked him.

"More places should have lots. Parallel parking is for the birds," he said flippantly.

"I've never seen a bird drive," she said with a laugh.

"What's got you all keyed up?" he asked after she turned the car off.

"I'm hoping this will finally be the break we need in this case," she told him.

Alex shrugged. "We still won't have a name, but maybe we can find some overlap between the victims."

Genevieve nodded. They walked up the steps to the precinct and went inside. An older man in a suit was waiting near the front desk. He had closely-cropped grey hair and a bit of a belly. She saw his detective's shield clipped to his belt and figured it must be Benson.

"Detectives?" he asked when they reached him.

"Runimoss and Viacorte," Alex said with a nod. "Thanks for meeting with us."

"No problem. I pulled the murder book for you. Would you rather look through it first or let me give you a run-down of the case?" Benson asked as he led them through the station.

"Go ahead and give us a summary. Then we can look through the book and come back with any follow-up questions," Alex suggested.

"Sounds good," he said and unlocked a door for them.

They followed him inside. Genevieve thought it looked a bit like an interrogation room. A large binder sat on the table in the middle of the room with two metal chairs on each side. She sat next to Alex while Benson sat alone on the opposite side of the table.

"So, this all happened something like fourteen, maybe fifteen months ago. Our vic was camping on his own one weekend. He normally called his wife each morning to check in, but Sunday morning came and went without a call. She tried to call him and couldn't reach him, so she used the Find My Phone feature to figure out where he was. It was pouring down rain when she arrived at the park and she had to beg her way inside. When she reached his camp site, it was deserted. His truck was still there and his tent, but there was no sign of him. It seemed like he had vanished.

"A day or two later, his body was found by a hiker near the cliff's base. Like I said, we got a ton of rain in a twenty-four-hour span, so the park had limited access to visitors as several of the trails were flooded or impassable. In fact, the wife had to wait up at his camp site for almost a day because the access road was blocked by fallen tree limbs and full trunks. Anyway, everyone assumed he must have slipped in the wet conditions and went over the edge," Benson explained. "However, once our ME had a look, he found some tissue under the guy's nails. He ran a DNA profile, but it wasn't in the system. It wasn't his DNA, so it seemed like he must have gotten in an altercation with someone. You can see how we conducted the investigation. We never found a suspect."

The older detective gave them a nod and then left the room, closing the door behind him. Genevieve felt some of her adrenaline fading. If the case was that old, it couldn't be the one Dureski had referenced on the phone. She pushed the thought aside and refocused on the task at hand. Alex pulled the binder closer to them and flipped it open to the first page.

"Sounds a lot like our scenario already," he remarked. "I wonder if their victim had a habit of camping by himself. He kind of implied that, right?"

"He did," Genevieve agreed. "Where should we start?"

"I want to read about the victim first," he said as he looked at the first page. "It says his name is Marshall Aguirre. He was in his sixties and Hispanic. He owned a little coffee shop."

"Small business owner, there's another commonality," she remarked.

"Pretty thin connection. Let's look at the interviews and see who they talked to," Alex told her.

He found the interview tab and turned to it. The first page listed the people interviewed during the investigation. He started with the first interview, which was the wife, not surprising since she reported him missing.

"The wife's interview reads much like Benson told us. Once she couldn't find him, she called the police, who contacted the ranger's office. It took them some time to clear the road and get to her. They looked through all his stuff but couldn't find any hint of where he might be," Alex said aloud, though Genevieve was reading the page without his assistance.

She pointed at the page. "The wife insisted he was nearby as his last known location on his phone had been around eight in the morning, right where they were. The phone had since died. Does it say if they found the phone anywhere?"

Alex flipped a few pages back to the evidence section. "Here it is. Yeah, it was in his pocket. The screen was cracked and they weren't able to recover anything from it as it got soaked in the rainstorm."

127

"Surely they got phone records though, right?" Genevieve asked.

He turned to the evidence list. "Says they did."

"Let's see if he got any calls during the time his phone was still on," she suggested.

Alex found the records. "They have some labels for some of these numbers. Pink is his wife; you can see her calls that afternoon, as she said, and then she also spoke with him the previous morning."

"Yellow is…a burner phone," she looked at Alex pointedly. "But the only one who called him once he was camping was his wife, assuming her timeline is accurate."

"She stated in her interview that he regularly went camping at that location…something like every other weekend," he told her. "The green phone number seems to be his business calling."

"It seems like the coffee shop called and then he called the burner number around the same time he left for his camping trip. How far back did they get his phone records?" she asked.

Alex paged through the binder. "It looks like they only printed those few days. I'm sure they at least got an entire month. Maybe they have that saved digitally somewhere."

"Let's hope so. Okay, who else did they interview?" Genevieve asked him.

"A son, several employees…the new owner…and some of his friends," Alex listed people off. He turned to the interviews and they started reading the summary of the son's comments in silence.

The younger Aguirre is not local, but still close with his dad. Always thought everyone loved his dad. Viewed father as friendly, successful, and easy-going. Can't think of ever seeing his dad get in an argument.

"The son wasn't much help," Genevieve observed.

"I'm going to guess most of these interviews went the same way. Everyone loved Marshall. Fun to be around, great boss, who couldn't like him…and so on and so on," Alex remarked as he turned the page.

"Well, maybe not. Look at this first employee's interview. The person mentioned Aguirre being frustrated about the city requiring some kind of landscaping upgrade," Genevieve ran her finger across the page.

"Someone's gonna kill a guy because he doesn't want to plant flowers?" Alex scoffed.

"Some people aren't sane," Genevieve reminded him. "I'm going to see if I can find the restroom. Do you need anything? Water? Snack?"

He shook his head. "I'm going to keep reading."

She exited the room and looked down the hallway. The men's and women's rooms were at the far end, in the opposite direction from where they entered. She didn't really need a restroom break. She wanted to at least text Dureski about the connected case. The women's room was empty when she stepped inside. She slipped into a stall and pulled out her cell phone.

We got a DNA hit in the Frobish case. Cold case. Marshall Aguirre from last year.

She waited to see if he'd respond quickly. Her phone screen lit up with a call from the special agent. She answered in as quiet of a voice as she could. She didn't want anyone eavesdropping from outside the restroom.

"Viacorte, what DNA?" Dureski asked after she said hello.

"Our ME found DNA under Frobish's nails. When he looked for a match in the system, he got a hit from an older case, not in Brenington. My partner and I are reviewing the murder book now. It has some overlap with our case," she paused. "Is it on your radar?"

"Aguirre?" he asked quickly. "Speak up. I can barely hear you."

"I'm in the restroom at the other precinct. I wasn't expecting you to call," she explained. "And, yes, Marshall Aguirre."

"Okay, yeah, he's on my list, but we didn't have any connections within that department, so we haven't pulled the case file. That's the only other case in the bunch that was ruled a homicide besides Frobish. I've been keeping tabs on it from the periphery, but it seemed like they'd kind of given up on it," Dureski told her. "The DNA matches with Frobish's attacker, but no one knows whose it is still."

"Yeah, but maybe we'll find some other connection that will help us find the guy," Genevieve said hopefully.

"Keep me posted."

The call ended and Genevieve stuffed the phone back into her pocket. She'd been gone long enough. She needed to get back to the interrogation room with Alex. She walked quickly down the hallway to the room and sat down by Alex.

"Everything come out okay?" he asked without looking up.

"I'm sorry?" she asked in confusion.

"That was a pretty long bathroom break," he remarked.

She pursed her lips. "Whatever. Did you find anything we can work with?"

"Besides the gardening complaint? Sort of, but not really," he responded.

"What do you mean?" she asked.

"They took the effort to look up and speak to each of the people who entered the park during the appropriate time frame. Everyone had an alibi. They'd been with friends and the friends vouched for their presence for the entire evening. One of the cars was a rental; even that guy had a friend who could attest to his whereabouts," Alex told her. "I do want to see the phone records from the whole month. They didn't follow up with the city about his landscaping beef either. It seems like a long shot, but it might be worth talking to some of the other business owners here to see what their experience was like with regards to the city's requests."

"Back to Benson to ask for the rest of the phone records?" she asked.

He nodded and got up from the table. "Let's go find him."

They left the interrogation room and retraced their steps through the precinct. Benson was typing on a computer when they exited the hallway. He heard them approach and looked up.

"Find everything you need?" he asked.

"Mostly," Alex nodded. "We were wondering if there's a full month of phone records for the vic? The book only has a few days' worth."

Benson nodded. "I have a digital file, yeah. I can email it, if you give me a card. I can send our digital case file too, if that helps."

Genevieve pulled one of her cards from her pocket and passed it to him. "That would be great. We read in one of the interviews that he had some sort of disagreement with the city about landscaping? Did you follow up on that?"

Benson looked at Alex before responding to her question. She knew he thought her question was outrageous, but she didn't care. "I don't think the city sent someone out to push him off the mountain, Detective."

She kept her face neutral. "Lotta crazies out there."

"Anything else?" Benson asked with a smirk.

Alex shook his head. "That's all we need. Thanks for the help."

Chapter 11

The last two codes on Robby's list had only numbers. Cari couldn't find anything relevant with the numbers or the dates attached to them. She wondered what made Robby include them or if he had more information that could make her research easier. She decided to risk sending him a text even though she knew there was a decent chance he wouldn't respond until he got off work.

I'm drawing a blank with these all-number codes. What else can you tell me about them?

With four deaths amongst the eight codes, Cari knew he was right. Something nefarious was going on and somehow his company was involved. She checked her watch and saw it was almost five. She closed her browser windows and shut down her work computer. After gathering all her belongings into her messenger bag, she made a beeline for the elevator. Bryson joined her before the car arrived.

"How's that article going?" he asked her while they waited.

She smiled. "Actually, Ollaman decided he had time to do it himself, so I sent him all my research earlier today."

"That has to be a load off your plate," he observed. He held the doors open so she could get on the elevator.

"Definitely. Now I can focus on Elaine Frobish and what led to her death," she agreed. "How's work for you this week?"

He shrugged. "I've made some progress on the 400-year celebration article. I have a couple City Hall meetings, and I need to interview some new people running for city government. They might hold a town hall meeting for people to ask questions and meet the candidates."

"Wow, I had forgotten it was an election year for the council and the mayor too," Cari remarked. They stepped off the elevator into the parking garage.

"Yeah, it's nice to see some friendly competition. I'm looking forward to covering it for the paper," he said. "Have a good night."

She waved goodbye and walked to her car. Now that she'd reviewed Robby's codes, she understood his fears a little more. It was more than a coincidence. She hoped he would listen to her and agree to speak with Genevieve about it. Her right hand rubbed her locket. She noticed and lowered her hand toward the start button of her car. She started the car and wove her way out of the garage to the street.

Cari bit her lip. Her grandmother always had good advice and Cari *had* already mentioned a potential story or source. It seemed duplicitous to talk to her about it in generic terms when the whole thing concerned somebody they both loved. She supposed this was why they usually made investigators recuse themselves from a case if a family member was involved. Her thumb hovered over the Bluetooth button. Unable to resist, she pressed it and placed the call to Grandmother.

"Well, hello, Cari! I wasn't expecting a call from you again today. How are you?" she asked with a cheerful voice.

Cari tried to keep her voice even. "Busy, but I'm hanging in there. Is it still Monday?"

Her grandmother laughed. "All day today. I can tell you're in the car. Where are you headed?"

"I'm eating at Bob's tonight. I couldn't talk my boss out of canceling the healthcare plan for our office, so I need to see what package I can afford on my own. Bob offered to help me go through my finances and see what my options are," she told her.

"That sounds like a headache," Grandmother retorted. "I hope it isn't a big change in cost for you. Is there any chance Bob could add you to his plan early?"

Cari hadn't thought of that. "Hmmm…I'm not sure. I think you usually have to be married first."

"Probably so," she agreed. "What else is on your mind, sweetheart? You've called me twice in as many days. It can't just be because of your health insurance. Is something happening with the other story you mentioned on Friday?"

Cari grimaced. "Yes, and now that I've looked into it some, I think they're right. I haven't been able to convince the person to bring their story to the police, though, I did find some more evidence confirming they were on the right track. Maybe when we speak again, they'll change their mind."

"That sounds rather frightening. I can understand their desire to stay in the shadows, but for the greater good…" she trailed off.

"Yeah, it's a hard situation," Cari admitted. "Well, I just made it to Bob's complex, so I need to hang up. Thanks for listening, Grandmother. I love you."

"I love you more," she said and ended the call.

Cari parked in the visitor spot at Bob's unit and got out of her car. Bob's vehicle was in his spot, so she made her way to his door. She gave a quick knock and tried the knob, but it was locked. She knew it would be; he was very safety conscious. The door opened moments later.

"Hey, Cari," Bob said as he let her inside.

She raised onto her toes to give him a quick kiss. "Hey, Bob. How was your day?"

"It was pretty busy. We ran the DNA from those fingernails through the system and it came back with a hit on another case," he told her.

Cari froze. "You have a suspect?"

He shook his head. "No, the other case is unsolved. It's a cold case from what I heard. Genevieve and Alex met with the lead detective from the case today," he paused. "Oh, I never responded to your text about the wedding planner. I'm sorry about that. You said Wednesday at eight?"

"No worries. It was the last thing on my mind today," Cari replied.

"Me too," he agreed. "Besides getting denied by Ollaman, how was your day?"

She hesitated. She'd already talked to Bob some about Robby's theory. Normally, if she had a source for a story, she wouldn't tell Bob the person's name. She looked at his face. He stared back at her with concern.

"What is it? Something more with Ollaman?" he asked. A knowing look entered his expression. "Robby."

"I'm hoping he'll call me tonight. I need to convince him to talk to Genevieve," Cari told him. "She's familiar to him, so maybe that will make it easier."

Bob's lips creased into a thin line. He sat down on the sofa but remained silent. He rubbed his hands together and then looked at her again. "Before I forget, what should we order for dinner?"

A realization dawned on Cari. Bob's quietness from Saturday evening began when she was talking about Robby's codes. It made him uncomfortable. She swallowed hard and sat down next to him.

"I feel like it's making you uncomfortable when I mention this thing with Robby. Is that true?" she asked him.

He tilted his head and took a deep breath. "You're right. It is making me uncomfortable. I know you have your job to do and part of that is protecting sources, but by not sharing this with the people I work with, you're limiting their abilities to do their jobs."

Cari started to respond defensively and stopped herself. She had asked him to share how he felt. "I understand. Is it better if I don't talk about it in front of you?"

He grabbed her hand and squeezed it. "I don't want that either. I get that it's different because it's Robby."

"That's true. It is different because it's my brother-in-law. I didn't totally believe his theory to begin with, but now it's becoming a very real...thing...and I see how it's awkward for you. I'm not trying to keep Genevieve and Alex from solving their case, but I really cannot be the one that brings this information to them," she explained.

"I know. Hopefully, Robby will agree to speak with law enforcement soon," he smiled at her. "I'm starving. What should we order?"

She smiled back. "How about Chinese? It's been a few days since we've had that."

"Works for me," Bob responded as he took out his phone. "I'll order through the app. It usually only takes a half hour or so for them to get it delivered."

Cari raised her messenger bag. "I brought my paperwork. Should we look at it while we wait?"

He nodded while he looked at his phone. "Do you want your usual?"

"Sure. I'm going to refill my water. Can I refill yours too?" she asked as she stood up.

"I'm having a beer tonight, please. It's in the fridge," he paused and pressed another button on the phone. "Order is placed."

"Cool. I'll get the drinks. I put my paperwork on the coffee table." She gestured toward it and then walked into the kitchen.

"Are you wanting to stay with the same provider?" he asked.

She set the beer bottle in front of him and sat down. "I don't know. Is that the cheapest option?"

"Let's see what they offer. The packet lists your current healthcare plan. I'll pull it up on my laptop and we can look at it," Bob responded.

He navigated to the website and found the page for individual plans. "It won't say an exact amount. We'll have to request a quote. I'm not sure how long it takes to get a quote back."

"I should probably request from multiple places, right?" she asked.

He slid the laptop over to her. "Why don't you enter your information? You're young and mostly healthy…when you aren't getting chased by crazy people."

She laughed. "Hopefully, I won't ever get run down by a speed boat while kayaking again. I can just ask for minimal coverage then, right? Sort of bank on the idea I won't need it very often?"

"Yeah, your deductible and your copay will be higher, but like you said, if you don't have to use it, it doesn't matter," he responded.

She typed in her information and submitted it on three different health insurance sites. She pushed the laptop back toward Bob just as her cell phone buzzed with an incoming call. *Robby.*

"Oh, it's Robby. I'll take it on your balcony?" she pointed toward the sliding glass door.

He nodded in confirmation and she answered the call while walking to the door.

"Hey, Robby. I'm glad you called. Did you get my text?" she asked him as she stepped outside.

"I did," he answered quickly. "I don't know what to tell you. I promise I copied the codes down exactly."

She tried a different angle. "Do you know the company who billed NTS for each of these codes? You actually gave me four codes with only numbers."

"I didn't write that part down. I was trying to be fast," he explained.

"Well, we can worry about that later. Of the eight codes you gave me, I found four deaths with matching initials to the codes," she told him. "That's Frobish, Manwith, and two others."

"Four?!" he exclaimed. "I was right. I'm going to jail. What am I going to tell Bea?"

"Stop panicking! You're not going to jail," Cari told him firmly. "You do need to talk to the police about this. You know Genevieve. She's not going to treat you badly or assume the worst about you, right?"

"Right," he said and let out a breath. "I just. This whole thing has me constantly looking over my shoulder. I don't know who's involved or what's happening, but I couldn't ignore what I was seeing."

"So, you'll meet with Genevieve? I can be there with you if you want, or you can do it alone," Cari offered.

"Yeah, I'll talk to her. I don't want to do it at the house. I don't know if they're watching me. Where can we meet besides the police station? I don't want to be seen going there either," he told her.

"How about my apartment? We're related. It's not weird for you to come see me, right?" she suggested.

"That...seems...okay," he said slowly. "Tonight?"

"If that's good for you, I can make it happen," she responded. "What time?"

"I want to wait until the kids are in bed. I'll tell Bea I have a late meeting again," he said.

"Robby, I know it isn't my place to give marriage advice, but—"

"I'm not telling her yet. I don't want to scare her," Robby interrupted.

Cari put up a hand even though he couldn't see it. "Fine. But when you do tell her, make sure you mention I suggested it happen sooner."

"Does nine o'clock work?" he asked with a sigh.

"I'll give her a call. See you soon, Robby," she said and ended the call.

She slid the balcony door open again and went back inside. Bob was taking the Chinese food from a delivery man. He closed the door and turned back to her.

"Good news?" he asked.

"Robby is willing to talk to Genevieve," Cari responded. "He wants to meet at my apartment later tonight. I need to call her and set it up."

* * * * *

Genevieve let Alex drive, so she could look through the digital version of the victim's phone records on their way back to Brenington. It wasn't ideal on her phone, but it was better than nothing. They could print it out at the station if needed. She scrolled through the call log.

"He called the burner number a few times in the last month he was alive. They called him too," Genevieve pointed out. "We should talk to the coffee shop and see if any of the employees remember the last phone call. It prompted him to call the burner number."

"Benson interviewed all the employees, though. He asked about the last phone call. Aguirre's people said it was just to get a summary of the final numbers for the day. He left early to get his camping gear together. If he wasn't there at the end of the day, they would call to report how closing went," Alex reminded her.

"I don't think the interview explicitly stated asking about phone calls the business received," Genevieve countered. "Maybe Benson assumed they would mention it if someone had called, but they felt like it was nothing, so they said nothing."

Alex shrugged. "We don't have any other leads, so I guess it's worth a shot."

She checked her watch. "We aren't getting back too late. Less than an hour past when our shift ended. We'll have to save this search for tomorrow though."

Alex grunted in response.

She was still scrolling through the phone records when a call came in from Cari. She swiped the screen to silence it. She could call her once she was by herself again. Never one to be patient, a text popped up from her friend.

I have a source who wants to talk about Frobish with you. They have info on several possibly related deaths too. Wants to meet TONIGHT.

Genevieve's eyes flashed in anticipation. She wondered if this could be the connection to Dureski's case. She looked at Alex with her peripheral vision. He was only paying attention to the road. She thumbed off her own response.

Where and when?

The response came back: **My apartment. 9 pm.**

"What's got you so jazzed?" Alex's voice startled her. Her phone jostled in her hands and she almost dropped it.

"Uh," Genevieve stalled. "I've been trying to do some work on the side for Dureski, my FBI contact."

"Is this that thing with Robby you mentioned at the race?" Alex asked.

Dureski said he wasn't sharing details with his whole team because of a possible mole. Genevieve hesitated again, which made Alex glance her way.

"It is, isn't it?" Alex asked in an accusatory tone. "Are you sworn to secrecy or what? I mean, c'mon, you already told me part of it."

"Dureski thinks he has a leak or a mole. He's parsing out information in a very limited manner," she told him.

Alex threw up a hand in surrender. "Whatever. If you want to do double the work, have at it."

He pulled into the parking lot for the station and returned the vehicle to its assigned location. Genevieve felt bad for keeping Alex in the dark, but she couldn't jeopardize her relationship with Dureski. It was already barely there to begin with. They got out of the cruiser and headed toward the entrance.

"First thing tomorrow, I'll follow up with the coffee shop about the phone call," Alex told her when they reached their desks. "You call over to their City Hall and see what you can find out about the landscaping requirements."

She nodded and started putting her things into her bag. "Sounds like a plan. See you tomorrow."

Genevieve waited until she was in her car to call Dureski. He picked up immediately.

"Viacorte, what did you find out?" he asked.

"I might have a source with info on one of your connected cases. I'm hopefully meeting with them tonight to learn more," she told him.

"From the cold case?" Dureski asked in confusion.

"No, it's related to Frobish. I've been told the source has information on Frobish's death and other *possibly connected* deaths," she said, emphasizing some of the words.

"You talked Rialto into coming in?" Dureski asked excitedly.

Genevieve felt an uneasiness creep into her stomach. *Could Cari's source be Robby?* "I'm not sure of the identity of the source yet. I'll keep you posted."

"What about the cold case?" he asked.

"We have a couple leads to chase down tomorrow. Hopefully, one of them pans out," she responded.

"If this source is legit, I need to know ASAP," he said and ended the call.

Genevieve rolled her eyes. She wondered if working for the FBI would always feel like you were the work horse and never the co-worker.

It wasn't quite seven o'clock yet, so she could still make some of her reserved time in the raised gardening beds on the roof of her apartment building. She hadn't expected to be getting off late and had reserved an hour that evening. She should have enough lettuce to put together a salad for dinner and maybe some of the not-quite-ripe tomatoes from Saturday would be ready to harvest now too. It would be a good way to keep her from pacing the floor until her meeting at Cari's apartment.

After collecting the lettuce and a tomato, she dug in her fridge for some feta cheese and a bell pepper to round out the salad. She found some thawed chicken that wasn't expired yet, so she got it out to sauté too. She pulled out a frying pan and drizzled some olive oil in it. Her phone buzzed with an incoming call before she could add the chicken to it.

"Hey, Chris. What's up?" she asked as she sprinkled the chicken with salt and pepper.

"I looked at the list of calls from the burner phone Alex gave us the other day. There was another frequently called number on it from early in its life," Chris told her.

"As in, some of the first calls made with the burner?" she asked for clarification.

"Yeah. The number traces back to a battery store of some sort. I'll text you the info if you want," Chris offered.

"That would be great. Thanks, Chris," Genevieve said. "Anything else?"

The call had already ended, but a text popped up with the information on the battery business. Genevieve scribbled it onto a scrap of paper and went back to cooking her chicken. Maybe they'd just identified another one of Dureski's cases or someone who knew more about the person using the burner phone. She ran a quick internet search on it and saw the business was under new ownership. The About section told her the company was in its fourth generation of ownership with the new owner being Kristina Manwith, the great-granddaughter of the business' founder and daughter of Horace Manwith. She ran a search on Horace and discovered he'd been killed when he stepped in front of a garbage truck last month. *And there's the connection.*

Chapter 12

When Cari returned to her apartment, she groaned. As usual, the place was a complete mess. She'd left dirty clothes on the bathroom floor, had some dishes in the sink, and the trash was close to overflowing. She tossed her messenger bag onto her bed and got to work. She wondered if Bob was ready for her messiness; he kept his apartment really neat and clean. Maybe his habits would rub off on her.

She gathered up the dirty clothes and threw them into her hamper. She didn't know if anyone would use her bathroom while they were meeting, but it was better to be safe than sorry. She quickly wiped all the toothpaste speckles off the mirror and silently congratulated herself for not having any on the counter. Satisfied her bathroom wouldn't make anyone feel sick, she went to the kitchen.

She quickly stuffed all the garbage into the bag and hauled it out the door to the trash compactor down the way. She was pretty sure the dishes in the dishwasher were dirty, so she slid the ones from the sink into empty spots and gave the sink a rinse. The dishwasher made a lot of noise when it was running, so she tried to make a mental note to turn it on later after the meeting. The carpet seemed clean enough, so she left the vacuum in the coat closet and looked around the rest of the apartment. The table was littered with mail, so she swooped it all into a pile and put it in her bedroom to look through later. Then she wiped the table down with a damp paper towel.

Her watch buzzed with three quick notifications. She set down the paper towel to check. Thankfully, it wasn't Robby canceling: she'd gotten quotes back from the insurance companies. She left the emails unread; she could save those for later too. She went to her bedroom to get her messenger bag and draped it over the back of a chair. A knock sounded from her door.

"It's Gen!" her friend called out.

She unlocked the door and let her in. "Thanks for coming."

Gen looked around the apartment. "Where's your source?"

"Not here, yet. You're early," Cari told her.

"Just a few minutes," she said with a shrug. "Did you just speed-clean your apartment?"

Cari blushed. "How did you know?"

"Let's see…there's a paper towel in the middle of the table. Your garbage can doesn't have a bag in it, and I can see a huge pile of mail on your bed. Should I go on?" she laughed.

"Guilty as charged," Cari confessed.

Another knock interrupted their laughter. "It's me," Robby whispered from the other side of the door.

Cari opened the door and turned to Genevieve. "I think you already know Robby, right?"

Genevieve looked a bit pale, but gave them both a confident smile. "Yeah, good to see you, Robby."

He nodded and looked at Cari. "So, how does this work?"

"We can sit at the kitchen table or on the couch. Where are you more comfortable?" Cari asked him.

"Couch, no…table," he said timidly.

"Relax. It's just us. Have a seat. Can I get anyone some water?" Cari asked.

Her two guests nodded in the affirmative, so she filled two glasses in the kitchen. Her water bottle was on the coffee table, so she grabbed it and then joined them at the table.

"Okay, Robby. Go ahead and tell Gen what you've told me. I can fill in the gaps from my side," Cari said, earning a confused glance from Gen.

Robby cleared his throat. "Before I start, I haven't talked to my wife…to Bea about any of this yet. I didn't want to scare her, so please don't rat me out."

Genevieve nodded. She had a notebook open and a pencil in her hand. "Got it. No problem."

"I haven't been with NTS long, but pretty quickly, I started noticing some funny things happening," Robby began.

Cari listened as he explained about the oddly timed phone calls and requests for payment by his boss. Genevieve kept her eyes on him for the most part, but occasionally jotted something down in her notebook.

"So, I had all these suspiciously timed payments and the codes started matching up with these people who had died. I brought it to Cari's attention first to see if she could prove to me I was crazy or paranoid, but…" he trailed off and looked Cari's way.

"I did some research of past obituaries on the dates in question. Several of the codes he gave me matched the initials of someone who died in the area on the same day. We've found four matches," Cari told Genevieve.

Her friend's hazel eyes widened. "Four?! Wow. Okay. Let me see what you've found."

Cari opened her laptop and logged in. "I have four names and dates, one of which is Elaine C. Frobish, who died last week. Here are the other names."

She turned the screen so Gen could see it better. Her friend scribbled down the names and dates.

"You sort of implied there were more than four codes. What's the story with the others?" Genevieve asked.

"I couldn't find a match with them. They only had numbers, so that was really confusing," Cari explained.

Robby opened and closed his hands into fists. "Am I going to get into trouble for all this?"

Genevieve's expression clouded. "For approving the payments?"

He nodded. "Like, am I liable too? Am I guilty in this?"

Genevieve put her hands up. "I'm not even sure we have a *this* right now. Clearly, you didn't have prior knowledge *and* you're cooperating. From my perspective, I don't see anything against you."

Robby nodded and then swallowed. "Cari suggested I look up the amount of the transactions for each of those as well as who we were paying, but...um...I haven't had a chance to do it, yet."

"Yeah, we need that. For all of these," Gen agreed.

Robby frowned. "It's just that, um, well, I'm worried someone is going to catch me looking this stuff up."

Genevieve frowned at him. "Aren't you the CFO or something? Isn't it part of your job to know who is getting paid and when?"

"I mean, sort of, yes," Robby admitted. "But some of these transactions are over six months old. Why do I need to keep referencing them?"

"Who do you think is watching?" Genevieve asked pointedly.

He shook his head and shrugged. "I don't know. It just feels like someone is."

Genevieve tapped her pencil on her notebook. "You've only been there eight or nine months, right?"

He nodded. "Yes."

"Could you look up something from before you started at NTS?" she asked.

"Before? What?" Cari asked in confusion.

"It's a hunch," Genevieve told them. "I can give you the initials and the date."

"I guess I could. When do you need this information?" he asked in a quiet voice.

"Can you do it now?" Genevieve asked.

He shook his head no emphatically. "No, I have to do it from the office. If I went in after hours to look this up, it would definitely draw suspicion."

"It's just that these codes and names...well, it doesn't really tell us much," Genevieve explained.

"But can't you look into their deaths? Find some sort of common factor or contact between each of them?" Robby asked.

"I can't just start inquiries into these deaths for no reason. Most of them aren't in my jurisdiction," Genevieve explained.

"No reason!" Robby exclaimed and then shrunk back. "Sorry. I'm just...really on edge lately."

"I get it," Genevieve nodded in understanding. "Tomorrow, I need you to get the rest of the information. Then, hopefully, we'll be able to see the bigger picture."

"Is it okay if I send it to Cari like before?" he asked. "I just don't want anyone to think I'm sharing information with the police. Texting my sister-in-law seems more normal."

Cari swallowed a laugh. She wasn't sure that was more normal, but he was willing to keep getting information for them. She didn't want to dissuade him now.

"That's fine," Genevieve told him. "You're doing the right thing here."

Cari watched Robby's face. His eyes widened some and he rubbed his forehead. "What do I tell Bea? I've been keeping this from her and now that I've told the police, I feel like I need to tell her."

Cari was nodding in agreement when Genevieve spoke up. "No. Don't tell her anything yet. It's not that I think she'll tell someone, but the fewer people who know, the better."

Cari frowned at her friend. "But, Bea's his wife. She deserves to know what's happening in his life."

Genevieve shook her head firmly. "Not yet. Soon, but not yet."

Robby's shoulders sank. "Okay, but you'll let me know when?"

Genevieve nodded. "Yes. We'll be in close contact."

He looked at his watch. "I need to go or she'll start to be suspicious and I'm running out of good lies to tell."

Genevieve nodded and Robby got up from the table before turning to Cari. "I'll text you tomorrow. Thanks for your help."

"Any time, Robby," Cari responded.

She closed the door behind him and looked at Genevieve. Her friend was gathering her things. "Is it really too thin to investigate at this point?"

Genevieve sighed. "I can't really get into it, Cari. This was a big help, but it doesn't really tell me who's involved. Once we get more information on the payments, I think it will be much clearer."

"Can't you just get a warrant for the records and leave Robby out of it?" Cari asked.

"We could try, but that would alert anyone involved that we're on to them. If we were denied, then we could lose them all together," Genevieve explained.

"I guess so. I'm worried about him. He seems really stressed," Cari told her friend.

"I don't know him as well as you do, but I have to agree. This is really weighing on him," she responded. "I'll try to look into these other names some before I go to bed tonight."

"I've done a little digging already too. If I find any connections, I'll send them your way," Cari offered.

"Perfect. I'm going to take off then. Thanks for the water. And for cleaning," she winked.

"I'd say any time, but I really hate cleaning, so you're welcome," Cari laughed.

* * * * *

Genevieve got back in her car and pulled out her phone. She sent a quick text to Dureski to tell him Robby Rialto was the source she met with and she had some evidence from him. Dureski immediately called.

"What kind of evidence, Viacorte?" he asked her.

"Mr. Rialto has a series of codes which correspond to different victims' names. Four victims and codes," she told him.

"Codes for what?" Dureski asked.

"I believe they're payment invoice codes issued by the company requesting payment," she said.

"I'm not sure I'm following…" Dureski said slowly.

"For example, last week, when Elaine C. Frobish died, he received an invoice request on the same day and the invoice code had her initials in it.

It's happened more than once and he started to feel uneasy about it," she explained.

"What company is requesting payment?" Dureski asked.

"That I don't know. He only looked up the date and the code. He's feeling a little paranoid and is worried someone is watching him, so he only looked up the bare minimum," she told him. "But don't worry. I explained to him we needed more, including the business name and the amount. He has a few other codes from requests made in irregular ways, so he's going to get the company name for all eight codes."

"Good. Which names?" Dureski asked her.

"Frobish, Horace Manwith, Aaron Roth, and Thomas Washburn," she recited.

"Not Aguirre?"

"I wondered about that too, so I gave him the initials and a timeframe. He's going to see if he can find a similar code. That happened before his time at the company though," Genevieve explained.

"Okay. What else?"

"I need to rope in my partner, Detective Runimoss on this. He doesn't have to know it's an FBI related matter, but our Frobish case is tied in and I can't keep parsing out what information I give him and what I keep to myself," she said boldly.

"Fine. When can I talk to Rialto?" he asked.

Genevieve hesitated. She wasn't sure Robby would meet with the FBI. "I'm not sure, sir. We had a liaison who connected us—"

"A liaison? You mean his sister-in-law?" Dureski barked.

"Yes, sir. I didn't think I should mention your case in front of them yet, so he doesn't know about you," she paused. "Like I said, he's a little nervous about looking stuff up at all. I don't know what he'll think if he hears the FBI is involved too."

"I don't care. If he wants to continue cooperating and not get lumped in with the other criminals, then he is going to have to talk to me," Dureski said pointedly.

Genevieve grimaced. "I honestly don't think he had any idea anything illegal was happening, sir. I do not believe he is involved."

"Again, I don't care. I want to talk to him tomorrow or the day after at the very latest. If threatening him with being charged gets him in front of me, then so be it," he said and ended the call.

Genevieve put her phone back in her bag and sighed. She didn't know Robby well, but threatening him was not something she felt good about doing. Hopefully, he would be open to meeting with the FBI. She turned on her SUV and pulled out of her parking spot. She wanted to look into these three other deaths before she went to bed tonight.

She thought about the names Robby and Cari had given her: Thomas Washburn, Horace Manwith, and Aaron Roth. These were in addition to Elaine Frobish and Marshall Aguirre. Dureski thought it related to business ownership, but she didn't see it that way.

She only had access to case files for Aguirre and Frobish, but maybe she could find the commonality between the two of them. She wasn't sure case files existed for the other three; they were considered accidental deaths. She steered her Expedition into her parking lot and parked. Something was tickling the back of her mind. Maybe if she looked through her notes on Frobish again, she'd see it. She grabbed her bag and headed up to her apartment on the second floor.

Once inside, she locked the door behind her and pulled out her laptop and notebook. She flipped through the pages and skimmed her notes. Both Aguirre and Frobish had employees who stated their bosses had received phone calls from some sort of angry person. In both cases, the number was linked to a burner phone. In Aguirre's case, the employee said he was mad about some sort of landscaping requirement, but what was it with the Frobish woman? She turned a few more pages and sighed. The employee who mentioned the angry caller hadn't known why the person was calling. She yawned. It was after ten o'clock now. She reluctantly put everything back in her bag and decided to get ready for bed.

* * * * *

Robby parked his car in the garage and gently closed his car door. The kids had been asleep for close to two hours and he didn't want to wake them up. Luckily, neither of their rooms were above the garage, so the noisy door shouldn't disturb their sleep. He reached for the door knob to the house when the door swung open. Bea stood inside with an angry expression on her face. Her mascara had run down her face and her eyes were red from crying. Her wavy blonde hair was askew and frizzed instead of being shiny and perfectly styled. He gulped.

"Tell me again. Where have you been this evening?" she hissed.

Robby felt the color leave his face. "At a work meeting."

Bea held up her phone. "I installed a new app on our phones over the weekend. It lets me track where you are and where Hilary is now that she has a phone too. You were not at your office. You were not at a restaurant. You were at *my sister's apartment!*"

Robby put his hands up. "I can explain—"

"Well, you better get started." Bea glared at him. She stayed in the doorway and didn't move to let him inside.

"They asked me to wait a few more days, though," he said sheepishly.

"Who? Who is they?" she asked through clenched teeth.

Robby looked around him. "Cari and Genevieve."

"Genevieve?! Detective Genevieve? *That* Genevieve?" her voice almost rose above a whisper.

Robby nodded and watched her face switch from anger to confusion. She looked up and then ran a hand over her hair, which only made it worse.

"What have you gotten us into, Robby?" she asked as fear crept into her eyes.

He swallowed hard. "I don't know. I'm so sorry. Can I, please, can I come inside?"

She stepped back and made a sweeping motion with her left arm. He stepped inside and pulled her into a hug. More tears poured from her eyes.

"I'm sorry, Bea. I'm trying to make it right. I still don't even know what *it* is, but I'm trying to stay ahead of it," he told her.

She pushed back from him and looked him in the eye. "Are we safe?"

"I hope so," he whispered.

Chapter 13

Cari went for a run the next morning. The stresses from the previous day kept her tossing and turning in the night. She'd taken a glance at the insurance quotes and knew the premiums were higher than she currently paid. The stipend Ollaman was offering wouldn't cover all of it. She didn't save much money each month as it was, but now she'd be saving zero.

She also couldn't stop thinking about Genevieve's reaction to Robby's information. She asked him not to say anything to Bea yet, and that seemed weird. Genevieve was hiding something; it almost seemed like she wasn't that surprised Robby was the source. Robby's anxiety about the whole thing must be contagious because Cari couldn't stop thinking of worst-case-scenarios where Robby got fired and Bea never talked to her again.

She pumped her legs faster and tried to enjoy the run. She willed herself to think about anything else…like…the wedding. It had been kind of fun to talk about wedding plans recently. She wondered who Bob would ask to be his best man. She knew Bea would be her matron of honor…assuming she didn't hate her for getting her husband fired.

Cari shook her head and ran the last block to her apartment complex. She wasn't sure if the run had helped clear her mind or not. She was ready to get to work and hoped Robby would get the additional information to her early in the day. She unlocked her apartment and went inside. After locking the door behind her, she grabbed her water bottle and took several drinks. The humidity was high and she was soaked with sweat. She paced through her apartment to cool down some more and then started her coffee maker. She could take a quick shower while the coffee brewed.

Running hadn't left her as refreshed as she had hoped, but the shower felt nice. She took her phone from the charger and checked to see if she'd missed any messages. The screen showed a missed call from Bob as well as a text asking her to call him back. She touched the call symbol and continued getting ready for work.

"Hey, Cari," Bob said when he picked up. "We didn't really get to finish talking about your finances last night. Did you get any quotes from those three places?"

"I did," she responded as she pulled on her blouse. "They're all a lot higher than I expected. Or maybe just higher than I hoped."

"Yeah, it isn't cheap," he agreed.

She sighed. "I don't save very much each month as it is, but this will completely eliminate any saving."

"Ugh," he commiserated. "I'm sorry to hear that. Maybe there are some other options we could consider. Free tonight?"

"Definitely. I'd love to hear some better options," she said with some curiosity. "What do you mean?"

"I have some ideas I can go over with you tonight at dinner. How about I cook something for you this time?" he suggested.

"Works for me. I'll see you then. Love you, Bob," Cari said.

"Love you too," he responded and ended the call.

Cari wondered what other options he could have for her and why he wouldn't have mentioned them already. Maybe he could get permission to add her to his benefits package before they were officially married. She shook her head. She'd worry about it later. She finished getting dressed and went to the kitchen to pour her coffee into her travel tumbler.

The four names she'd connected to Robby's codes floated through her head as she drove to her office. She hadn't done a lot of reading about the two newest names yet and wondered if their lives had intersected or what else they might have in common. Frobish and Manwith had almost nothing in common other than being small business owners, but owning a business wasn't that unique. There had to be something else that linked these four strangers. She parked her car in the parking garage and grabbed her messenger bag. Bryson Millar pulled into the spot next to hers and waved.

"Good morning, Turnlyle. How's the suspicious death story rolling?" he asked with a smile.

"It's kind of...expanding, I think," she said vaguely.

His face grew serious. "That sounds ominous."

She gave a half-hearted shrug. "It's still early. No reason to sound the alarm bells yet."

He held the door for her. "Well, that's good. You met with Ollaman already, right?"

She nodded. "I couldn't talk him into getting a smaller healthcare package for us."

"Yeah, I didn't even try. I've been on this ride once already. I know how it ends," he said and frowned. "I hoped the Beagle would be different, but I guess I was wrong."

"What will you do? You have kids, right?" she asked him.

"I have two boys, yes, but their mom still has good insurance," he explained.

"I didn't realize you were married," Cari said as they stepped onto the elevator.

"I don't wear a ring. People make certain assumptions when you wear a wedding band," he explained. "My wife is used to it."

Cari blinked in confusion. "I guess if it works for you, then that's all that matters."

"Exactly," he said. "Well, happy hunting with your story. And good luck with the health insurance search too."

Cari smiled her thanks and walked to her desk. She settled into her chair and pulled out her notebook. After turning to a new page, she wrote each of the victim's initials across the top and drew lines between them. She wrote "occupation", "age", "town", and "death date" in the margin. She tapped her pencil on the page. She needed more than these basic characteristics to find a connection. Two of the people had died months ago. She wondered how their family members would take a phone call about their deaths now, but she needed more information and that required speaking with family. She booted up her computer to look up their names. Hopefully, she wasn't going to spend the entire morning making awkward phone calls.

* * * * *

It seemed like the computer was running slower than usual. Robby ran a hand over his short hair and looked out the small window in his office door again. No one was outside his office. Still, he felt like someone was watching him. The system finally finished logging him in. He had the initials and date from Genevieve in his pocket. He glanced again at the window before retrieving it. Satisfied that no one was lurking outside, he pulled the note from his pocket.

He set it on his desk and went to the search function in the accounting system. He typed in the date and hit enter. Just as the results starting appearing on the screen, footsteps sounded in the hallway. He minimized the screen and opened his work email program instead. He had an email from Follard about the client from lunch on Monday. He opened it as the footsteps grew quieter. He pretended to read it, but the words weren't registering as his mind went through various scenarios of how he would respond if someone knocked on his door. He waited half a minute before looking out the window again. It was clear, so he enlarged the accounting program again. Several transactions occurred on the date in question. He scrolled through them, looking for one with the letters MDA. Halfway down the page, he saw it. He quickly scrawled the code onto the note from his pocket and then clicked on the line item to open the details.

He blinked and rubbed his eyes. The transaction was for a consulting fee paid. It was categorized as programming and was a payment of $7500. He wrote down the name, amount, and category on the note and added two question marks. Then he took out his personal cell phone and snapped a photo to text to Cari. Maybe she could make sense of it. As soon as he sent it, his office phone rang. He closed the accounting system and looked at the caller ID. It was Follard on the line. He wiped his sweaty hands off on his pants and picked up the receiver to answer the call.

"Hi, Damien. What's up?" Robby said as calmly as he could into the phone.

"Hey, Robby. I just wanted to let you know I just spoke with the potential client from lunch yesterday. He was really impressed with our company and plans to sign on," Follard said enthusiastically.

"That's great to hear," Robby responded. He wasn't sure why Follard needed to call him to tell him this.

"Everything okay with you? You've seemed a little uptight the last few days," Follard commented.

Robby looked over his shoulder again and swallowed. No one was outside his office. No one was suspicious. He was fine.

"I stayed up later than usual over the weekend doing family stuff. Guess I'm getting old and don't quite bounce back like I used to," he responded.

Follard laughed. "Kids will definitely take it out of you. Well, keep up the good work!"

The call ended. Robby replaced the receiver and opened the accounting program again. He just needed to look up a few more things for Cari and Detective Viacorte and then he could go back to business as usual.

* * * * *

151

Genevieve rubbed her eyes and yawned. She had tossed and turned all night. She wanted to get the information for Dureski, but she didn't want to scare Robby off or possibly put him in harm's way. She had brainstormed ways to approach Robby, but nothing seemed right.

"Late night, Sleeping Beauty?" Alex asked her from his desk.

"Funny. Not really…I just didn't sleep well," she said and yawned again.

"If you would leave work at work, you'd sleep a lot better," Alex advised.

"Sure. I'll just turn my brain off and call it a night," she joked.

"Since you obviously kept working the case last night, what's new?" Alex asked her.

"Okay, keep an open mind before I say anything," she cautioned.

"Let me guess. You met with Turnlyle last night," Alex surmised.

She nodded. "She's smart and helpful. I met with Cari and a…source of hers last night."

"A *source?*" Alex scoffed. "C'mon, Gen. Don't give me that."

"You'll probably find out who it is later, but for right now, it's a source," she said firmly.

"Fine," Alex grumbled. "What does the source know?"

Before she could answer, her desk phone rang. The caller ID read *CSU Luvenon.*

"It's Chris. Maybe he finally got something with all the license plates," she guessed. "Hey, Chris. I've got you on speaker."

"I finally finished going through all the footage from the state park. Several single-passenger-vehicles exited, so it took me longer than I expected," he told them. "I have six names for you. One was a rental and the company just got back to me with the driver's information. Check your inbox for the details."

"Thanks, Chris. Hey, what about the puzzle?" Genevieve asked.

"The trash puzzle?" Chris asked in an annoyed tone.

"That's the one," she responded. "Did you find all the pieces?"

"Maybe?" he said uncertainly. "Something in the trash was wet and several pieces of paper had deteriorated or lost their shape entirely. We couldn't really make anything from it."

"Not even a name or business letterhead?" she asked hopefully.

"I honestly think it was just on plain, white paper, but it's impossible to say," he answered. "Sorry."

"That's okay. Thanks for trying," Genevieve told him.

"Anything else?" Alex asked.

"That's all I've got for now. Laters."

The call ended and Genevieve replaced the receiver in the cradle.

"Rather than compromise your *source*," Alex said snottily. "Why don't we look into these six drivers?"

She shrugged. "Works for me."

They both pulled up the file from their email accounts.

"You take the first three and I'll take the last three," Alex instructed.

The first name on the list was Tate Goldlum. Genevieve entered his name into the search bar of the database and clicked enter. His phone number popped up with his driver's license. He was a retired army sergeant and had a completely clean record. He'd been married fifty-two years, but his wife was deceased. Genevieve checked the date. It had been over six years since she'd died. The man was close to eighty; she had a hard time believing he could force anyone over the side of a cliff.

"The first guy is almost 80. I'm not sure he can even get up to the top of the cliff," Genevieve told Alex.

"I started with the last name. I figured that was the rental car guy and I was right. Check this out." He turned his screen so she could see it better.

The man in the driver's license photo had closely cropped dark brown hair, dark brown eyes, and pale skin. Genevieve had never seen him before. She put her hands up and shrugged.

"Who am I looking at?" she asked.

"Oh, right! You didn't see the photos in the other murder book. You were in the bathroom. This guy looks a lot like the other rental car guy from the Aguirre file," Alex explained.

"Wait a second. They had DNA in the Aguirre case too. Why not just swab everyone to rule them out?" Genevieve asked.

Alex frowned. "Good question. They definitely should have done that instead of rely on alibis. I think I read something in the case notes…"

"Benson gave us a digital copy of the case. Let's take a look," she suggested. "I've got it in my email. Just a sec."

She scrolled through the messages until she found Benson's name. She double-clicked on the attachment and waited for it to open. It took half a minute for the computer to open the large file. She scrolled through it to the case notes.

"Here it is. They did swab everyone who was local, but the car rental guy was out of state. He had an air-tight alibi from their perspective anyway, so they let it drop," she told Alex.

"Scroll to the driver's license photos. You'll definitely recognize the guy," Alex said confidently.

She found the images and started clicking through them. "Oh, you're right. This looks a lot like the guy from the other license. What's the name? This one says Scott Holman."

Alex looked back at his screen. "Nope. John Benally…from Maryland. Wasn't the other guy from Florida?"

Genevieve nodded. "We need to find out who this guy really is."

"Not to state the obvious, but we can't exactly pick someone up from these other states," Alex said.

"Let's talk to Grusky. I think my FBI contact might be able to help, but I don't want to go over Grusky's head on this," Genevieve responded.

They stood up to go knock on the lieutenant's door. Genevieve's cell phone vibrated with an incoming call before they reached his office. It was Dureski again.

"I need to take this. Hopefully, it will be quick. You get started with Grusky," she told Alex.

She walked quickly to the exit and then swiped her thumb across the screen to take the call. "This is Detective Viacorte."

"I haven't heard from you about Rialto yet. Did he get you the info? Is he coming in?" Dureksi asked her.

"I've been tracking down a different lead this morning and haven't heard from him yet," she explained. "My partner and I may have found a connection between the older case and the Frobish case. We were just about to check in with our lieutenant and then I might need to call you for a favor."

"A favor?" Dureski asked skeptically.

"Yeah, we might need you to send agents to pick someone up. Can I call you back in a few minutes?" she asked.

"Fine," Dureski grumbled and ended the call.

Genevieve hurried back inside. Alex motioned from Grusky's office window to come on in. She slipped inside and waited for the lieutenant to speak.

"Alex was just explaining about your person of interest. John or Scott or whatever," he said. "How sure are you that he's involved?"

"He has been in a rental vehicle near the scene of two different *accidents* that we know aren't really accidents. The license photos are not identical, but they are very similar," Alex said.

"Let me see for myself," Grusky said.

He followed them to their desks. They each turned their screen to face him. He looked from one to the other and back a few times.

"Two different states, but I agree. This could definitely be the same person. His face is a little fuller in the Maryland photo and his hair is a little lighter in the Florida photo. Which one is more recent?" Grusky asked.

"Maryland is from the Frobish case," Genevieve responded.

"I don't really know anyone in Maryland," Grusky mused. "We need to call the local police there and get them read in. We don't have jurisdiction there."

"I might have a solution, sir," Genevieve offered.

"Let's hear it," he encouraged her to continue.

"My contact with the FBI could send agents to both locations," she proposed.

"We should verify the addresses are real first," Alex suggested.

"Correct. Runimoss, you look up the addresses and validate them. Viacorte, call your guy and see if he'll help us out," Grusky instructed. "Keep me posted."

He walked back to his office and slammed the door.

"Want me to do one address?" Genevieve asked Alex.

"You can probably find both of them faster than I can find one, but sure. I'll take Maryland. You take Florida," he told her.

She sat down at her desk and opened her web browser. She typed in the address and waited for the map to load. After changing the view to satellite, she zoomed in to see what the location looked like. It was an apartment complex with twelve buildings. The address listed his unit as #1032, making her think he was probably in building ten. It seemed at least plausible that the location was a residence.

"Florida address is an apartment like it shows on his license," she told Alex.

"The map is showing a house at the Maryland address, so it looks legit too," he said. "The FBI should be able to verify someone with that name actually lives there."

"Agreed. Let me call Dureski," she said and pulled out her phone. The screen showed she had an unread text, but she ignored it for now.

"Agent Dureski, it's Detective Viacorte. I have two addresses for you. First, can you verify the owner's or renter's name with the address? We confirmed the locations but hoped you could access who really lives there," she explained.

"Text me the information. I'll get back to you. It might take me some time to connect with our offices in those areas. Call me as soon as you hear from Rialto," he said and ended the call.

"He's going to get the ball rolling on it and get back to me," she told Alex.

"Sounds like it's time for a coffee break then," Alex remarked. "Coffee truck?"

"If you're buying," she said with a laugh.

Chapter 14

The image on the phone screen started to darken, so Cari tapped it to keep her screen on. Robby had texted her about the date Gen requested from over a year ago. She looked at his note again. *Consulting fee. Pierce Construction and Landscaping. $7500.*

She opened her web browser and typed in Pierce Construction and Landscaping. Maybe there was another company with the same name? The familiar link from her previous research showed up. Cari scrolled through the first page of search results, but no other company existed in their area with that name. She frowned. Why would a landscaping company charge Robby's company such a large consulting fee?

Before she looked into it more, she needed to send it along to Gen. Hopefully, Robby would get the rest of the information to her soon. She texted the image to Gen, but didn't add any of her extra information. It just didn't make sense. Admittedly, she didn't actually know the man, but everything she'd read about him made him seem like a good person.

The revelation stymied her for a few minutes. She tried to come up with reasonable possibilities to explain why the friendly landscaping man would be charging a technology company a large consulting fee. Nothing came to mind. She needed to come at it from a different angle.

Cari had only read a little bit about the deaths of Thomas Washburn and Aaron Roth. Maybe something within their stories would help her connect the dots to Pierce. She pulled up the obituary of Thomas Isaac Washburn again. He was survived by a wife, a son, and a daughter. She found his wife, Ellen Washburn in LexisNexis and jotted down her phone number before punching it into her desk phone keypad.

"Um, hello?" a female voice said in a questioning tone.

"Hi, Mrs. Washburn?" Cari began. "This is Cari Turnlyle with the Brenington Beagle. I'm doing some…research about local construction companies and came across your husband's business. Do you have time for a few questions?"

"Oh, you must be mistaken. My husband died and we sold his business recently. I can get you their number. Just one moment," Mrs. Washburn replied.

"Actually, I would like to talk to you, Mrs. Washburn. Could we meet for coffee?" Cari interjected.

"I…guess so. Can you come to my house? I haven't gotten out much since…well, since Thomas died. Leaving the house is…hard," Mrs. Washburn said sadly.

"I understand. Can I bring you a coffee?" Cari offered.

"I suppose that would be fine. I just take it black. Nothing fancy. I guess you know my address?" she asked.

Cari recited the address from her computer screen for confirmation. "It will take me about half an hour to get to you. Is that okay?"

"That's just fine. I'll be here either way," the older woman assured her.

"See you soon," Cari said and replaced the receiver.

She locked her workstation and gathered up her belongings. As she walked back to the elevator, she thumbed off a text to Michelle to tell her she was chasing down a lead and would be back soon. She hurried out to her car and used her phone to find a coffee place on the route to the Washburn's home. She hoped she wasn't wasting her time.

* * * * *

Genevieve opened the text from Cari. She'd never heard of Pierce Construction and Landscaping and wondered why a consulting fee would be so high. She could feel Alex watching her, so she turned the screen toward him.

"Since I know you're trying to read over my shoulder anyway…take a closer look," she offered.

"What is this? Pierce Construction and Landscaping? That's a consulting fee? What am I looking at?" Alex spewed out questions faster than she could respond.

She laughed. "One at a time, Alex. Remember how I told you I met with one of Cari's sources last night?"

Alex nodded. "He's a landscaper?"

"No," she shook her head. "This is the company who charged his company on the same day that the Aguirre man was killed."

"Oh, well, now I understand perfectly. What?" Alex shook his head in confusion.

"It's a little convoluted. An accountant—"

Alex interrupted. "It's Robby. I know who your source is."

She pursed her lips at him before continuing. "As I was saying, an *accountant* recently noticed some of the billing codes he was asked to approve had some letters which coincided with the initials of people in the area who died from accidental...events."

Alex frowned but motioned for her to go on.

"In the past seven or eight months, he was asked to approve or process payments for eight different charges or payments at irregular times," she explained.

"What? Irregular times?" Alex raised his eyebrows.

"I'm not an accountant. I don't work in the corporate world. I'm just telling you, in these eight instances, things were handled differently and it raised his suspicion," Genevieve said curtly.

"Okay, fair enough. Are you telling me we have nine victims here, counting Aguirre?" Alex's eyes grew wide.

She waved his question off with both hands. "No. Just eight codes. Only four of them connected to a death which also matched the person's initials...well five if you count Aguirre."

"Still...five victims. That's a lot. How does the landscaping company fit in?" he asked.

"Well, I'm actually not sure. This information pertains to the Aguirre case. I asked him to look up the date Aguirre died to see if there was a code with his initials and if there was...who was asking for payment and what were they being paid for," she said and pointed at the phone's screen. "Oh...and how much were they paid."

"This landscaping fee is exorbitant unless the business has a significant amount of property. Something is off here," Alex agreed. "What about the four other codes?"

She frowned. "He hasn't gotten the information for us yet. Let's look up Pierce Construction and Landscaping and see what we can find. Maybe the owner looks like the guy we're trying to find and we can wrap this up finally."

She opened her web browser and typed in the business name into the search bar.

She clicked through the website. "The company is really involved in the community...here's a photo of Pierce. He doesn't look like the rental car guy. Let's see...it says they sponsor girls and boys little league teams every summer, amongst other things."

"I know we're pretending I don't know who your source is, but doesn't Robby work for some sort of tech company? Why do they need a landscaping consultant?" Alex asked, annoyed.

"Exactly. It smells a bit like money laundering, but why? What could Pierce be into that's dirty?" she asked herself as much as Alex.

"Well, like you said earlier, you still need to hear from him about the other four codes. Maybe they were charges from someone or something else," Alex suggested.

Genevieve's cell phone buzzed before she could respond. "It's Dureski."

Alex motioned for her to take it. She rolled her eyes. Of course she was going to take the call.

"Agent Dureski?" she said after accepting the call.

"We checked the names on those two residences. The apartment is not being rented by anyone with either of those names, so that's a bust. The home is owned by a Scott Holman, but the man is much older, not to mention the little hair he does have is white," Dureski informed her.

Genevieve groaned. "Ugh. So, whoever this guy really is, he's definitely involved somehow."

"We're using facial recognition software to see if we get any hits. It's completely possible his fake licenses will show up, though, and his real identity will still elude us. What's the story with Rialto?" Dureski asked the question she was hoping to avoid.

"I haven't gotten to talk to him yet," Genevieve said in an effort to stall the confrontation. "I'll keep you posted."

"Get him on the phone soon," Dureski ordered and ended the call.

Alex was watching her from his desk. "Bad news?"

"The addresses and identities are not a match, so we still don't know who that guy is," Genevieve told him.

"Seems like we need to talk to Robby," Alex said, echoing Dureski's request.

"If only it were that easy," she mumbled.

"What?" Alex asked.

"Nothing. He's scared. We have to wait for him to get us the rest of the information. Hopefully, we'll hear from him soon," she said with less confidence than she felt.

* * * * *

Cari pulled alongside the curb of Ellen Washburn's home. She could see the older woman watching for her from the front window. She turned off her car and grabbed her messenger bag. She slung her bag over her shoulder and then grabbed the two coffees. Before she had her door closed, the woman had opened her front door to wave her into the house.

"Come on in," she said as Cari approached the porch. "We can sit at the kitchen table."

"Thanks," Cari said as she stepped inside.

Mrs. Washburn locked the door behind her and guided her to the kitchen. The white and black checkered backsplash was set off by cherry-red hand towels hanging from the white cabinets below. The countertops were made of white and black marbled granite. Cari wasn't sure anyone ever cooked in the kitchen; it was spotless. She took a seat across the table from Mrs. Washburn.

"Thank you for the coffee, Ms. Turnlyle," Mrs. Washburn said as she took a sip.

"Please, call me Cari. And you're welcome. Thanks for meeting with me," Cari responded.

"You can call me Ellen," she said amicably. "You said you wanted to talk to me about Thomas' business?"

"Yes," she paused. "How long had Thomas owned the construction business?"

"He started doing some work for neighbors when he was a teenager. Fence repair, gutter stuff, um…replacing window shutters. Simple stuff early on. He found he really enjoyed it, so when he went to college, he studied construction science or something like that. He did some projects with a larger company right out of college, but eventually, he came back to his hometown and opened his own company. People remembered him and he got a lot of customers right away. It was a lucrative business for us," Ellen told her.

"Did he ever run into any challenges?" Cari asked.

"I mean, it was never easy. Long days and long projects, but he always enjoyed the work, so it didn't bother him," Ellen said matter-of-factly.

"He didn't have any frustrating customers or bureaucracy struggles at any point?" Cari asked in an effort to steer the conversation.

Ellen started to shake her head, then stopped. "Well, you know, right before he died, he was complaining to me pretty often about a new city policy regarding landscaping."

Cari blinked and had to struggle not to gasp. "Landscaping? What do you mean?"

"Well, let me think. It seemed pretty ridiculous, and I don't know why he cared, but he would sometimes make up his mind on something and just not want to budge," she started to explain. "I think the city wanted everyone to have similar store front landscaping. Same flowers, same colors, that sort of thing. They had a company who was going around to plant these flowers or whatever and the businesses had to pay a fee to cover some of the cost.

"Thomas wanted to do it himself and not pay, but they said all the flowers had to be planted at the same time and come from the same greenhouse and so on and so on," she continued. "Thomas told me it was ludicrous. He could do it for almost no cost and he shouldn't have to pay for it. He was still trying to fight it when he died. The city told him this landscaping firm had offered them a great deal to do all the businesses at once and there was no fighting it. I still can't believe he's gone some days. He probably jumped fifty car batteries in his life. The medical examiner said he mixed up the diodes or…well, I don't know what they're called. Thomas always took care of those things. Anyway, I guess you know. He shocked himself and it killed him."

"How terrible. I'm so sorry, Ellen." Cari reached across the table and squeezed the older woman's hand.

"Thankfully, his business sold for plenty of money. I'll be taken care of and won't have to go to the poor house yet," she said with a half-hearted smile.

Cari returned the expression. "I appreciate you meeting with me, Ellen. You've been really helpful."

"Have I? You said you were researching construction businesses or something?" Ellen asked in a confused tone.

"Something like that. I'll let you know when I get the story finished. Thank you again," Cari said and stood up from the table.

"Have a nice morning," Ellen said.

"Thank you. You too," Cari said.

Ellen walked her to the front door and stood on the porch while Cari walked to her car. She hadn't asked which company the city was using for the landscaping project. She knew it had to be Pierce. She just didn't know why. She needed to look into Aaron Roth's death to confirm the connection, but something more was at play.

Cari didn't want to concern Ellen by sitting in front of her house while she looked up the details surrounding Aaron Roth's death. She waved goodbye and then drove out of the neighborhood to a nearby diner she'd passed earlier. She could grab brunch and do some reading about Roth at the same time.

She took a seat in the back booth and almost laughed at how she was following Genevieve's lead with her seat selection. After placing her order with the waitress, she pulled out her laptop and used her cell phone as a hotspot to run some searches. Aaron Roth had drowned about four months ago. The obituary said he was survived by his wife, Dora and son, Trent, both of whom lived in the area. The son was unmarried as far as she could tell from the obituary. Cari figured meeting with the wife would be easiest, but her search revealed the woman was living in a memory care facility. She looked up Trent Roth next. He lived in a townhouse about an hour from where she was eating lunch, but his employment was listed as a sales associate for a men's clothing store in the mall.

Cari checked her watch. It was almost eleven o'clock. Maybe Trent could spare a few minutes to speak with her. She found his phone number and entered it into her cell phone. She hit the call button and it went immediately to his voice mail. *He must have some kind of call screener.* She decided to leave a message.

"Hello, Mr. Roth. My name is Cari Turnlyle with the Brenington Beagle and I'm calling in regards to a business which used to be in your family. Socket-To-Me. If you could return my call at your earliest convenience, I would appreciate it."

She ended the call and drummed her fingers on the table. The waitress stopped by to refill her water glass and offer her the check. Cari fished her credit card out of her wallet for the bill. She closed her laptop and put it back into her messenger bag. After signing the bill, she gathered up her things and went back out to her car. It was time to do some research on Randall Pierce.

* * * * *

Robby wiped sweat from his forehead and scrolled through the accounting system to the next code. He could feel dampness on his back and under his arms and hoped it wasn't visible to anyone passing by. Maybe he should turn down the thermostat so he could cool off a bit. He didn't want to risk walking away from his desk to the wall with the control panel. He picked up a file from his desk and fanned himself once. He felt like an old woman and set it back down. *Breathe. You're almost finished.*

163

He had made it through the four important codes. Genevieve had only asked him to do the four which coincided with people's deaths, but when all of those had the same business listed as the recipient, he got curious. It was risky, but he had to know. All the remaining codes weren't for payments NTS made to another company, but money paid to NTS. When he found the first "non-death" code, as he'd started referring to them, he remembered how Follard had never given him the paperwork for the payment. He had put it on the back burner to check the account for the payor's information.

His sticky note was creased from hiding in his wallet for the past day or so, but he still had room to add the details. He pressed his index finger along the creases to flatten in more as he logged into the bank account. Hopefully, he could get the information for these four payments quickly and be done with it. He felt no less anxious with this step even though it was something he had planned to do before he met with Cari and Genevieve.

His desk phone rang and made him drop his pen. He closed the accounting system and the bank account window and quickly answered the call without looking at the caller ID.

"New Technology Systems. This is Robby speaking," he said.

"They're about to start the party. Are you coming?" his co-worker Jesse asked him.

"Party...?" Robby started to ask. "Oh, the baby shower thing for Bridget. I completely forgot."

"So, are you coming? Basically, everyone in accounting is here and people are kind of wondering where you are," Jesse told him.

"Yes. I'll be right down. I was just finishing up with some statements. Give me two minutes to run down the stairs," Robby responded.

"See you," Jesse said and ended the call.

Robby double-checked that nothing was open on his computer besides his work email, then locked the workstation. He grabbed his sticky note and shoved it in his pocket. It bothered him not to hide it in his wallet again, but he needed to get downstairs and he couldn't leave it out. He pulled the office door closed and checked to make sure it locked behind him as usual. He rushed to the stairwell and took the steps two-at-a-time down to the third floor where their entry level accountants worked. The party was in the conference room. He tried to slip in quietly, but everyone had been watching for him to arrive.

"Finally! You didn't have to actually run down the stairs, man. You're almost sweaty," Jesse told him and made a face.

"Sorry I'm late. Congratulations, Bridget!" he said to the woman seated near a large stroller with a bow on it.

"No worries. I know you're busy. Thanks for the stroller. It's a really nice one," Bridget said cheerfully.

"You picked it out. We just paid for it," another woman a few chairs over said with a laugh.

Bridget laughed. "True! I do have good taste."

Another woman was cutting slices of cake and passing out cups of what Robby assumed was some kind of punch. He waved off the cake and feigned being full from breakfast still. In reality, his stomach could not tolerate any food. It was in a state of revolt after the stress of sneaking through the ledgers to find information without his boss knowing. He didn't know how people lied their way through life. He'd been lying to Bea for a few months; now he was lying to his boss and his co-worker. He needed to get all of this behind him. Accounting was supposed to be boring.

"Earth to Robby. You want any punch?" Jesse asked him.

"None for me. Thanks, though," Robby responded.

"Is today your last day, Bridget?" someone asked from the other side of the room.

She nodded and patted her round stomach. "Yeah, my due date is tomorrow, so even if she isn't here yet, I'm taking some time to get everything ready."

Robby let the conversation fade into the background. He turned back to Jesse. "This is my first baby shower. How long do we usually stay?"

Jesse snorted. "This isn't even a real baby shower. There was only one gift and she didn't even really need to unwrap it."

Robby looked at him with frustration in his eyes. "So, like ten minutes?"

"Hey, you're the boss of us. You can leave whenever you want," Jesse laughed. "But, at least sign a card first."

Jesse pointed at the table with the cake. Robby saw several light pink envelopes next to a pile of white index cards. Several envelopes were sealed and in a wicker basket near the edge of the table.

"We didn't sign a card in advance?" Robby asked hesitantly.

"It's kind of a good luck, advice, best wishes sort of thing. Like, you write something with parenting advice and stick it in an envelope. The card with the gift was just signed "from the accounting department" by one of the secretaries or something," Jesse explained.

Robby went over to the cards and picked up a blank one. No one had thought to leave a pen for this little activity, or someone had absconded with the designated pen before he arrived. He patted his pockets in search of a pen. He found a mechanical pencil in his pants pocket and pulled it out.

"You dropped this," a woman said to him. He couldn't remember her name.

He looked to see what she was holding out for him and almost gagged. The little sticky note. It was still folded and she didn't seem interested in it. He grabbed it from her hand and put it in his other pocket.

"Thanks," he said and went back to his index card.

His palms were sweating. He had easily been able to read the name Pierce on the sticky note when the woman handed it to him. He felt foolish for not remembering it was there. He swallowed and tried to clear his head.

"You don't need to be Aristotle or anything. Just write something. You have kids. Surely, you can think of something," Jesse's voice startled him and he almost dropped the index card.

"I've never done this before. Don't want to look like an idiot," Robby quipped. He hoped Jesse didn't notice his uneasiness.

Robby scrawled something about sticking to a schedule and signed his name. He put the card into an envelope and debated about writing Bridget on the back or not. Some of the others were blank, so he quickly licked the edge and sealed it closed. Now, maybe he could leave without looking rude.

He put a hand up to get Bridget's attention. "Congratulations again. I hate not to stay longer, but I need to get back to work. Best wishes with everything."

Jesse nodded and joined him in leaving. Luckily, Jesse worked on three and not five, so he couldn't follow Robby for long. Robby opted for the elevator for his return trip. He paused in front of it without pushing the up button.

"Thanks for the tips, Jesse. Hopefully, I'll be less awkward next time," Robby said and smiled.

"I doubt it," Jesse laughed. "You are an accountant. No one expects you to be smooth."

Robby's smile widened. "See you around."

He pushed the elevator button and waited for it to arrive. He was almost home free. His anxiety couldn't take much more of these stealth-mode shenanigans.

He made it to the fifth floor and went straight to his office. Once inside, he pulled his sticky note from his pocket again and unlocked his workstation. He quickly logged into the accounting system and then the company's bank account. He put the two windows side-by-side so he could refer to them at the same time. After locating the payment, he jotted down the time stamp and the amount on the sticky note. The oldest payment code wasn't quite six months old yet, so thankfully, he didn't need to download any old statements to see the history. He clicked through several pages of the account until he got to the correct date range. The amount was $7500 again. He felt like an idiot for not noticing the parallel of it before this, but pushed the thought aside. He just needed to get the information and get out of the system. His eyes scanned the amounts in the bank account history until he found the round number. He opened the line item and blinked. He'd expected to see Pierce Construction and Landscaping as the payor, but it read Phoebe Alexis Hale, LLC. He scribbled it down and repeated the process for the next four codes. The same name popped up again and again as the payor. He'd never heard of Phoebe Hale and couldn't imagine why her company would be paying NTS this much money four different times in the last six months. Robby swallowed. He just needed to take a photo and text it to Cari. Then, his undercover work was complete.

* * * * *

The LexisNexis file on Randall Pierce was lengthy. Cari had taken two pages of notes already and felt like she'd barely scratched the surface. She remembered reading on his company website that he was Canadian and had relocated to the United States for college. Rather than focus on his personal history first, she went straight to his financials. LexisNexis listed his philanthropic contributions centering around local boys' and girls' baseball or softball teams. Cari pursed her lips; clearly, he was willing to support other programs financially. *Why not the newspaper?*

She didn't have to look much further to get an answer to her question. Randall Pierce had a lot of debt. In fact, she wasn't sure how he managed to be a youth team sponsor every summer. He had credit card debt, a mortgage he'd refinanced more than once, and several small loans where it appeared he was only paying the interest each month. For a business owner who had completed numerous projects in the area in the same time frame, he sure wasn't staying in the black very well. She wasn't able to view the transaction history, but none of this looked good for Pierce.

167

Cari went to his employment history and almost gasped. He wasn't listed as the owner of Pierce Construction and Landscaping; he was the manager. She opened a new tab and navigated to the business webpage. The website spoke of him as though he was the owner, but clearly, he wasn't. She clicked on the business on the LexisNexis listing. Pierce Construction and Landscaping was owned by Phoebe A. Hale. She looked up the woman's information. Ms. Hale was Pierce's wife; she just didn't take his name when they got married. Cari went back to Pierce. He was a Canadian citizen, not an American citizen. She wondered why he hadn't at least obtained dual-citizenship. Maybe it was cheaper tax-wise for his wife to own the business.

She decided to look up the couple on social media next. While people rarely posted about being close to filing for bankruptcy, maybe she could gain some insight into how he spent his time. Pierce and his wife shared social media accounts and looked happy in all their photos. Their children were adults, but none of the accounts were public, so she couldn't figure out where they lived.

Her phone buzzed. She looked at her watch and saw Robby had texted her an image. She pulled out her phone and opened the message. She needed to call Genevieve. After forwarding the image to her friend, she closed the messaging app and hit the call button for Gen's number.

"I didn't expect you to call. What's up?" Gen asked.

"Robby sent me another update. I'm at a loss. I just sent the image to you, but it doesn't make any sense," Cari told her.

"I'm opening it now," Genevieve said to her. "Hmm…so his company made payments to this landscaping company at basically the same time these five people died…and they got payment from some other small business at some point in between? What? And who is Phoebe A. Hale?"

"That is Randall Pierce's wife. She *owns* the landscaping business, well her corporation does or whatever," Cari explained.

"Ahh…okay. So, this husband and wife are somehow teaming up to kill people over…landscaping?" Genevieve said with doubt in her voice.

"Yeah, I can't quite wrap my mind around it. Something else is going on. I talked to Thomas Washburn's wife. She told me that before he died, he had been arguing with their City Hall about some sort of new landscaping project. He wanted to do it himself and they said it needed to be uniform and they had an agreement with another company to complete it," Cari responded.

"The other company must be Pierce, but I still don't see why they'd kill him," Genevieve mused. "You know what? Aguirre's file mentioned something about him having a disagreement with the city about landscaping too."

"Aguirre is the extra case?" Cari asked for clarification.

"Yes, we got a DNA match with his case," Geneveive told her.

"Frobish…" Cari said aloud as she thought about her conversations with the woman's employees.

"Yeah, that's the case we have the DNA match to Aguirre's," Genevieve confirmed.

"No, I was just thinking about something her employees told me," Cari began. "They said Frobish was working on having a medical spa or pool or something put in for some of their clients to use after their workouts. That's construction-related too."

"True," Genevieve said slowly. "I'm not sure how it fits. Was she working with Pierce to have it done?"

"I don't know. They didn't say," Cari said. "But! Horace Manwith's front desk guy had a similar story. Someone was calling repeatedly and the front desk guy found them to be rude."

Cari flipped through her notebook to find what the man had told her. She summarized her interview for Gen. "The guy at the front desk told me two interesting things. One- someone made the angry phone calls and wouldn't leave their name and two- he wanted to expand the building, but the construction hadn't started yet. He wasn't sure how far along the plans were."

"Hmm…well, that's a little thin, but I'll make a note. I think we need to bring this Pierce guy in," Genevieve commented. "Anything else, Cari? I've gotta go."

"That's all I've got for now. Keep me posted?" she asked.

"I'll do what I can," Genevieve said vaguely and ended the call.

Cari drummed her fingers on her desk. She hoped Aaron Roth's son would call her back soon. Maybe he could provide the connection they were missing.

Chapter 15

Alex looked at Genevieve with interest. "What did my favorite journalist have for us today?"

Genevieve gave him the side eye. "I can't tell if you're being sarcastic or not."

"Just tell me already," he complained.

"Robby got the payment info for the other four codes *plus* four more," Genevieve started to say.

"Okay, so these other four codes. What do they tell us?" Alex asked.

Genevieve showed him the image. "These four are for payment received and the payment was from the LLC which owns the landscaping company, Pierce Construction and Landscaping."

"Okay, so the landscaping company is using Robby's company as a go-between. They're not paying whoever it is directly or something?" Alex asked.

"Or something. I think we need to talk to this Pierce guy. He definitely knows about these payments," Genevieve told Alex.

"Let's go find him. He's probably at work, right?" Alex proposed.

"More than likely. It's possible he's at a job site, but I think we should start at the business front and see if we can catch him there," Genevieve said. "I need to make a phone call first."

Alex frowned. "Okay, but make it quick."

She ignored his irritation and walked to the exit. She wanted to get an update to Dureski. She knew it would probably lead to him demanding *and getting* a meeting with Robby, but she couldn't keep the information from him. She hit the call button next to his number. He answered immediately.

"I hope you're calling to give me details for a meeting with Rialto," Dureski said.

"First, I have an update in the case. Mr. Rialto was able to get the information on the payment codes to us. We have five which coincide with the deaths of five small business owners and four others were payments to

NTS in the same amount within hours of Rialto being notified of a payment request," she told him.

"Okay, I need all of this in writing. I need print outs and evidence. I need to speak with Rialto," Dureski said sharply.

"I'm sure he'll be able to get you a print out or hard copy of this information, but he would probably rather speak with you first. He's a little paranoid about someone watching his movements right now," Genevieve explained.

"Call him up and ask him to meet us for lunch," Dureski suggested.

Genevieve looked at her watch. "I'll text you the details. He's in the city, so we should probably meet there."

"I'll be waiting for your text," Dureski responded and ended the call.

Genevieve bit her lip. She wasn't sure of the best way to reach Robby mid-morning. Bea had given her both of their cell phone numbers when she watched their kids, so she decided to try his cell phone first. Worst case, she could just go to his office and say she had a meeting with him. She found the phone number and hit the call button. His voice mail picked up after four rings.

"Robby, this is Genevieve. We need to talk. Call me back as soon as you get this," she said into the phone.

She sent him a text with the same message and waited for him to respond. She knew Alex was inside growing more and more annoyed with her by the second, but she had no choice. She had to get this set up for Dureski. Her phone screen lit up with an incoming call. She breathed a sigh of relief.

"Robby, I need you to meet with me and another law enforcement person for lunch," she told him quickly.

"What? I gave you everything…what's happening?" he asked with fear in his voice.

"This is no big deal," she said calmly. "You did a good job getting everything we asked for. This investigation is a lot bigger than we initially thought. Name a place you can meet us for lunch," she instructed.

"Who is us?" Robby asked.

"I'll introduce you when we all get there, okay? I trust the person. It's not a big deal. Where are we meeting?" Genevieve asked again.

"There's a bistro down the street from me. I'll text you the name. Can you be here by noon?" he asked.

She checked her watch. If she left in the next twenty minutes, she could swing it. "I can do it. Send me the information. I'll see you there."

She ended the call and waited for his text to come through. She wasn't familiar with the bistro, but she could find it easily enough. She forwarded the text to Dureski and pocketed her phone on her way back inside.

"Finally," Alex said when she got back to their desks.

"Change of plans," she told him. "I need to meet Dureski for lunch. I should be back by one or so. We can go pick up Pierce then."

"What does Dureski have to do with this?" Alex asked. "Did he find the guy from Maryland or Florida?"

Genevieve had forgotten Dureski was supposedly running a facial recognition search using the man's two driver's licenses. "Uh, no. This is for something else. Maybe he'll have an update on that for me too."

"I guess Pierce doesn't know we're onto him yet, so it's fine to wait. I'll see if I can look up some more background on Pierce," Alex responded. "I'm going to call each of the cities and see what I can find out about the landscaping stuff too."

"Cari might have something for you, if you want to call her. I know she was looking into Pierce too," Genevieve suggested.

Alex rolled his eyes.

"Work smarter, not harder, remember?" Genevieve said with a smirk.

"I'll consider it," he grumbled.

She grabbed her bag and patted him on the shoulder. "Change is hard. I know you can do it. I'll be in touch."

* * * * *

Robby locked his office door and went to the elevator. The hallway was deserted, which was a relief. He didn't want to talk about his lunch plans. He hoped no one else planned to eat at the bistro today. Maybe he could request a table in the back.

He stepped off the elevator and tried to walk casually out the front doors. He couldn't remember if he usually waved to the security person at the front desk or not, but it was easier to keep his eyes forward than it was to speak to someone. He wasn't good at small talk. He let out a breath when he reached the sidewalk. The bistro was two blocks away. He didn't see anyone familiar outside, which relieved him even more. Two short blocks, then he could hide inside the restaurant.

He kept his head down and made it to the bistro within two minutes. He assumed Genevieve and whomever else he was meeting would be inside getting a table, so he went straight inside. The hostess smiled at him.

"Table for one?" she asked.

"Uh, I'm meeting some people. They might already be here," he said and craned his neck to look around her.

Genevieve was sitting in a back booth. She raised a hand to signal him over to her. A man with dark brown, close-cropped hair sat across from her. The man wasn't tall enough to be her partner, Runimoss. Robby wondered who it was. He gestured toward their booth.

"I see my party. Thanks," he said to the hostess.

Genevieve stood up from the booth before Robby reached it. "Mr. Rialto, this is Special Agent Dureski with the FBI. Agent Dureksi, meet Robby Rialto."

Dureski got out of the booth to shake Robby's hand. "Have a seat."

Robby started to sit by Genevieve, but Dureski moved to the opposite side of the table first. This was starting to feel like an interrogation rather than a casual lunch. He swallowed and sat down.

"Mr. Rialto, you look nervous. Let me assure you, you've done nothing wrong. Coming to us was the right decision. Let's order some lunch and then I have a few questions for you," Dureski said quickly. He put up a hand to signal to the waitress.

Robby glanced at the menu. He was thankful the restaurant was familiar, so he didn't have to ask for more time to decide what to order.

"What can I get for everyone today?" the waitress asked.

Dureski spoke first. "I'll get an iced tea, unsweet…and the cheeseburger. Medium. With fries."

"I'll have the spinach wrap with chicken and an ice water, please," Genevieve said next.

Robby's appetite was weak. "Um, water for me too and…a cheeseburger with everything on it. And fries."

"How would you like that cooked?" she asked.

"Well, please," Robby said and his voice cracked.

"Coming right up," she said cheerfully. She collected the menus and walked back to the kitchen.

"Okay, so my understanding is your boss asked you to process some payments and in doing so, he strayed from the normal way your company handles invoices or whatever," Dureski said to Robby.

"Correct. Normally, I get an email with an invoice attached and I issue the payment. If it's payment we're receiving from another business or client, I also get an email with the payment information," Robby told him. "Several times, my boss has called and given me an invoice code over the phone.

Sometimes it's been at night and sometimes it's during the work day. He also gives me a client code to file it under. That code will reference the business name in our accounting system."

"So, you hadn't realized all these payments were going to the same business until Detective Viacorte asked for that information?" Dureski asked for clarification.

Robby felt his hands start to sweat. He swallowed. "That's right. It seems dumb that I wouldn't recognize the client code when I'm a numbers guy, but I guess the requests were infrequent enough; it just didn't register."

"I can't even remember my own phone number sometimes. Don't sweat it," Dureski said with a laugh.

Robby smiled awkwardly. Before anyone else could speak, the waitress arrived with their drinks and food. She placed them in front of each of them.

"Can I get anyone anything else?" she asked.

Dureski waved her off. "We're good. Thanks."

She smiled and walked away. Robby picked up a fry from his plate and took a bite even though his appetite had completely vanished. Dureski chomped down on his cheeseburger and washed it down with a swig of his iced tea.

"Viacorte told me you also had some abnormal deposits show up in your system," Dureski prompted.

"Yes, within a day of each of these invoice requests from Follard, uh, that's my boss, a deposit would show up in our account for an equal amount," Robby explained.

"And what was the amount?" Dureski asked.

"Seventy-five hundred dollars," Robby told him.

"Does Pierce Construction and Landscaping do work for your company?" Dureski asked.

Robby shrugged. "We're a technology company. We have computer scientists and software engineers on our payroll. Our building is surrounded by sidewalks, though there is a fountain in the atrium."

"Was it recently installed?" Dureski asked.

Robby shook his head. "No, I haven't seen anyone working on it either. It's always just running whenever I see it."

"So, you can't give me a valid reason your company would be paying a landscaping company?" Dureski asked.

"Not at all," Robby confirmed.

"Viacorte showed me your handwritten note with the codes and dates and so forth. I really need a hard copy from you with all of this," Dureski told him.

Robby took a drink of water to delay his response. "Okay, um, I, um, I'm not sure I can do that without someone finding out."

"I understand you feel unsafe," Dureski acknowledged. "That's completely reasonable considering what we know. I still need the information."

Genevieve put her hand up. "Would it be possible for you to bring in Mr. Follard for a talk so Mr. Rialto could get the accounting statements to you without the fear of his boss seeing him?"

Dureski took a bite and chewed slowly. "Hmm...I would have to kind of bluff about having the evidence, but with the phone records of these calls Follard made to you, I could swing it. I'll get my assistant to pull the records if you give me your phone number as well as Follard's, Mr. Rialto. She can get them in less than an hour."

"So, should I just go back to work like nothing happened?" Robby asked.

"Yeah, just finish up your lunch here and go back to your office. I'll let you know when we've picked up your boss. Then you can go about getting these files to me," he pulled a card from his pocket. "This is my email. This is my cell phone."

Robby slid the card into his front shirt pocket. "Okay. I guess I'll go back to work now, if that's okay."

Dureski waved his hand in agreement. "Go right ahead. Lunch is on the bureau."

"Thanks," Robby said without glancing at his uneaten cheeseburger. "I guess I'll talk to you later."

He put his napkin on the table and slid out of the booth. This nightmare was almost over. By the end of the day, he could put this all behind him.

* * * * *

Genevieve waited for Dureski to finish signing the receipt. She figured he wasn't going to include her in his interview with Follard, but didn't want to leave without checking. He'd moved to the opposite side of the booth after Robby left.

"My partner and I plan to pick up Pierce and speak with him this afternoon," she told Dureski.

He nodded slowly. "That works. I'm going to call one of my agents to join me in picking up Follard. Our office isn't far from here."

"A few days ago, you theorized this had to do with the businesses changing hands or something. I think it's something else. We've seen a pattern with some of these business owners who died or were killed. Several of them had complained about some new landscaping requirements brought down by the city where their businesses are," she said, hoping she wasn't offending him by challenging his perspective.

Dureski scratched his head. "All of the victims had landscaping issues?"

"No, two of them were looking into some remodeling or expansion projects. Construction-related projects," she clarified.

"That is interesting. Hopefully, Follard or Pierce can shed some more light on it," he said without agreeing or disagreeing with her.

"One more question. Did you get any hits with facial rec for the rental car guy?" she asked him.

He shook his head. "Nothing. I'm not sure where they guy got his DMV photos made, but the two licenses are the only places we could find him and we know those are fake."

"Bummer. Well, I'll let you know what we get from Pierce, if anything," she said and got up from the booth.

"Good work, Viacorte," Dureski said as she turned to walk away.

She turned back to acknowledge the compliment. "Thanks, sir."

Her vehicle was parked a few blocks away in a public lot. Thankfully, she'd paid for enough time in advance and didn't need to worry about a parking violation. She reached her car and pulled out her cell phone to call Alex.

"I'm on my way back. Any luck with Pierce's background or the landscaping thing?" she asked him.

"His finances suck," Alex said bluntly.

"Did you talk to Cari?" she asked, knowing he would say no.

"No. I can do my own research," he snapped. "The guy has several credit cards with high balances. He's only paying interest on some loans he took out. Things are not going well for Mr. Pierce."

"What else?" she asked as she drove down the road back to Brenington.

"He's a Canadian citizen," Alex said. "I bet that's why his wife is technically the business owner. I think the taxes are higher otherwise. They might get a discount because the business is owned by a woman too."

"Does he have a record of any sort?" Genevieve asked.

"He seems pretty squeaky-clean. I read some of the reviews of the work his company does. Everyone says he does *exemplary* work."

"Wow, your vocabulary is expanding every day," she teased.

"So funny. Let's see. What else did I find?" he paused and she could hear him flipping pages. "He donates to youth sports regularly."

"We found that together. Old news," she reminded him.

"I'm just saying from the surface, he looks like a nice guy," Alex remarked. "I called Pfinning, Lander, and Brenington. They all confirmed implementing uniformed landscaping for businesses. The same company did it for all three locations: Pierce's company...are you almost here or what?"

"I'm getting closer every second," she quipped.

"Seriously. How much longer?" he asked.

"Fifteen minutes. Go grab a taco. I'll be there before you know it," she told him and ended the call.

She called Cari next. She felt a bit guilty for pulling Robby in front of the FBI without warning her friend first.

"Hey, Gen. What's up?" Cari asked.

Genevieve sighed. "We've been making a bit of progress over here, but I wanted to let you know Dureski demanded to meet with Robby. We had lunch about half an hour ago."

"Robby met with the FBI?" Cari asked with alarm.

"Yes, I would have called before, but Dureski is constantly worried about leaks and moles, so I just joined them for lunch," she explained.

"I still don't know if he's told Bea anything. I feel like she'd call if she was worried, but I don't know. We aren't the closest sisters in the world," Cari lamented.

"Well, Dureski is going to bring Follard in for questioning. That will allow Robby some freedom to get hard copies of these invoices and payments. He's felt pretty paranoid about it, as you know," Genevieve told her friend.

"Do you think Robby will have to testify at some point?" Cari asked with concern.

"I don't know, Cari. It's way too early to be thinking about a trial. We still don't have the whole picture," she responded.

"Did you talk to Pierce?" Cari asked.

"That's next on the list. I'm on my way back to the precinct so Alex and I can go pick him up," Genevieve replied.

"Okay, well, I'll let you know if I find anything else in the meantime," Cari said.

"Thanks. I appreciate it," Genevieve said. "Talk to you later."

"Yep," Cari said and ended the call.

Genevieve pulled back into the station's parking lot and parked her vehicle. It had been a long day already and it was just barely after one o'clock. She locked the Expedition and went inside.

As soon as Alex saw her, he stood up and grabbed the keys to the cruiser. "Let's do this."

"Give me a minute to catch my breath," she said to him with a laugh. "I literally just got out of the car. I'm going to run to the restroom, then we can go."

Alex rolled his eyes and sat back down. She put her bag in her desk chair then went to the women's restroom. Her conversation with Cari was still fresh in her mind. She knew better than to guarantee Robby was safe, but it seemed unlikely anyone else involved in this elaborate payment scheme would know he was their source. If they needed him to testify, that would be a different story. It seemed like Follard could fill that testimony position, though. He would know more direct knowledge too. She nodded to herself as she walked back to her desk.

"Ready now?" Alex asked impatiently.

"Yeah, I take it you're driving?"

He held up the keys. "Your turn to navigate."

Genevieve looked up directions to the business on their way out to the vehicle. "It's over in the warehouse district...near that pool supply store from last fall."

"Ha ha ha. I wonder if that place is still in business," Alex laughed as he started the car. "That guy was such a pain. I can't believe he tried to run."

"Not his best moment," Genevieve agreed.

"Okay, so...we'll go in and ask for Pierce. If he's not there, I think there's a good chance they'll call him and warn him we're looking for him," Alex pointed out.

"You're probably right. Let's just hope he's there. I have no idea where they have projects..." Genevieve trailed off.

"What?" Alex asked.

"Cari mentioned something the other day about an article the editor assigned her regarding new businesses and new construction in town. She might have a list of where he'd be if he's not at the store front," Genevieve hypothesized.

"How many projects could they have going at once?" Alex asked.

"Beats me. I don't know anything about construction," Genevieve told him. "Let me call Cari back...see, I told you it was useful to be nice to her!"

Alex grumbled something unintelligible as she pulled up Cari's number.

"Hey, Gen! Did you find something already?" her friend asked earnestly.

"Not exactly, but I need a favor. You mentioned an article you were writing about new builds or something in the area?" Genevieve asked.

"Yeah, but Ollaman decided to do it himself," Cari told her.

Her shoulders slumped. "Any chance you know what projects Pierce has going on right now?"

"Oh, I can look that up. I still have the files," Cari responded. "Let me see. He's doing some work at the rec center. I think it's a new restroom facility. And then...they're doing landscaping outside of the Pfinning Library...one town over?"

"I know Pfinning," Genevieve said. "Anything else?"

"It looks like everything else is finished," Cari answered.

"Cool. Thanks, girl," Genevieve said and ended the call. "We've got three options for Pierce: the business, the Pfinning Library, or the local recreation center."

"Call Grusky and ask him to send some officers over to watch those two locations. They can stop him if they see him and wait for us to arrive if he's not at the office," Alex instructed.

"Dialing him now," Genevieve responded. "Hey, LT. We're on our way to pick up a person of interest in the Frobish case. We aren't sure if he'll be at his office or a work site. Could you send a couple officers to two locations? I'll text you the addresses."

"Who are you picking up?" Grusky asked.

"Randall Pierce," Genevieve responded. "We don't think he killed anyone, but he's involved somehow, so we need to speak with him."

"Okay. Send me the addresses and I'll have someone there," Grusky assured her.

"One address is in Pfinning," Genevieve warned him.

"I'll call over there and see if they can spare someone. They'll be able to get there faster," Grusky told her.

"Thanks, LT," she said and ended the call.

"We don't have an arrest warrant, so if he doesn't want to come in, we don't have a lot of options," Alex told her as she texted the two addresses to their boss.

"Yeah, and we don't really have enough to get a warrant either," Genevieve agreed.

"Maybe we should try to leverage his wife," Alex suggested.

"Say more," Genevieve prompted him.

"It's possible his wife is pulling the strings here, though, I doubt it. However, he might be involved without her knowledge. We can mention our plans to go speak with her as she is the business owner. Maybe it will get him to cooperate," Alex explained.

"Worth a shot," Genevieve said with a nod.

Alex pulled into the parking area near the landscaping office. Genevieve took out her pencil and pocket notebook after they got out of the car. Alex slowed his pace so she could catch up to him. He opened the door and held it for her with a smirk. She rolled her eyes and went inside. A middle-aged man sat behind the counter. He was wearing a headset and typing on a computer. He looked up in response to the bell from the door opening.

"Welcome to Pierce Construction and Landscaping. How can I help you today?" he asked cheerfully.

Genevieve glanced at his name badge. "Good afternoon, Linus. I'm Detective Viacorte and this is my partner, Detective Runimoss. We were hoping to speak with your boss, Randall Pierce."

Linus smacked his lips before responding. "Randy's out at the rec center overseeing the new bathroom facility. Should I call him in? This seems serious."

"No, thank you. We can find him," Genevieve said and smiled.

Alex leaned forward and whispered something to Linus who swallowed.

"No problem, Detective. I've got plenty to do right here," he said pointing at the computer.

"Perfect," Alex said and then nodded toward the door.

Once they were back in the vehicle, Genevieve put her hand on his arm. "What did you whisper to Linus?"

"I told him it would be better for all of us if he didn't call his boss and warn him we were coming," Alex told her.

"Think he'll listen?" Genevieve asked.

"Who knows? Did you text Grusky that we're headed to the rec center?" he asked.

She held up her phone and gave it a little shake. "Done and done. Let's go find Randy."

Chapter 16

Staring at the notebook didn't make the answer any clearer. Cari had scrawled some notes about the five cases onto the paper. She had a timeline across the middle with each victim's name and the date they died. *Were killed.* She corrected herself. She had added the payment codes as other hashmarks along the line. It seemed like the incoming payment showed up shortly before the outgoing payment. If she didn't know about the deaths, the payments would almost look like a money laundering scheme as the amount coming in was equal to the amount going out. The deaths painted things in a different light.

She surmised Genevieve and Alex must have decided to bring Pierce in for questioning. She didn't know what his role was in all of this, but the money trail definitely went through his business. Her cell phone buzzed with an incoming call. She recognized the number from entering it earlier that day: Trent Roth.

"This is Cari Turnlyle," she said into her cell phone.

"Ms. Turnlyle. It's Trent Roth. I'm returning your call. In your message you said you wanted to talk about Dad's business. How can I help?" Trent asked.

Cari could hear the curiosity in his voice. "Thank you for returning my call, Mr. Roth. Please, call me Cari."

"You can call me Trent," he mirrored her statement.

"Okay, Trent. I've been doing some research on businesses which have changed hands this calendar year and came across your dad's," she said. *It was mostly true.*

"It's been a few months since I've heard anyone mention Socket-To-Me," Trent told her.

"Several of the businesses I'm looking at have mentioned the previous owner was about to have some construction completed before the business changed hands. Was that true with your dad?" Cari asked. She didn't want to tell him she thought his dad had been murdered, especially since no one really understood why these business owners were targeted.

"Uh…hmm…I can't really think of anything," Trent said after a moment of silence. "Well, unless you count the landscaping thing."

Cari felt the hairs on the back of her neck start to rise. "Landscaping?"

"I didn't get involved much in the business, so I don't know if this was resolved or not," Trent began. "A month or so before he died, I met dad for lunch at mom's place. Uh, sorry. My mom is in a memory care facility. She has early onset dementia…it's been hard. Uh, sorry. What was I saying?"

"You met your dad for lunch…" Cari prompted him.

"Right. While we were eating, his cell phone rang and he cursed under his breath. I asked him what was going on. He said the city was making him put in some sort of flower arrangement in front of the business. He never liked change and didn't want to deal with it. I think they wanted him to pay some sort of convenience fee too. I don't know. He was mad about it," Trent explained. "I'd kind of forgotten about it. I'm pretty sure the flower beds were installed a week or so after he died. Seemed a little disrespectful, but I never understood his issue with it in the first place."

"His business is in Lander?" Cari asked to confirm her notes.

"That's correct," Trent said. "Has this landscaping thing come up a lot?"

"I've heard it from a few businesses. I guess it must be fairly common for cities to want a uniform look to their downtown storefronts," Cari said.

"Probably so. Did you have any other questions?" Trent asked.

"I think that's it. Thanks again for returning my call," Cari said more cheerfully than she felt.

"No problem. Have a good one," Trent said and ended the call.

Cari felt a bit guilty for not being honest with Roth's son. She hoped he wouldn't hold it against her later once they knew what was happening. She added the landscaping connection to her timeline. It seemed like three businesses were frustrated by a forced landscaping change while two had plans for construction that weren't completed as well as calls from some sort of angry client or service person. Pierce's company did both landscaping and construction, though it seemed like landscaping was the bigger portion of their business. She texted Gen with her latest finding. Hopefully, her friend was learning something useful from Randall Pierce.

* * * * *

The metal gate to the recreation center ball fields was open, but a Brenington police cruiser was blocking it. The officer had positioned the vehicle so no one could get in or out of the facility unless he moved. He waved at the two detectives as they approached the entrance. Alex double-parked their cruiser by the other one and they got out of the vehicle. The officer rolled his window down.

"They asked me to keep anyone from leaving here until you arrived, so this was the best I could do," he told them.

"This is perfect. Can you hang out for a few minutes longer?" Alex asked him.

"Sure. No problem," he responded.

They walked toward the group of construction workers who were pulling boards away from a concrete slab. Genevieve guessed it was the foundation for the new restroom facility. Alex put two fingers in his mouth and whistled to get their attention. All their heads snapped up to see who was whistling. He pointed to a blond man who fit Pierce's description and Genevieve nodded.

"Mr. Pierce, could you join us for a moment?" Alex called out.

Pierce's face registered surprise, but he walked over to them. "What can I help you with?"

"Mr. Pierce, we've been investigating a series of deaths associated with some payments made to your company. We were hoping you could come in and explain the significance," Genevieve told him pointedly.

The man's face visibly paled when he heard her statement. "Payments? For what?"

"We were hoping you could tell us," Alex said. "We'd have more privacy at the station."

"Am I under arrest?" Pierce asked in an aggravated tone.

They both shook their heads. "No, sir. You are a person of interest...you and your business."

"Then I don't have to talk to you," Pierce said and started to turn back to the workers. The group had been watching the exchange but pretended to get back to work at that moment.

"We realize your wife owns the business, so maybe she could answer our questions more easily," Alex said quickly.

Pierce froze. "My wife?"

Genevieve nodded. "This concerns her too as the business owner."

"Phoebe doesn't know anything about the business. She's an owner in name only," he told them. "How long is this going to take?"

"That depends. How honest are you going to be with us?" Alex asked him.

"He means that rhetorically," Genevieve stated.

"Fine. Can I drive myself?" Pierce asked.

"We'd rather you ride with us. We wouldn't want you to get lost or anything on the way there," Alex told him.

He gestured toward their vehicle and they walked alongside him. Alex gave the other officer a nod and the man maneuvered his cruiser away from the entrance. Alex unlocked their cruiser and Genevieve opened the back door for Pierce.

"Mr. Pierce, as we said, you aren't under arrest," Genevieve told him. "I did get the impression you are aware of the payments I mentioned."

Alex started the car and pulled away from the rec center. "Why are you making these payments?"

"Can we not do this in the car?" Pierce whined. "Can I call a lawyer?"

"It's completely within your rights to call your attorney, Mr. Pierce," Genevieve assured him. She turned toward the backseat to face him. "Did you want to call one?"

"I don't even have a lawyer. I mean, I know some lawyers, but..." he paused. "This is such a mess."

"Are we calling an attorney or...?" Alex asked, his dark eyes raised to the rearview mirror.

"No," Pierce said with a sigh. "How long does it take to get to the station?"

"Just a few more minutes," Genevieve told him. "Are you sure you don't want to chat on the way?"

"I just...I need you to keep my wife out of this. That's the whole point. She can't know. I'll lose everything," he said shakily.

"Why is that, Mr. Pierce?" Alex asked.

"Can you...can you just call me Randy?" Pierce whined some more.

"Sure, Randy. What is it you don't want your wife to know?" Alex asked.

"About the payments. She thinks the business is fine. She doesn't look at our accounts...like, ever. She just spends money and that's the end of her involvement," Pierce said.

"Who are you paying?" Genevieve asked.

"I'd rather not talk about it in the car," Pierce said again.

"Are you afraid of someone, Randy?" Alex asked. "You're perfectly safe with us."

"I just think it's better if we're inside for the discussion. I can clear this up and then get back to work," he said and rubbed his hands on his thighs.

184

Alex shrugged and continued driving. Genevieve turned around to face forward in her seat again. They rode in silence for a few minutes until the police station came into view.

"Finally," Pierce muttered under his breath.

"I'm sorry, what was that?" Alex asked and pointed at his ear.

"Nothing. Sorry," Pierce said.

They helped him out of the car and walked him inside to an interrogation room.

"Can we get you something to drink or a snack of some sort?" Genevieve offered.

"No. Let's just talk," Pierce said waving her off. "What is it you want to know?"

Genevieve took a seat across from Pierce and pulled out a folder with five photographs inside. She laid the photos out to face Pierce one by one. "Randy, do you recognize any of these people?"

His eyes darted from hers to the photos and back. She knew he recognized one if not all five people. He pushed the photos toward her.

"No. Who are they?" he said.

"Are you sure?" she asked and straightened the photos. "Like this one? Elaine Frobish is her name. I think you're familiar with her."

"Uh, I, uh, I might recognize the name," Pierce stuttered.

Genevieve pulled Horace Manwith's photo from the bunch so it was in full view. "Or this one? Horace Manwith? You know who Horace is, right?"

She could see Pierce starting to sweat. He swallowed hard, but still shook his head. "I don't know him. Why?"

Alex spoke up from the corner. "As we mentioned in the car, some people have died under somewhat mysterious circumstances. Your company seems to have a connection. Like I said before, it might be simpler to just talk to your wife as she is the owner of the business."

Pierce threw up his hands in defeat. "Enough! You want to know about the money. Here's the thing. A few months ago, well, over a year ago, I was having an affair."

"An extramarital affair, Randy?" Alex asked with his pencil raised.

Pierce reddened. "Yes, an extramarital affair with a woman several years younger than me. We met at a job site. She happened to be jogging by every morning and...I didn't mean for it to happen."

"I understand," Alex said. "Continue. You had an affair. How long did it last?"

"A few months, I guess. At some point, this guy came by the same job site with an envelope for me. He actually put it under the windshield wiper on my car. I saw him do it and was baffled, but in the back of my mind, I kind of knew it must be related to the affair," he said and grimaced. "I thought we'd been really discreet, but…well, anyway. There were photos. And a letter. And a burner phone. The letter gave me instructions about my wife's LLC occasionally paying some tech company and then my business would get the money back by the next day. It was a net zero for me and my wife wouldn't find out about the affair, but as I kept reading, I realized it was still going to cost me."

"I mean, obviously whoever was wanting you to move money around for them like this isn't doing something legal, right?" Genevieve said with a look of disdain.

"Yes, of course, but my wife owns the business! If she found out I was having an affair, she'd take the business. I have no way of stopping her," Pierce pouted.

"Right. That's so hard on you," Alex rolled his eyes. "What else did the letter say?"

"Okay, so I'm reading the letter and having some hesitation about the amount of money and possibly making a deposit from one company to the other and it's like the guy expected it," Pierce said in an annoyed tone. "The letter went on to say my wife's company would get a payment for *services rendered* in the same amount a few days before the request would come in for me to pay the tech company. Then within twenty-four hours, I'd usually get a payment to my business from the tech company for the same amount."

"But you'd still be even and then you'd get paid again, so it seems like you should have made almost $40k from this setup," Alex said.

"Right, except there was more. Several cities in the area were in the process of taking bids to upgrade the landscaping of their downtown storefronts. I was to make an incredibly low bid, one that would eliminate virtually any profit margin, to ensure they would offer my business the contract," Pierce explained further. "And what's more, I had to transfer the money from the tech company to another account after it cleared my bank. I've lost a ton of money. My business is barely alive right now. On top of all of that, I also had to withdraw five hundred in cash from my account and leave it under a bench in the city park every week. Every. Single. Week."

"When did the affair end?" Alex asked.

"I haven't seen her since the envelope showed up on my car," Pierce said. "Which is good. I couldn't say no to her...she had a...power over me."

"What was her name?" Genevieve asked.

Pierce reddened. "I only know her first name."

Alex narrowed his eyes. "And? What is it?"

"Shelly," Pierce said, continuing to blush.

"Do you have her phone number? Or how did you, uh, connect with her?" Genevieve asked.

Alex snorted in the corner.

"Like I told you, she used to jog by my work sites and then one day, she was getting coffee where I get coffee and...we shared more than coffee that day," he said and reddened some more.

"Must have been some good coffee," Alex said with a smirk. Genevieve gave him a look.

"Do you find it at all strange that *Shelly* disappeared after you started getting blackmailed?" Genevieve asked.

"Obviously, I'm an idiot. You don't need to rub it in," Pierce said and sulked.

"So, you don't have a phone number?" Alex asked. "Just to be clear."

"No. I'd meet her for...coffee a couple times a week," Pierce explained. "It's kind of humiliating. I actually went to that coffee shop every day hoping she would be there too, but it didn't always work out that way."

"What did she look like?" Genevieve asked him, her own eyes narrowing in disgust.

"She was really, um, she was...her hair was, uh, blonde and her eyes were maybe brown? Or blue? And she was...uh...really fit," Pierce stuttered again.

"And you've never seen her again since?" Alex asked.

"No. It's been a year or whatever and I'm glad she's out of my life. I should have never turned my head..." he said and ran a hand through his hair.

"Do you still have the letter?" Genevieve asked.

"It's locked in my safety deposit box," Pierce said with a nod.

"We're going to need that account number," Alex said. "How often have you done this?"

"I don't know, maybe four, five, possibly six times," he said glumly. "Oh, one other thing. The payments I made to this tech company had to have specific codes. Those were texted to me on the burner phone. The letter was very explicit about it."

"Let's go pick up your letter," Genevieve said and stood up. "Where's the burner phone?"

"I have it right here," Pierce said and pulled it out of his pocket. "The texts come in from a hidden number, so it's not going to give you much."

"We're going to need to copy everything off that phone. We'll give it back to you, in case your letter writer reaches out again," Alex told him. "Chris can do that in a few minutes."

They escorted Pierce down to CSU. Both Chris and Bob were at their stations when they entered through the double doors. Genevieve held up the little burner phone.

"Hey, can one of you copy the contents of this for us?" she asked as she waved at them with the phone.

Bob motioned her over to his desk. "I can do it. Do you have a cord?"

Genevieve looked at Pierce, who shook his head no. "No problem, I have a whole drawer full. Let's see it."

She passed him the phone and he dug through his drawer of miscellaneous cords. "This should do it," he said with satisfaction. "You want everything? Contacts? Calls? Texts? Photos?"

"There aren't any photos," Pierce said flatly.

"Everything," Alex said from behind them.

"Coming right up," Bob said.

He connected the phone to his computer and opened a program from the start menu. After selecting a few commands, a progress bar appeared on the screen. Bob's computer dinged when the process was complete.

"Done," Bob said and unplugged the phone. "Should I email these files to you?"

"Perfect. Thanks, Bob," Genevieve said. "We also need you to see if you can trace any of the numbers on the call list. Let us know who they belong to."

"Will do," Bob said and opened the file on his computer.

"Now we can go to the bank," Genevieve said to Pierce and pointed toward the exit.

Alex led the way back upstairs and out to the cruiser. He tossed Genevieve the keys. She caught them and smiled.

"Randy, which bank are we going to?" she asked him.

"It's a few blocks over on Grand Avenue," Pierce said as he buckled his seatbelt. "I feel like a criminal back here."

"Newsflash. You *are* a criminal, Mr. Pierce," Alex said bluntly.

Genevieve saw the man's shoulders slump as she pulled onto the street. "You're cooperating though. Maybe the district attorney will be lenient with you."

"I can't believe this is happening," Pierce whined. "I've ruined my life, haven't I?"

"It doesn't look good," Alex said without empathy.

Genevieve shot him a look and then spoke to Pierce again. "Is this your bank, Randy?"

He looked out the window and nodded. Genevieve parked on the street in front of the building. They got out of the vehicle and she locked it.

"Did your company do the landscaping out here? If it's any consolation, it looks nice," Alex said with a smirk.

Pierce looked away and followed Genevieve into the bank. He walked up to a teller and pulled out his wallet.

"Hi there. I'm Randall Pierce and I need to access my safety deposit box," he told the young man behind the counter.

"Can I see your ID?" the young man asked.

Pierce passed it to him.

The teller returned it. "Right this way, Mr. Pierce. Will your friends be joining us?"

"We will be," Alex said quickly before Pierce could say otherwise.

"It's a party," the teller said cheerfully. He seemed oblivious to Pierce's somber mood.

"Box 569 is right…here," the teller said and pulled out his key. "Do you have your key, Mr. Pierce?"

Pierce held up his key chain. They each inserted a key and the teller removed the box. He placed it on the table.

"And if you'll sign right here," the teller asked holding up an electronic device. "We have to document every time it's accessed."

Pierce signed the screen and the teller left the room with the device. Pierce opened the box and lifted a large envelope. Underneath the envelope was a single sheet of paper. He pointed at the envelope after removing the sheet of paper.

"The photos are in here. I don't know why I saved them," Pierce said dumbly. "This is the letter."

Genevieve took a photo of the letter before reading it. It was just as the man described. The sender had outlined very detailed instructions. If Pierce didn't do as he said, the person would send another set of photos to his wife.

"What do you remember about the person who put this envelope on your car?" she asked him.

"It's stupid, but almost nothing. It was winter, so he had on a coat with the hood up. He was wearing gloves, which wasn't weird because, again, winter," Pierce told her.

"You're sure it was a man?" Alex asked.

"He carried himself in a masculine way and he was pretty tall," Pierce said confidently.

"We probably can't get any CCTV at this point since it was a year or more ago, right?" Alex asked.

"Are you asking me for the time frame?" Pierce asked.

"No, you already told us that," Alex said to him. "Viacorte?"

"I don't think they keep it for over a year," Genevieve agreed.

"Bummer. Well, maybe Bob will find something from the phone's history," Alex said hopefully.

"What happens with me?" Pierce asked. "Are we done with the box?"

"We need the envelope and the letter," Alex said and held out an evidence bag.

Pierce slipped them inside and then closed his box. He pushed it back into the wall and turned around to look at them. Genevieve almost felt sorry for him, except it was his own actions which got him into this mess.

"Well, Randy, I think we're going to take you back to work," Alex said and Genevieve nodded. "We need you to behave as though nothing is going on. Basically, just keep telling the same lies you've been telling."

"Am I safe? What if the guy contacts me again?" Pierce asked as they exited the bank.

"Did you feel safe before?" Alex asked.

Pierce frowned. "Well, yeah, but I didn't know people were getting killed."

"I think whomever is putting the screws to you needs you alive to funnel his payments through your businesses. You're most likely fine," Alex said.

"Good job using whomever," Genevieve said to Alex and laughed.

"How are you both so chill?!" Pierce asked loudly from the backseat.

"Dude, we'll keep an eye on you, okay? If something feels unsafe, just give us a call," Alex said and handed him a business card.

Pierce rolled his eyes. "Whatever."

Genevieve stopped the cruiser outside the entrance of the rec center. "We'll be in touch when we know more. Thanks for your time."

She opened the back door and let the saddened man out of the cruiser. He brushed invisible dirt off his clothes and lifted his head. She was glad he seemed to be able to pull off a look of confidence. She waited until he was back on the concrete slab and then got back in the cruiser.

"So, what now?" Alex asked her.

"I think we need to keep an eye on him. He definitely recognized some faces from the photos I showed him. We can't put a tracker on him or anything, but I think we should watch his vehicle and see if anyone leaves him any more gifts," she suggested.

"You think the guy pulling the strings is going to contact him again?" Alex asked with his eyebrows raised.

"I do. I'm not sure what will trigger this person's attention, but he—or she—seems to have a finger on everyone's activities," Genevieve responded.

"Think Grusky will approve it?" Alex asked.

"No, but I'm going to do it anyway," she told him pointedly.

Chapter 17

Cari parked her car outside of Bob's apartment. She grabbed her messenger bag and got out of the car. She knew Bob was planning to talk about her finances and health insurance, but she also wanted to talk about meeting with the wedding planner the next day. It felt like it would be rude to meet her and have literally no idea what they wanted to do. She knocked on his apartment door. She could hear some pots and pans rattling inside and wondered what he was cooking. He came to the door wearing a black apron and holding a wooden spoon.

"Looks like you've been busy already," she said after kissing his cheek. "What's on the menu, Chef?"

"I'm making a reduction sauce to pour over our filet steaks. I threw together a salad with arugula, feta, pecans, and some poached apricots, too," Bob said as he hurried back to the kitchen.

"Is that all?" Cari asked with a grin. "Can I help with anything?"

He looked at the skillet in front of him and then back at her. "Uh, I got a bottle of wine. Can you pour us each a glass and maybe get us some water too?"

"I've been relegated to drink duty?" she laughed and gave him a kiss on the cheek. "No, it's fine. I do not belong in a kitchen. I can barely flip pancakes on Saturdays."

He laughed too. "It's almost ready, I'm just letting the shallots soften a little bit more. Then we can eat."

"I'll get some plates too," she said and reached around him in the kitchen. "It smells delicious."

"Thanks," he said and smiled. "It's one of my favorite meals. Oh, can you pull the bread from the oven? I didn't make it; I'm just warming it up."

"I'll do that first so it doesn't burn," she said and pulled out two oven mitts from a drawer. "Does this have a special plate or basket or can I just put it on the table?"

He grinned at her. "Any plate is fine. The salad is in the fridge with the wine."

Cari filled drinks and set the table while Bob finished cooking the main course. He brought the steaks over one at a time and then drizzled his sauce on top of each of them. Cari was impressed.

"I guess if science fails you, you can always work in a restaurant," Cari told him.

"Science never fails anyone," he said confidently. "But thank you. Shall we?"

She lifted her wine glass. "Cheers!"

"Cheers!" he said and clinked his glass against hers. "Is it okay if I bounce some ideas off you while we eat?"

"Of course. What do you have for me?" she asked him.

"Well, one sort of rushed decision would be to just get married legally now and add you to my health plan," he said and then took a bite.

"What?!" she said with alarm.

He chewed and swallowed then put up a hand. "I said it would be rushed. It's our fallback option, okay?"

"Okay. What are some other options?" she asked and then took another bite.

"Well, like you said, the new arrangement will basically eliminate your ability to save any money from one month to the next. How long are you willing to live like that?" he asked gently.

"I don't know. It doesn't leave me feeling very stable," she admitted.

"I know we agreed to not rush into wedding planning, but what if we moved in together? Shared an apartment? That would save you money on rent," he suggested.

She nodded slowly. "It would, but I never really saw myself as a cohabitating before marriage type person. I know lots of people do it and we did go on vacation together already, but I'm not sure that's the step I want to take."

Bob grabbed her hand. "I get that and it's not really how I saw my life progressing either. What if we sped up our wedding plans a bit? We could get married in, say…January and then you'd only have four months of careful spending to get through."

"Well, that does tie in a bit with something else I wanted to talk about," she said. Bob turned his head in a questioning manner while he continued to eat. "We're meeting with the wedding planner tomorrow. Aspen Wilson. We should at least have a few ideas of what we want for our wedding before sitting down with her, right?"

"For sure," Bob agreed. "What ideas do you have?"

"I kind of thought we might want an outdoor wedding, but now that we're talking January, I think we should stick with indoors," she suggested.

"Seems wise. Have you thought about where?" he asked.

"When we were at church last Sunday, I tried to envision getting married there, but I couldn't see it," she said and shrugged.

"And now? You still feel that way or...?" Bob asked.

"You know, we know a lot of people there, well, at least a lot from the group we volunteer with. It's a nice space and we said we didn't want a big wedding, right? Maybe the church is the right place," she told him. "I like the pastor. I guess he might require pre-marital counseling. We should ask."

"Good idea. I can call him tomorrow if you want. You don't have to do everything yourself," he offered.

"That would be great. Hopefully the wedding planner is on board with a sort of short planning window," Cari said.

"I'm sure she's had to plan quicker weddings. We can make it work," Bob assured her and then laughed.

"What?" she asked with concern.

"Our moms are going to be beside themselves when we tell them we're setting our sights on January for the wedding. After begging for a date for the last few weeks, they might faint from shock when we say it's only six months away," he laughed.

"Six months, wow! I can't believe we're going to be married by this time next year. Crazy. I love you, Bob Hursley," she said and smiled.

"I love you too, Cari," he said and smiled back.

* * * * *

Genevieve shifted awkwardly in her seat. Even though she was small, it was hard to sit low in the seat and stay comfortable. Alex had the passenger seat reclined and pushed all the way back. He was taking a nap while she watched Pierce's house and vehicle. Pierce lived in a corner lot, so she'd parked her Expedition on the opposite side of the cross street. They could see the front door and his car from their position. She grabbed an apple from the snack bag and took a bite. Alex stirred awake.

"What?" he asked groggily.

She quickly chewed the bite and swallowed. "Sorry, I didn't realize you were such a light sleeper. Next time we stake out a house, I'll slice the apple in advance so it's quieter to eat."

"Or you could just eat a candy bar like a normal person," he suggested. "I'm awake now. Any movement?"

"Nothing yet," she answered. "Pierce came outside around midnight and double-checked that his car doors were locked, then went back in."

Alex nodded. "Sophia likes you, but you better hope something comes from this or she might not make you a scarf ever again."

"Shh," she hushed him. "I saw a car just turn off its lights as it was coming down the street toward us. See it?"

Alex looked out the windshield. "Oh, yeah. The porch lights just reflected off of it. Okay, they're turning onto Pierce's street..."

Genevieve watched the vehicle slowly pass Pierce's house. The car drove to the end of the block and turned around. She put her binoculars up to her face to see if she could see the driver. She elbowed Alex.

"Take a look," she said to him. "I can't tell if it looks like the rental car guy Scott or John or whatever his name really is."

He took the binoculars from her. "Maybe. The guy looked different in both DMV photos, so maybe he has ways of altering his looks depending on the day."

"He turned up the street. Are there alleys over here?" she asked, worried they might lose track of the mystery driver.

"Nah. It's a green space past all these homes. Look, he parked about a block ahead of us. He's getting out of the car now. He thought ahead. The dome light didn't come on," Alex pointed out. "He's got another large envelope in his hand."

"I'm taking photos. Once we see him leave the envelope on Pierce's vehicle, I think we need to pick him up," she told Alex.

"You think this guy is *the* guy?" Alex asked with a frown.

"Uh...I don't know, but this matches with everything Pierce told us happened before except this time, it's the middle of the night. Okay, he put the envelope on the windshield. He's crossing the yard," Genevieve observed. "Ready to go after him?"

Alex put up his seat. "Start the car. I'll be ready to jump out, so don't drive too fast."

Genevieve turned on her car, but kept her eyes on the man. The sound of the engine turning over made his head whip their way. She put the car in drive and pressed lightly on the gas. The man broke out into a run.

"Not too fast, not too fast," Alex reminded her frantically.

"I'm basically idling. We're not even at ten miles an hour yet," she said to him. "He thinks he can reach his car before we get to him."

"Not today, sir," Alex said as Genevieve took her foot off the gas and let the car slow on its own.

Alex wrenched open his door and jumped out as she slowed to a stop. He stumbled a little but was able to stay on his feet. The man was in an all-out sprint to his car. Alex's long legs easily closed the distance between them. Genevieve put the vehicle in park and turned on her hazard lights. She stuck her bubble light on top and flipped it on.

Alex grabbed the man's shoulder just as he reached the back bumper of his car. It caused the man to trip and fall to the ground. Genevieve laughed when she heard Alex swear under his breath. He pulled out his handcuffs and started reciting the Miranda warning to the man. Once the suspect was cuffed, she jogged over to Pierce's vehicle and carefully removed the envelope from underneath the wiper blade.

"Do you understand these rights as I've explained them to you?" Alex asked him.

"What did I do? Why am I under arrest?" the man asked as he looked from one detective to the other.

"I think the contents of this envelope will answer that question for all of us," Genevieve said as she slid the envelope into an evidence bag.

"That's not mine. I've never seen it before!" the man exclaimed.

"We literally just watched you put it on the windshield, man," Alex told him.

The man glared at Alex. "Prove it."

Genevieve walked over to the Expedition and pulled out the camera she'd used to take photos. She turned the screen toward him. "This is you here walking across the lawn. And here you are passing behind the vehicle of interest. And here you are putting this envelope onto the windshield and under the wiper blade. And here you are crossing the lawn again. I think it's all pretty clear, sir."

His shoulders slumped. "You're going to regret this."

"Is that a threat, sir?" Genevieve asked pointedly.

"I guess you'll find out," he said derisively.

Alex pulled the man by the handcuffs to the Expedition. "Call it in?"

"As we speak," she said with her phone up to her ear. "Lieutenant, it's Viacorte. We just apprehended a man with another envelope at the Pierce residence."

"Wow. I thought you'd be spinning your wheels all night. Good call, Viacorte. Still not paying you overtime," he told her.

"Runimoss will get over it," she said with a laugh. "We're bringing him in now."

"You got a name?" Grusky asked her.

She turned to Alex. "Name on this guy?"

Alex patted the man's pockets and found a wallet. "Anderson Stenoway of Brenington, New York."

"Did you catch that?" she asked the lieutenant.

"Got it. I'll meet you at the station. Tell Runimoss if it makes him feel any better, I don't get paid overtime either," he said and ended the call.

Alex rode in the back with Mr. Stenoway while Genevieve drove to the police station. She could feel the man glaring at her, but didn't give him the satisfaction of looking in the rearview mirror.

"Is Grusky at least going to give us the day off tomorrow?" Alex asked.

"It *is* tomorrow, Runimoss," she said with a laugh.

They drove the rest of the way in silence. Grusky was waiting for them in the parking lot when they arrived at the precinct. His shirt was untucked and he was wearing glasses. Genevieve hadn't realized he wore contacts to begin with. Alex helped Stenoway out of the backseat once they were parked.

"I have interrogation one set up for you," Grusky said as they walked inside. "Let me know if you need anything."

Alex removed one handcuff from Stenoway's wrist and re-cuffed him to the table. "Do you need something to drink or eat?"

Stenoway shook his head no.

"Suit yourself. We'll be back in a bit," Alex told him.

Chapter 18

The two detectives walked back to their desks. Genevieve logged the envelope as evidence and then added her initials to indicate she was opening it. She folded the tabs of the brads on the envelope and peeled the flap loose to open it. Then she slid the contents out onto her desk. A new disposable cell phone slid out as well as another one-page letter. She read the letter aloud to Alex.

"Don't talk to the police again. Get rid of the old phone. Smash it and trash it. If I discover you've talked to the police again, your wife will see the photos I sent you. Our arrangement is working well as long as you don't mess it up. Be smart and you'll keep your business."

"Fairly straightforward," Alex remarked after she finished.

"Let's look him up before we speak with him," Genevieve suggested.

She logged into her computer and opened the database. She typed Anderson Stenoway into the search bar along with Brenington, NY, as his residence. One result appeared on the screen. She double-clicked it to open it.

"Anderson Stenoway of Brenington, New York…employed by the City of Brenington. Interesting. No priors. It looks like he works for the city…uh…issuing permits," she read from the screen.

"Hmm…so, he would know if someone was wanting to add on to their business or do any sort of remodeling," Alex surmised. "He somewhat resembles the rental car guy."

"A little bit, but Dureski said they didn't get a match when they ran the images from the two licenses through facial recognition software," Genevieve countered. "But he might be the person you talk to if you're upset about the city imposing things on you."

"What's the asterisk mean?" Alex asked and pointed at the screen.

Genevieve scanned the screen. "Oh, it says he's a shared city employee. He works a week each month at Brenington and Lander and then two weeks of the month at Pfinning City Hall."

"Doing the same thing?" Alex asked.

"Yep. Permits for all three locations," she told him.

"So, he could have spoken to all five of our victims," Alex mused.

"Seems likely," she said slowly. "Let's go talk to him."

"You seem hesitant," Alex observed. "What is it?"

"I mean, he's clearly a desk guy. Don't get me wrong, he's not out of shape or something, but he's a low-level city employee. I expected someone…smarter."

"Who says city employees aren't smart?" Alex feigned hurt.

She gently punched his arm. "You know what I mean."

He nodded and then opened the interrogation room door. "Mr. Stenoway. Let's have a chat."

He took his usual position in the corner while Genevieve sat across from Stenoway. The man looked at them with a bored expression.

Genevieve laid the large envelope on the table. "We found some interesting things in here, Mr. Stenoway."

The man continued to stare at her.

"A phone and a letter. Pretty cut and dry instructions you laid out for Mr. Pierce. Even a guy like that couldn't screw it up, right?" she asked him.

No response.

"We looked you up, Mr. Stenoway. You work for the city. And not just our city…several cities. You really get around. Is it a program through the county or state? Save some money somehow?" she asked with genuine curiosity.

"They're always cutting…" Stenoway started to respond and then closed his mouth.

"I'm sorry? You don't have to talk to me. I do need to go through a few more things here," she explained and pulled out the folder with the photos.

"Do you know any of these people? Elaine Frobish? Horace Manwith? Aaron Roth? Thomas Washburn? Let's see…Marshall Aguirre?" she asked as she laid each photo down in front of him one by one.

The man blinked once and swallowed hard. Then much like Pierce, he pushed the photos away.

"I'll take that as a yes," she said and narrowed her eyes.

"What? I didn't say anything," Stenoway objected.

"Oh, so you want to talk now?" Genevieve asked calmly.

"I don't recognize those people. Don't put words in my mouth," he told her.

"No problem," she agreed. "If you'll just excuse me one moment. I need to make a quick phone call."

199

She nodded at Alex on her way out of the room. She took out her cell phone and found Dureski's number. She hoped he wouldn't be too angry for the three-a.m. phone call.

"Viacorte, this better be good," Dureski said sleepily.

"We've brought in a suspect," she explained. "Anderson Stenoway."

"Tell me about him," Dureski requested.

Genevieve explained his connections to each city as well as how he was associated with the money coming from Pierce. Dureski listened without interrupting for once.

"Hmm…I guess I had it wrong this whole time. It's not about the businesses. It's about the money. It's always about the money," he lamented. "You're at your precinct with him now?"

"Yes, sir," Genevieve responded.

"I'm coming in. I'll be there in half an hour or so," he said and ended the call.

Grusky touched her shoulder after she put her phone in her pocket. She turned around to face him.

"I've filled out a warrant to get Stenoway's financial information and his DNA. We can ask for a swab. He might give one voluntarily," Grusky suggested.

Genevieve shrugged. "He seems pretty smug, but I'll go ask…" she paused. "Um, sir?"

Grusky rolled one hand over the other in a 'get on with it' gesture.

"I told you earlier about getting help from my FBI contact with this case. As it turns out, they've taken an interest in the deaths too. My contact, uh, his name is Agent Dureski. He's on his way here," she stammered.

Grusky's face clouded. "He's taking over our case?"

Genevieve put her hands up. "No, nothing like that. He wants to be a part of the interview process. It's possible…at the end of the day…they'll end up taking this guy into custody."

"Less expense for us," Grusky said with a nod. "Go see if you can get the DNA swab."

"Thanks, LT."

She rejoined the two men in the interrogation room and took her seat at the table. "Mr. Stenoway, we have some DNA evidence in our case. Would you agree to a swab voluntarily? If you're innocent as you claim, this will clear your name."

The man ran his right hand lightly down his left arm which was still handcuffed to the table. He dropped the hand when he noticed Genevieve watching him. "No, and I'm requesting an attorney."

"That's fine. Is there one we can call for you?" she asked.

"His card is in my wallet, but I have the number memorized. I can write it down for you," he said and smiled like a cat.

She tore a sheet from her notebook and passed it to him with a pencil. "We'll call him right now."

Alex pushed away from the wall and followed Genevieve back out of the room. She went to her desk to dial the number Stenoway had written on the paper. The call connected and rang three times before someone answered.

"Logan Salzer, attorney at law. Who do I need to represent?" an older man's voice asked.

"This is Detective Viacorte with the Brenington PD. Mr. Anderson Stenoway is requesting your services."

Genevieve thought she heard the man inhale sharply, but couldn't be certain since she couldn't see him. He didn't speak for a few moments. He clicked his tongue twice and made a sucking sound through his teeth.

"Well, Miss Viacorte—" he began.

"Detective," she corrected him.

"Right. I'm still half asleep. Forgive me. I'm old. Detective then. I'll be at the station shortly. What is my client being accused of?" Salzer asked.

"Murder. Five counts of murder," she said firmly.

"Okay. I'll see you there," he responded and ended the call.

She replaced the receiver in the cradle and looked at Alex. "I guess we just keep him in interrogation for now."

"Works for me. Can we go home and shower or sleep for an hour or more?" he grumbled.

She looked at her watch and yawned. "You go ahead. Dureski is coming in and Grusky is here. I need to coordinate that, but you go see Sophia. Tell her I'm sorry for keeping you out late."

"I'm not leaving. Are you kidding? Sophia is asleep. She'll be so mad if I come home now and wake her up. Nah, I'll see this through," he told her.

The doors to the detective's bay swung open and in walked Special Agent Dureski. His hair was wild and shot off to the left. His shirt was only partially tucked in and he hadn't shaved either. Genevieve hoped he at least said hello to his toothbrush.

"Viacorte. Where's the guy?" he asked as he marched over to their desks.

"He's in interrogation one, but he just lawyered up. His lawyer said he'd be here shortly," Genevieve said gently.

Dureski groaned and threw his head back. "Ugh. I was hoping to get here before he did that. Well, he can still be interrogated with the lawyer present. Did you find anything to tie him to Rialto's company?"

"Just the admittance by Pierce that he was sending and receiving money from NTS, though he referred to them as the 'tech' company when he spoke with us," Genevieve told him.

The doors opened again and another man walked in. He looked like he was just stepping out from a night at the theater. His attire was polished from his navy pinstripe suit to his shiny brown wingtips. He smiled at the three law enforcement members.

"Greetings. I'm Logan Salzer and I'm here to see my client, Anderson Stenoway. Could I trouble one of you for some water?"

Genevieve nodded and went to retrieve a bottle from the break room. The three men were still standing silently when she returned. She handed two bottles of water to Salzer.

"I thought your client might be thirsty too," she explained.

"Thank you, *Detective*," he replied.

"Right this way. We still want to question Mr. Stenoway, but you are allowed to meet with him first," Alex told the lawyer.

"I know the law, good sir," Salzer said sweetly.

They let him into the interrogation room and Salzer turned back to them before taking a seat.

"Please uncuff my client," he requested.

Alex stepped forward and removed the handcuffs. "Anything else?"

"That will be all. I'll knock on the door when we're ready to speak with the three of you," Salzer told him and closed the door.

Alex locked it just in case the lawyer had plans to sneak his client out. Then they walked back to the desks. Grusky was waiting for them.

"The judge approved the warrant for two of Stenoway's accounts. The account number Pierce gave us doesn't seem to have Stenoway's name on it. They said they'll look into the ownership of that one more before granting us access. The judge also wants to see more evidence before he'll sign the one for the DNA," Grusky told them.

"We already have his DNA," Alex stated.

Genevieve looked at him with her eyebrows raised before it hit her. "The envelope. He probably licked it to seal it. Will the adhesive alter it though?"

"Again, Gen. Zero science here. Green's team is good. I'm sure it will be fine," Alex told her.

"Well, swab it already," Dureski told them.

"I think it would be better if we get someone from CSU to do it," Genevieve suggested. "We don't want to contaminate the sample or something."

"That's probably best," Grusky agreed. "Get it back in the evidence bag and I'll take it down to the lab. I'm not sure anyone is on call tonight, but they'll be here in a few hours."

Grusky grabbed the evidence bag from Genevieve and headed toward the stairs. Alex pulled a chair from a neighboring desk for Dureski to use.

"I guess I never introduced myself," Dureski said. "I'm Special Agent Dureski with the FBI."

Alex leaned forward to shake his hand. "Alex Runimoss, detective. I take it you're more familiar with this case than just running down some addresses and identities for us?"

Dureski cleared his throat before responding. "Yes, I'm sorry if it seems like we've been keeping you in the dark. Maybe I'm being paranoid, but I've had several cases get away from me in the past year or so. It seems like I'm more than a step behind each time, so I think I have a leak in my department."

"No problem. Viacorte told me you were picking up the owner of NTS earlier today. We're both curious how that went," Alex responded.

"He's cooperating. He was pretty surprised we knew about the payments," Dureski told them.

"You never told me how you came to suspect NTS in the first place," Genevieve interjected.

"One of my analysts noticed a lot of turnover in business ownership in this area," Dureski began. "When they looked into it, three of the business owners had also recently died. Then a couple months later, Manwith was hit by the garbage truck. None of the deaths were necessarily suspicious, but none of the people were elderly. They were in their fifties or sixties and in good health for the most part. All of the new business owners opened an account with NTS immediately after acquiring the small business."

Genevieve could tell by the look on Alex's face he thought the evidence was pretty thin. "NTS is pretty widely used for data management by companies in this region," she argued.

Dureski nodded. "That is true, but we felt like it was worth looking into. We had just started looking into their financials around the same time the Frobish woman died."

"But we've heard her daughter is getting her business," Alex pointed out. "That's not really new ownership."

"It's a new name, so it fit the criteria. They haven't opened an account with NTS yet, so we weren't certain her case was part of the bigger picture," he explained. "I was working with a thin group to tease this out, so it was pretty slow going. The other three deaths weren't even ones that warranted investigations because they seemed like accidents, so I couldn't call on a local PD to sniff around. When your department got a hit on the DNA, it really made things progress."

"Not to mention Rialto giving you more of the inside financial story," Alex remarked.

"True," Dureski agreed. "Anyway, Follard was also being blackmailed, much like Pierce. You told me Pierce was seduced by a woman named Shelly, right?"

The two detectives nodded.

"Same story with Follard. The biggest difference with NTS is his wife only co-owns the business with him. Regardless, she could take it all away if she had grounds for a divorce," Dureski said plainly.

"Which apparently she does," Alex remarked. "What happens with Follard and Pierce now?"

"I can hold Follard for twenty-four hours before I have to bring him in for an arraignment," Dureski said. "I'd like to speak with Mr. Stenoway first. We might be able to offer some leniency for these two idiots if they'll testify against Stenoway."

A loud knock sounded from down the hall. "Ask and you shall receive, huh, detectives?" Dureski said as he got up from the chair.

They walked over to the interrogation room. Genevieve could feel the anticipation rolling off both men as they reached the door. Alex unlocked it and turned the knob. The lawyer was retaking his seat next to Stenoway. She noticed sweat stains on his shirt that weren't there when they spoke to him earlier.

"Against my advice, Mr. Stenoway would like to provide a full confession," Salzer announced.

Genevieve paused mid-step. "Full confession?"

Stenoway nodded. "I've had my fun, but you caught me. The jig is up, as they say."

Alex went back to his preferred spot in the corner while Dureski and Genevieve sat across the table from the other two men.

"Mr. Stenoway, this is our colleague from the FBI, Special Agent Dureski. He'll be joining us for your interview this evening," Genevieve explained.

"Start at the beginning," Dureski instructed.

"Well, as you know, my job is to issue permits for three cities in the area: Brenington, Lander, and Pfinning. I'd hoped to get added to Green Mountain too, but they have a lifer in the role, so I've been waiting him out for retirement," Stenoway said easily. "My job gives me access to all kinds of information. I discovered a few businesses here are actually owned by the perceived owner's wife. I thought there was a chance I could get these men to stray from their wedding vows with the right persuasion."

"You mean Shelly," Genevieve commented.

"Sure. Shelly. Don't worry about her. You'll never find her. She's long since moved on and had no idea why she was asked to seduce these two men," Stenoway told them quickly. "She's a nobody. Anyway. It was easier than I ever dreamed it would be. I know you're onto Pierce, so I'm guessing you know about Follard too. I was getting a grand a week between the two of them for the past year and change. It's not a lot of money, but it basically doubles my government wages."

"You're being very casual, Mr. Stenoway," Dureski observed. "At what point did you start killing people?"

"Well, we both know I've killed five people," Stenoway said as though it were nothing. "Relax, big guy. I can see your jaw dropping in my periphery. I said full confession and I meant it. Shall I continue?"

The three investigators nodded.

"Okay. Where was I? Right, killing. Some of these people got a little too curious about my scheme. I had the landscaping guy doing all this work for basically free and he couldn't get away from it. I couldn't twist the screws on NTS as much because the man was a co-owner of the business and he ended the affair before I'd instructed Shelly to leave him hanging. I was worried he might grow a conscience and tell his wife himself. If he'd complained about the blackmail payments, I probably would have let him quit making them.

"As I was saying, some of the business owners got angry about having to pay a fee for these landscaping projects. They would call the city to complain. Those calls would often come through my desk, but there were always memos about the complaints, so I knew every time they lodged a complaint. When they got to the point of asking for permits and if it was *legal* for the cities to require this of them, I had to step in. I'd start by making some harassing phone calls, telling them it was in their best interest to just comply. They never saw it my way, so I watched them and learned their habits. Then I waited for them to show up in one of their habitual locations and I'd cause a fatal accident.

"I pushed one guy in front of a garbage truck while he was on the phone with me. I got the Frobish woman on the phone while she was near the cliff edge. Pushed her over. She was a fighter, but I'm stronger and she wasn't expecting me to be there. I rigged another guy's car battery so it seemed dead, but it wasn't and it electrocuted him. Thankfully, I didn't have to watch that happen."

Genevieve forced herself not to gag as he continued to describe the ways he led people to their deaths. He seemed so detached from the reality of his actions. He was a murderer, but he acted like it was all one big game. He seemed to know all the details, but something felt off to her.

"Mr. Stenoway, when we first picked you up, you threatened us. You said we'd regret it, yet now, you're happy to share every little detail with us. What changed?" she asked him.

"I realized if you had Pierce, then you probably had Follard and my scheme was about to come to a screeching halt. No more payouts, no more blackmail. I lost. I swung for the fences and I lost," he said with a shrug.

"Tell me what triggered you to go after Manwith and Frobish," Genevieve challenged. "They weren't part of the group complaining about landscaping."

"Ah yes. Two outliers or so it seems. Both business owners reached out to local construction companies for bids on some additions they hoped to make. Pierce fouled up his bid somehow. I think he was so used to putting in low numbers like he did for the city projects…by the way, did I mention those little projects were my idea too? Brilliant, right? Anyway. Pierce initially put in super low bids for both projects and tried to retract, but the two owners felt like it was a bait and switch. They called the city to report him and they both called to get his permit history to see if he'd done anything similar to other customers. I couldn't allow them to uncover my little scheme, so they had to go," he said and mimicked a person walking with his fingers.

Genevieve slid a notepad across the table. We need you to write it all down and then sign it," she told him.

"It might take me a few minutes," he said. "I never thought I'd garner the attention of the FBI with this. In some ways, that's a win in and of itself."

"Could you excuse us for a moment, Agent Dureski?" Genevieve asked.

He waved her away without looking up. She locked eyes with Alex and tilted her head toward the door. He followed her out.

"What's up?" he asked.

"Something about this feels too easy," she said with a frown. "I don't think Stenoway looks like the guy who left DNA behind at the two scenes. Something is off."

Alex shook his head. "Don't do that, Gen. Don't second guess yourself. This guy is proud of his handiwork. He was basically bragging about it. He's been getting extra money; maybe he had his face worked on. He knew all the details and laid it all out for us. It's done. Case closed. We probably won't even have to have a trial since he's writing out a confession. He'll go to some federal prison your guy Dureski picks out for him and we'll never see him again."

"It looked like he was sweating in there," she pointed out.

"Maybe he gets hot flashes," Alex joked.

"This isn't funny, Alex. I think someone is making him confess."

Grusky cleared his throat and startled both of them. "What's the problem, Viacorte?"

Alex put his hand up. "No problem, sir. We were both just surprised by Stenoway's *full* confession just now."

Genevieve fumed. "We were surprised because it seems too good to be true, sir."

"What do you mean, Detective?" Grusky asked.

"Stenoway told us 'You're going to regret this' when we arrested him. Now he's spilling every secret about the case like it isn't a big deal. He's sweating like he's scared and he doesn't look like the guy who rented the car. We should at least run his DNA to confirm he's the killer," Genevieve argued.

"Once he's booked in the system, we can probably do that. Right now, we have to wait for the judge to order it," Grusky told her.

"But we might have his DNA downstairs!" she objected loudly.

"Calm down, Detective. We aren't going to spend money on that if we already have a confession," he explained. "I think you should take your wins where you find them. Not every case will come with a full confession."

She sighed. "I understand, sir."

* * * * *

Cari woke up to her phone buzzing. She grabbed it and swiped to answer the call before it went to voice mail.

"This is Cari," she said and yawned.

"I didn't think I'd wake you up. Sorry about that," Gen apologized. "I have a pretty big update for you."

Cari sat up in bed and threw back her sheets. "Let me get my notebook, just a sec."

She padded out to her living room and pulled her notebook from her messenger bag. "Okay, I'm ready."

"It's pretty detailed, but we arrested someone for the murders," Genevieve said. "He made a full confession, so Robby won't have to testify."

"He must be relieved," Cari remarked.

"I'm calling him next," Genevieve said. "I thought you probably woke up before he did, but I guess I was wrong."

"No problem," Cari said. "Tell me the story."

She listened as Genevieve recounted the tale of blackmail, seduction, and murder. She was shocked to learn it was a city employee.

"I knew I didn't like that place," she said, only half-joking. "So, the FBI has him in custody for now?"

"Yeah, I'm guessing he'll agree to plead guilty and forego a trial. It wrapped up more easily than I expected," Genevieve admitted.

"I'm surprised he slipped up by trying to deliver that envelope himself. It seems like he would have been more careful after all the scheming he did over the past year and a half," Cari commented.

"Yeah, that bothers me some, but the FBI people think he just got tired of the charade," Genevieve told her. "He's facing five murder counts."

"The whole thing almost feels too easy, though. This whole investigation we both struggled to find evidence and suddenly, he just gives us everything?" Cari asked.

"I don't disagree with you, but no one sees it that way. Both Grusky and the FBI say it's done. Case closed. Even Alex signed off," Genevieve groused. "I plan to continue to monitor his finances. Follow the money, find the *real* bad guy."

"But you think Robby's safe? No one's looking for the guy who shed light on all of this?" Cari asked with concern.

"My gut says yes. If I'm right and this guy is taking the fall for someone else or even multiple people, then they aren't looking to cast blame elsewhere. I'm not going to stop following up on things. If I get wind of anything that makes me think Robby is in danger, we'll get him protection immediately," she said confidently.

"Well, thanks for letting me know. Keep me updated on that. Is it okay if I write this up for the paper?" she asked.

"Yeah, I can send you an official brief later when we finish getting our reports together. It will be in the afternoon, though. I've been up all night and I need to sleep first," she said with exhaustion in her voice.

"Get some sleep. I appreciate the phone call," she said.

Her friend ended the call. Cari walked into her kitchen to start the coffee maker. Right as she clicked it over to brew, her phone alarm went off. She quickly silenced it. She went to her closet to pick out her clothes for the day and then jumped in the shower. She hated to admit it, but she was kind of excited to meet with the wedding planner.

Forty-five minutes later, Cari pulled into a spot outside of Aspen Wilson's office. She saw Bob waiting in his car a few places down and wasn't surprised he beat her to the meeting. He got out and waved. She met him halfway, even though it meant walking away from the entrance to Ms. Wilson's office.

"Good morning," she said with a smile.

He bent down to kiss her on her cheek. "Ready to plan our future?"

She grabbed his hand. "Definitely."

"I'm guessing Genevieve already called you, but just in case, they made an arrest last night," Bob said.

"Yeah, she called before seven to tell me," Cari said and yawned. "I'm sure Robby is relieved, but it kind of feels unsettled to me."

Bob gave her a concerned look. "I heard Genevieve wasn't sold on it either, but the feds disagreed, so what's done is done."

"Genevieve is going to keep investigating on her own. She promised to keep me updated," Cari told him.

"They were going to have us do some DNA testing, but then the guy full out confessed, so they don't need it anymore," Bob told her.

"Did they get a DNA sample from him?" Cari asked.

209

"I don't think he submitted one, but we might have his DNA from an envelope," Bob explained.

"You should run it!"

"You know I can't do that, right?" Bob asked and then looked at his watch.

"I know. At least reassure me the sample is getting saved in case it does need to be run later," she begged.

Bob put his hand on her shoulder and gave it a squeeze. "It's all saved, super sleuth. Ready to go inside?"

She nodded. Bob opened the door for her with his free hand. She squeezed his hand. Life finally felt like it was on track again.

Epilogue

Four Weeks Later

Genevieve took a sip of her coffee and logged into her computer in the precinct. Her email inbox showed eleven new messages. She scanned the names of the senders and paused when she saw one from one of the clerks at the courthouse. She clicked on it first and started skimming the message.

"Finally!" she exclaimed and threw a fist in the air.

"What?" Alex said with almost no enthusiasm. "It's barely eight in the morning. You need to tone it down a bit."

She rolled her eyes. "We *finally* got approved to access and monitor Stenoway's other account. You know, the one Pierce wired money to after each, uh, hit?"

"I didn't realize we were still waiting for that. What took so long?" Alex asked.

She scanned the email again. "It took them some time to find his name associated with the account."

"Is someone else's name on it?" he asked.

She read the email again. "Some sort of business name, but now we can see the rest of the story."

Alex shrugged. "You just will not let this go, huh? The guy confessed. He did it. Case closed."

"Yeah, and he's in a cushy prison with all sorts of freedoms even though he told us he *killed* five people!" Genevieve almost shouted at him.

"Woah. Again, it's still early. Chill," Alex said with exhaustion in his voice.

"Well, I don't think he was working alone. I think he's covering for someone else," she opened a browser window so she could use the information provided to access Stenoway's account. "The feds should have been able to freeze this account once he was arrested, but the courts took forever to sign off on the warrant."

"Whatever. I'm going to get more coffee. Need anything?" Alex asked as he stood up.

She waved him off as she entered the digits into the boxes on the screen. After a few verification steps, Stenoway's account summary appeared on her screen. She frowned. In the transaction history, she could see the transfers Pierce wired over, but no money had been withdrawn since Stenoway was arrested. Something was not adding up. She had been monitoring his other bank account for the past four weeks. He had recurring withdrawals for rent and utilities, but nothing else. She opened another tab to look at the other account again.

"You should just bookmark that site. You visit it every day," Alex remarked.

Genevieve's hand went to her chest. "I didn't hear you get back. You scared me."

Alex laughed with satisfaction. "You look like you found something interesting this time."

"He didn't spend any of the money in this account," Genevieve said and pointed at the screen.

"He's in prison," Alex said, stating the obvious.

"Thanks, Sherlock. But how is he paying his lawyer? Surely he had some legal fees for dragging that guy out here in the middle of the night, right?" Genevieve asked.

"Maybe he has the guy on retainer and late-night call outs are included," Alex proposed. "Nobody is reopening this case, Gen. You have to let it go."

"This isn't over. You know I'm right," Genevieve said with anger in her eyes. "I need to make a phone call. I'll be back."

She pushed back from her desk and walked out of the station. Maybe Alex didn't believe her, but she knew someone who would. She scrolled through her contacts and hit the call button.

"Gen! I wasn't expecting to hear from you this morning. What's up?" Cari asked cheerfully.

"I got access to Stenoway's other account. None of the money has gone anywhere. I can see the transfers from Pierce, but that's it. He didn't spend any of it. He still hasn't even paid his lawyer!" Genevieve told her.

"Are you reopening the investigation?" Cari asked with interest.

"I can't even get Alex to believe me that this is meaningful, but I don't think he acted alone. He was just another puppet. We're still looking for the puppeteer."

The End

If you enjoyed the book, please consider leaving a review.

Ready for more Cari, Genevieve, Bob, and Alex? Stay tuned for book 7, summer 2025! Here's a snippet to whet your appetite:

Genevieve has continued to investigate Anderson Stenoway and monitor his finances since his imprisonment. Since her superiors don't support her theory, she is left keeping an eye on his accounts on her own time. She's certain the real killer is still on the loose, but can she get the evidence to prove it? Meanwhile, Cari is neck-deep in wedding plans when a young woman contacts her about her sister's disappearance. The woman says her sister made it to the connecting airport, but somehow missed the final flight. She isn't answering her phone and no one has heard from her in over twelve hours. Cari feels inadequate; she's only a journalist, not an investigator. The woman is relentless and begs Cari for help. Can Cari find the sister before something terrible happens to her?

Keep up to date with all things Cari: https://leslieapiggott.com

Acknowledgments

Thank you to my wonderful editor, Jennie Rosenblum! You make each book better. Thank you for all you do, especially for supporting my books in so many ways.

To my friend Desiree: you're an amazing friend. Thank you for always reading my drafts, finding typos, and giving me feedback.

To my sister-in-law, Stacy: thanks for the tips on accounting terminology

To Dr. Ted Pate: Congrats on winning my little contest! Hope you enjoyed your role as the park ranger.

To all of the authors and crew with Indies United Publishing House, you are fantastic! Thank you for your support and encouragement. Best of luck with all of your future books.

And finally, to my beautiful family: Brad, Abby, and Simon. You make my world go 'round. I love you so much.

About the Author

Leslie A. Piggott lives in the Austin, Texas area with her husband and their two children. She is a scientist-turned-mom who received her doctorate in Biomedical Sciences from the University of Texas Health Science Center at Houston. In addition to writing, she also enjoys running marathons, quilting, knitting, singing in the church choir, and watercolor painting. She has previously published two watercolor and poetry books, both in 2021: *Poems in the Pandemic*, and *Art in Words*. Her first novel, *Rising Pressure* was published in January of 2022. She began publishing her first mystery series with *Chasing the Edge, book 1 of the Cari Turnlyle Series* in July of 2022. To sign up for her newsletter, you can visit her website at https://leslieapiggott.com.